DOOM'S CHAMPION

BY MATTHEW CULVER

2015

This story is dedicated with love to my mother, Jill.

Chapter 1

It was a dark day in the castle, a day the king spent on his throne as he often did. He wasn't truly sitting on the throne, though; sitting would imply some measure of comfort. He was positioned in his throne, much like a wooden toy might be. The king was in his late fifties, but his face was wrinkled like that of a man much older. Why had he aged like this? There was something inside of him that was draining him of his vitality, wringing him out like a sponge: it was fear. He had been afraid for so long, writhing in this illogical fear. Surely there was nothing to be afraid of.

The door opened and smashed against the wall, its jarring sound soon followed by the equally dissonant clanging of the guard's metal-plated boots as he hurried into the room. The king looked down from the throne.

"Your Majesty!" shouted the guard. The king gripped the armrests tightly as his gaze intensified into a baleful stare.

"What is it now?!" he spit. "Why must you disturb me like this?"

"Your Majesty! A man's here to see you!"

"Someone's here to see me? What business does he have here?"

"He…"

"I have a proposition for you, sir," interrupted a new, gruff voice. The man pushed the guard aside and entered the room. He was tall and fairly well-built, and he wore dark, simple clothing. A curly red mustache was all that softened the appearance of his chiseled, angular face. At least the soles of his shoes were made of a softer material; the metal clanging of the guard's shoes was agitating enough.

"You would do well to address me as Your Majesty. Now, what is so important that you must barge in here without proper permission?"

The man stared up at the king.

"Five-hundred thousand gold pieces. That is what I am willing to give you."

"For what? What do you mean?" The king began to fidget around if he had suddenly become extremely uncomfortable in his seat. Even more uncomfortable than he had been before, if that were even possible.

"I believe you know *exactly* what I am talking about, Your Majesty."

The king leapt up out of the throne.

"What do you mean!?"

"I believe you know exa…"

"I know what you're here for. You're here for the Golden Egg, right? Well that's not enough for it!"

"Eight-hundred thousand, then." The king stepped towards the man.

"It's not for sale," he spit under his clenched teeth. "The Golden Egg is a valuable family heirloom. It is *quite* priceless. Guards! GUARDS!!!! Escort this man out of the throne room at once!"

"Wait!" shouted the man, his confidence suddenly gone. "Wait! I'll pay you more! It means nothing to you!" Guards surrounded him and grabbed him by the arms. "You have no idea what you're doing!"

"A pleasure, sir. Good afternoon."

"Wait!"

"A *pleasure*, sir."

"Wait! You don't understand the forces at play here! I'll give you…" The man was dragged out of the throne room and down the hallway as the king returned to his seat. It was suddenly quiet. Things had calmed down for a moment.

"Guards, you will not let that man on the premises

again. Do I make myself quite clear?"

"Of course, Your Majesty."

"Very good."

A few minutes passed.

The king remained silent in thought, his face wrinklier than ever. Tension was building. He couldn't hold himself back any longer; it was time. He stood up slowly and walked around the back of the throne, kneeling down to access a hidden chest. He hadn't opened it in years, but he just couldn't stop himself. It was time for him to see it with his own eyes and make sure it was still in there.
The Golden Egg was still in there.

"Your Majesty, are you ready for dinner?" The king pried his hands away from the Golden Egg, latched the chest shut, and looked up.

"Yes. Yes. Quite ready."
He quickly walked off. It would be the last meal he would ever eat.

Despite the king's exhaustion, there would be no sleep for him that night. He needed to open the chest again and see it again. One more time, just to make sure it was still there. His wrinkly body crawled out of bed. Was he wearing his crown? Good. He needed the crown. He slinked across the dark, shadowy bedroom and crept down the short hallway into the pitch black throne room. It was so dark and cold. It was strange how unfamiliar this place became when the lights were put out.

He felt the chest with his hands; it was still locked, just as he expected it would be. Or did he expect it? It was dark. Everything seemed so unfamiliar. Maybe he couldn't expect anything anymore.

Chapter 2

"So you're saying the killer entered through the window?" asked Prince Lucio.

"It's the only way!" replied the frantic guard. "We were stationed at the door all night! Nobody came through!"

"Who is *we*?"

"Me and one other chap. I didn't know who he was, couldn't see his face past the helmet."

"So neither of you saw or heard anything at all?"

"Well, I *did* leave to take a wee at one point. Actually it was exactly when the murder took place, wouldn't ya know it. But the other guard was still there! He wouldn't have let anyone through!"

"Who else was stationed at the door!?" shouted the prince to the other guards assembled in the room. Nobody answered, and the prince stomped his foot. "You blasted idiot! It was all a setup!"

"That still doesn't explain the fact that the window is broken, or that there's blood all over the windowsill," said General Richmond, one of the royal family's most trusted advisors. "The walls outside of the window are stained with bloody marks as well. The glass is spread into the room, so it is likely that the window was smashed from the outside. Whoever or whatever did this must have left through the window and probably also entered through it."

"Yes, that appears the case, indeed," muttered the prince. "I suppose it's possible that multiple perpetrators were working together on this job." He then stomped his foot on the ground again. "Damn it! Why the hell did this happen?! How did you idiots let this happen?! Does anyone have anything to say about this?!" There was no immediate response. Everyone was still stunned by the gruesome scene before them: the king's body lay in a bloody heap near the throne, his head severed in half and his brain removed. His royal crown was also missing. The once-sturdy wooden chest behind the throne was smashed into pieces, its contents stolen.

"Does this mean you become king?" asked one of the guards.

"Have some respect for my father, you ingrate! Thanks to your incompetence, he has just been murdered! There shouldn't be anything else on your mind right now!" The prince turned around to face the window. "And no, I cannot become king until we recover the crown. That crown is a symbol of Victory City, and tradition says that the king's successor cannot ascend to the throne without it. You knew that already. Obviously, I am quite annoyed that you moron guards allowed someone to walk right out of here with the crown!" The guards looked down at the floor.

"Do you know who could have committed this horrible crime?" asked a nobleman who had entered the room relatively recently.

"It was those damn, pig-face orcs, no doubt!" spit Prince Lucio. "I'm sure of it! Those murderous creatures, breeding in the mountains like vermin and attacking anyone they see. It sickens me to even think about them. We should have dealt with them long ago." General Richmond suddenly stepped forward.

"You think the orcs are responsible for this? Hmm." The general turned to the door guard. "What did the other door watchman look like? Did he have green skin or a pig nose?"
"Can't tell. He was wearin' a full suit of arma."
"Was he big? Did he have the build of an orc?"

"A big chap he was indeed! Pretty tall, at least. Pro'ly six feet or so. Six-one. Didn't look much like an orc, though."

"Did you notice anything unusual about him?"

"Nope." The general paced around.

"Orcs are usually at least six feet tall. And they're very muscular."

"Well, this man was quite muscular, but no more so than meself, a' course. Course, not many are!"

"Don't humor yourself," muttered the general as he turned back to face the prince. "Now, if this man's description is correct, it appears very unlikely that the false guard was an orc. Orcs are very muscular, not to mention they wouldn't easily fit in a man's suit of armor. Their body structure is different. And an orc's constant snorting and slobbering would have raised suspicion as well."

"Yes, you make a point, General," responded the prince. "But only someone with great strength could have been responsible for this brutality, strength few men know. And scouts have reported that the orcs are mobilizing along our borders. This is unlikely to be a coincidence, I think!"

Just then, a messenger burst into the room.

"My Prince! Yohannis has reported a small group of orcs encamped within sight of Victory City walls. What are your orders?"

"We will move to strike!" replied the prince. "We must recover the crown and avenge my father's death at once!"

"That's good, because Yohannis is already on his way to fight them!"

"Die, vile creatures!" screamed Yohannis as he ran at full speed towards the orcs, longbow in hand. "Villains! King killers! Feel the sting of my arrows, you vile, despicable creatures!" He was a very well-built man in his late twenties, with long blond hair and a handsome face that seemed to have a perpetual angry look to it. A continuous stream of arrows flowed out of his weapon towards the orc encampment. The orcs finally noticed him, and they immediately readied their weapons.

"Yohannis! Wait for backup!" cried General Richmond from the city walls.

"Justice waits for no one!"

"Grrr… pink-skins want some punishin'!" shouted a charging orc. "Die!" Yohannis shot several arrows at the orc, with one of them hitting the orc's arm and the rest missing. The muscular, gray-green skinned creature, who had a pig snout, big ears, and large tusks protruding from the bottom of his mouth, continued his charge until Yohannis felled him with an arrow to the chest.

"Yohannis, wait! We're coming!" General Richmond and several other soldiers rode up on horseback. A second orc ran up to attack them but was cut down by the general's lance as he arrived. The remaining orcs abandoned their camp and began retreating up the hill, into the sunrise.

"Cowards! Come back!" shrieked Yohannis. "Cowards, all!"

"Cut off their retreat!" commanded the general. The orcs managed to escape into dense woods before the soldiers could catch up with them.

"Into the brush!" wailed Yohannis. "These murderous cowards cannot get away from us so easily!" As the others climbed off their horses, Yohannis stormed ahead by himself. His fluttering blond hair was the last thing the soldiers saw of him before he disappeared into the forest.

"I think the orcs are too deep into the woods," said one of the soldiers. "There's no point in chasing them now."

"Not so fast! Watch out!" General Richmond shoved the soldier out of the way of an incoming arrow. There, directly above them, were two huge orcs balancing on a large branch.

One orc sat down holding a longbow, evidently responsible for the arrow attack. The other orc, the larger of the two, was unlike anything the soldiers had ever seen before: he had pale white skin. This orc crouched on the branch and held a large trident, apparently ready to jump off and strike at any moment.

"Don't move!" shouted the white orc. "My buddy here has a bead on your head, Commander." The general had no choice but to freeze while his soldiers readied their bows and aimed at the two orcs, forcing a standoff.

"Are you the ones responsible for the attack on our king last night!?" shouted the general. The white orc looked around.

"I did not know of any attack. I cannot speak for the others, though."

The men looked at each other, thrown off guard by the brute's surprisingly forthright-sounding answer.

"Come down from there and we'll take you in for further questioning. There's no need for bloodshed." The general motioned for his soldiers to lower their bows. As soon as they were down, though, the green-skinned orc took the opportunity to fire! The arrow missed; the soldiers quickly returned fire, killing the shooter but missing the white orc, who swung down on a vine and kicked one of the soldiers to the ground. A different soldier prepared to launch another arrow but the orc reeled back and smashed that soldier in the side of the head with the shaft of his trident.

"Drop your weapon!" shouted General Richmond, but the orc ignored him and ran back into the underbrush. The two soldiers stood up, shaken but not seriously injured.

"Into the woods, sir?"

"No. We'll stay here for now."

"Shouldn't we look for Yohannis, though?"

"The orcs may be ready with an ambush, or they may

have the woods booby-trapped. I don't think we'll be able to catch them at this point anyway, and I think Yohannis can take care of himself." They waited there for him for a short while and then turned back to the city empty-handed.

"At least I *hope* Yohannis can take care of himself," muttered the general.

Chapter 3

Victory City was a fairly large city that had recently become a major commercial power in the area. This recent success could largely be attributed to the sudden chaos that had arisen three years earlier with the violent overthrow of the governments of Redcloud and Stormtree, two rival cities located several days of travel south in the Sandstorm Desert. As the years progressed, several small cities and towns surrounding Victory City had sworn oaths of fealty to their larger neighbor and had been accumulated into Victory City as it expanded in size. Residents believed strongly in order and justice and were extremely loyal to their ruling family; thus they were deeply shaken by the news of the king's death and felt the need to take immediate and decisive action against those responsible.

Fifteen hours had passed since the skirmish with the orcs, and Yohannis was still nowhere to be found. It was dark. General Richmond arrived in the war room of the castle, where he had been summoned by Prince Lucio.

"So nice of you to join us, General," said the prince. He was a very handsome man, with dark bangs that curled around his deep blue eyes, high cheekbones, and a pronounced chin. He was not alone; at the prince's left stood a very shapely, attractive woman with long reddish brown hair, white pants, a white shirt and a cape. Her name was Crista, and she was the prince's personal attendant and errand-girl. At his right stood Milkbone, a somewhat unattractive but nonetheless well-regarded nobleman who was wearing a blue cloak and a white, feathered hat.

"So, I hear that you were unable to procure any information from the orcs, General!" blabbered Milkbone. "A fine job you must have done out there! How much are you being paid for this buffoonery?"

"Sir Milkbone, I hope you will keep your insults to yourself," quipped the prince. "General Richmond has a long history of success as both a soldier and military commander, and his expertise in handling all facets of war goes without question. To suggest anything else would be simply incorrect."

"We did obtain some information," said the general. "One of the orcs we encountered told us that he personally didn't attack the king, but that he couldn't speak for the others."

"Oh, that tells us a hell of a lot!" cried Milkbone, clapping his hands together and laughing to himself. "You'd have to be a bloody idiot to take an orc at his word! I'll wager that very orc was the murderer! The very same one!"

"I think it's important to discuss the possible motivation for this attack," said the prince. "The act of murder itself and the gruesome manner in which it was accomplished may have been meant as a scare tactic, but I doubt that was the sole reason. Also, the crown is a historical relic that is worth nothing unless it is on the head of a royal family member. I'm sure the orcs, or whoever was responsible, have little use for it unless they plan on using it to obtain ransom money. I think there were bigger plans at work here."

"What other explanation can there be, Your Lordship?" asked General Richmond. "I'm not sure we should be so quick to dismiss those possibilities." The prince paced back and forth.

"I don't know, General. I believe there is only one thing the orcs could have wanted."

"What? Really?"

"They killed him for the Golden Egg of Gotty Gottya!" stated the prince.   "An artifact of tremendous magical power, one of only three in existence… it must be the reason. My family was in possession of one of them; it was among the items stolen during the raid."

"What kind of magical power?"

"Would you care to answer the general's question, Milkbone?"

"I wish I could, My Prince, but it appears this is one of the few topics where I'm just as ignorant as the general!"

"You'll keep your baseless insults to yourself, Sir Milkbone."

"So what magical properties are there, then, Prince Lucio?" asked the general. "What makes these things so special?"

"I don't know, either," responded the prince. "Nobody knows. All that is known is that there is vast untapped magical power within each of the three Golden Eggs."

General Richmond twirled his short, gray beard in thought and eased back in his chair. He was a middle-aged man of considerable physical strength, and his dark eyes glowed with deep wisdom.

"That brings us to why I have invited Sir Milkbone to this meeting," the prince continued. "In his years of collecting rare trinkets from across the land, the esteemed nobleman in our company here has inadvertently acquired one of the three Golden Eggs as well."

"What!?" shouted Milkbone. "I have no idea what you're talking about! I mean, naturally I do have my fair share of golden, egg-shaped objects, but…"

"Crista, if you please…" The prince's attendant unbuckled a pouch on her belt and took out a shining gold egg that was only a little bit larger than a chicken's egg. "Does this look familiar to you?" asked the prince. Milkbone looked stunned.

"Why, you're nothing but a common thief, Prince Lucio!"

screamed Milkbone in outrage. "How did you get that out of my house!?"

"It wasn't hard at all for my agent here."

"My trust is betrayed. I am utterly stunned and appalled by your behavior, Prince Lucio."

"Don't worry, Sir Milkbone. You can have it back. Crista, please return Sir Milkbone's Golden Egg of Gotty Gottya to him."

"Well I didn't know it was magical or anything," mumbled Milkbone as he snatched the egg out of the attendant's hand. "I bought it from a man who said he found it on the body of a dead dwarf. It wasn't as expensive as many of my other treasures." He gazed at the egg in his hand. "It *is* quite shiny, however."

"Yes, of course it is," said the prince. "General, whoever killed my father will be coming after this one, as well. I want you to set up a guard around his estate."

"Don't even think about it, My Prince!" shouted Milkbone. "I'd rather not have your minions, with their filthy, thieving hands, anywhere near my house again! What priceless treasures will they steal this time?!" Milkbone stormed out of the room.

"I will dispatch guards to his house within the hour," said the general.

"That's for the best, General Richmond. Sir Milkbone has made his inventory of luxury items well known through his many business collaborations, so his ownership of the second Egg is virtually common knowledge."

"But, what of the third Egg, My Lord? Where is that one located?"

"The high elves of Elkanshire are in control of it. Lord Eliazer himself holds it. I doubt that they will be easy prey to the murderer in the short term, but even still we must take serious measures to ensure that neither Golden Egg of Gotty Gottya ever falls into the wrong hands."

"Agreed, My Prince."

"That will be all for now, General Richmond." The general nodded his head and left the room.

The guards arrived at Milkbone's house later that night, but by that point they were no longer needed. Milkbone's blood-covered body lay on the floor just inside the front entrance to his house; the door had been smashed open. The top of his head had been cut off and his brain was missing. The second Golden Egg had already been taken.

Chapter 4

It was the mid afternoon. General Richmond sat at the table, slowly sipping a glass of red wine as he looked out the window. Sitting next to him was his eighteen-year-old son, William, who was tall like his father but somewhat thinner and not as well-muscled. He had recently followed after his father and joined the army. They sat without saying anything for a couple of minutes until a middle-aged woman entered the room carrying a pot of soup and placing it on the table. The general and his son poured themselves bowls and began to eat.

"Delicious as always, Helen. Delicious as always."

"It's your favorite, Charles. Tomato and chicken."

"I know, I know. I smelled it from here while it was cooking. Delicious." He continued to eagerly swallow spoonfuls of his wife's soup. "You have no idea what a relief it is to come home and share a delicious meal with my family after everything I've had to go through the past week."

"Are you any closer to finding out who the killer is?"

"No, Helen." The general shook his head. "I have no idea who did this. Nobody does, but still everyone rushes to blame the orcs."

"Why wouldn't it be the orcs? You know what they're capable of, Charles. Need I remind you that your own father was killed in an orcish attack twenty years ago?"

"I'll never forget what happened to my father. But still, we simply cannot rush to conclusions without a more thorough investigation."

"Didn't the killer rip down Milkbone's steel-reinforced front door like it wasn't even there, Dad? Didn't you say that?"

"Yes. But, I don't even think an orc would be capable of such strength. It's baffling, really." Helen Richmond left the room and returned shortly afterwards with a plate of biscuits. She was in her mid fifties and had gray hair but still retained much of the beauty from her youth. The general grabbed one of the biscuits like an eager kid and began to munch on it.

"Just promise me you'll be careful, Charles. Don't underestimate the cruelty of the orcs. They're not like us; they're unpredictable." The general looked his wife in the eyes.

"It's all right. Don't worry about me."

"Remember what happened to King Lucius and Sir Milkbone. I just don't want you to end up like they did. I don't want to see you with your head cut open and your brain missing. We all need you too much here." She glared at him sternly. He quickly finished eating and got up from his seat.

"Don't fill your head with such horrible thoughts. I apologize again for having to leave so early, but I have to prepare for the big meeting tonight." The general wiped his mouth with his napkin and walked over to his wife, giving her a quick kiss on a cheek. He turned to leave.

"Promise me you won't be the next victim, Charles!" she called after him. But the general had already left the house.

Chapter 5

The fortress of the orcs was located inside of a huge cave; actually, it could better be described as a complex system of tunnels dug inside of a tall mountain. It was not far from Victory City but, due to its position in the mountains and the presence of heavy forests and maze-like rivers all around, it was nearly impenetrable to attacks. The tunnels were lit by torches set up around the cave, and carved-out rooms were abundant. The largest of these rooms belonged to Molar-Licker, the tribe's shaman, and as usual he had been spending the entire day sitting alone inside of the room.

The white orc, whose name was Angroo, appeared in the entrance and looked down at the shaman. He was carrying his trident with him; it seemed like he couldn't go anywhere without his weapon of choice.

"What did you call me in here for?" he asked.

Molar-Licker turned around to face him but didn't respond.

"You know, that potion that you gave me still hasn't kicked in!" Angroo banged his arm onto the cave wall. "It's been almost three weeks! No relief!"

"The results will come," answered Molar-Licker. He was very big – even bigger than Angroo, who was himself oversized for an orc – and wore a bear-skin cloak over his head as he brooded in the dark corner. Angroo scratched his right arm.

"Well, they haven't. My skin still burns all the time."

"I said that the results would come. Just wait." Angroo was disappointed by the shaman's concise answer, but he couldn't say that he expected much else. He had known Molar-Licker for many years and knew that he always kept his word, so he decided against saying anything else on the subject.

Molar-Licker was perhaps the only orc Angroo truly felt comfortable around. Most of the others were too unpredictable for him, and their cruelness and lack of civility disillusioned him to some extent. He needed to be on his toes all the time because, as one of the tribe's highest ranking commanders, it was his responsibility to put others in their places. Although he differed from most of his tribe in mannerisms and especially in appearance, Angroo had eventually earned the respect of his tribesman through his proven tactical ingenuity in battle and, more importantly, his extreme level of skill in fighting; in fact, the only orc in the entire tribe who could have possibly stood a chance against him in one-on-one combat was Tooth-Licker, the chieftain of the tribe and the older brother of Molar-Licker. Tooth-Licker was an ambitious and bloodthirsty warrior who preferred to act first and think later. He had attained the position of chieftain by slaying the tribe's previous chieftain, and his authority went unchallenged afterwards; he and Angroo deeply disliked each other but shared a mutual appreciation for each others' skills and coexisted well enough as a result. Molar-Licker was second-in-command, and except for their similar physical appearance he seemed nothing at all like his brother. Angroo looked down at him as he continued to sit on the floor.

"You still haven't told me why you called me in here," he said after a while.

"I called you in here to notify you of our plans to attack Victory City," answered Molar-Licker. Angroo's eyes widened as he looked around.

"Why are *you* telling me this? Does everyone else know about it already?"

"Yes, everyone knows. Everyone important, anyway."

"Whose idea was this!? What reason do we have to risk

our lives? Is it our so-called *lust for blood* that, as orcs, we all share?"

"I wanted to tell you in private so that I could fully explain it to you. Angroo, *they* attacked *us* first. You saw it with your own two eyes."

"Don't pretend that we weren't readying ourselves to attack them before that little skirmish. What choice did they have?"

"You sound like you're one of them, Angroo. They want to exterminate all orcs. That's why we must strike first."

"That's not the reason. We're just attacking them because we're *savages*. It's practically our job to attack somebody!"

"So are you saying that you want them to kill us? You want them to kill all of your brethren?" Angroo squinted in disgust.

"Of course not!" he spit. "Nothing could be further from the truth! I'd give everything to protect my kin! You know that."

"And you also know that they have the capability to wipe us out, don't you?" There was a short silence.

"Yes. They are capable of doing that. But that doesn't mean…"

"You knew that it was coming to this anyway, didn't you?"

"Yes, I did. I guess I knew it all along."

"Sometimes it's hard to do what's necessary for your survival and the survival of your people. But it's something that has to be done, and tonight's the night. The humans are currently meeting with elven and dwarven representatives to discuss their plan of attack. If we strike tonight, we will hit them when they are most vulnerable. We will strike at dusk."

Just then, a four-year-old orc child crawled into the room. He was very fat and was naked except for a shirt made from animal skin.

"Orkianu! What are you doing in here!?"

"Dudududududududududust seein what yor ddddooin in here mista!"

"We have important matters to discuss. Your childish blabbering has no place in our conversation."

"Ooooo okay dere mista! I dust wanded to help in duh stwike adddd dddusk!" Orkianu banged some rocks together for a while and then crawled out of the room, leaving a trail of feces behind him.

"Stupid kid. He'll grow up to be a doofus like the rest of his family. Nothing but a little fat nuisance. Now anyway, Angroo, do you understand why we are doing this then?"

"Yes. I already said yes."

"Good. Then you will put everything you have into the battle?"

Angroo nodded.

"We need you. May the spirits guide your step." Angroo nodded again and left the room, contemplating what the shaman had just told him. Outside, in a different area of the cave, various orcs were running around and readying their weapons. He was starting to get a little bit of a headache as he walked past his tribesmen.

"Heh! We's gonna kill us some pink-skins!" chuckled one of the orcs. Angroo didn't like to hear that.

"You make it sound like some sort of game. This is a very serious matter, Grokk…" The orc suddenly turned and stared confrontationally at him. Angroo returned his stare but suddenly twisted his head around when he thought he heard something move behind him; seeing nothing, he turned back.

"You sound like one of them, white-skin!" responded the orc.

"Hey, I heard what you said to ol' Grokk there. You

make Klork angry. What you have to say for yourself?!"

"You going to give us speech, philosopher?"

"Hurr!! He not saying anything!"

"You think you better than us?"

"No one can challenge my right to kill puny humans!"

"Yah! You listen to what Krugg say! No one challenge our right to kill!"

"Enough, all of you!" shouted Angroo. "This will be a highly strategic strike. It's not for your personal entertainment."

"Has anyone seen young Orkianu!?" yelled an obese female orc. "He not in bed, and it be way past little baby's bedtime!"

"He was crawling around here somewhere. He'll show up." Angroo turned around. "Now, warriors, continue battle preparations. Save the fighting for tonight and prepare to march. We will strike in three hours – at dusk."

Chapter 6

"I bet you're all wondering why you're gathered here," stated Prince Lucio.

"Ya bet we are, fruit cup!" shouted the gruff dwarf. He had a long gray and brown beard, wore heavy, green-tinted metal armor from his head to his feet, and carried a two-handed battleaxe. "Ya better have a good reason fer draggin ol' McDuff all the way up here!"

"I'm sure there's a perfectly good explanation, McDuff."

"Thank you, Lord Eliazer. Yes, Lord McDuff, there is a very good reason why you and your troops are here." The prince looked around at the others in the room. McDuff and several of his dwarves leaned on their weapons; they were obviously all tired and bored. McDuff, known to his followers as McDuff the Great, was a fearsome fighter who was the leader of a large clan of belligerent dwarves hailing from the south. Eliazer, the king of the elves from the city of Elkanshire, had long blond hair and carried a quarterstaff that he used as a weapon. He was accompanied by his teenage daughter, Princess Silara, and a handful of elven soldiers. Also present were Crista, General Richmond, and numerous Victory City soldiers and officials.

"Yes..."

"As you have no doubt heard, my father, King Lucius, was murdered last week. And the esteemed Sir Milkbone, one of the most well-respected noblemen in the whole city, was also murdered in the same foul manner. The poor men were found with their brains missing."

"I've heard of a brain drain, but that's just absurd, lad!"

"Please keep your comments to yourself, Lord McDuff. Now where was I? Our scouts have reported that orcs are mobilizing around our borders. I have no doubt that they are responsible for these grisly murders that have shaken the very foundations of our fine city!"

"Orcs are a pestilence indeed!" said Eliazer. "But Prince Lucio, what makes you believe that they are the ones responsible?"

"Responsible er not, we dwarves have better things ta do than risk our life and limb helpin' ya fight them!" shouted McDuff.

"Yey!" roared the dwarves.

"But they have our royal crown!" shouted Lucio. "Our royal crown! Tradition states that a new king cannot be appointed without the crown, and our city will be thrown into disarray as long as it's in the orcs' possession!"

"My fist's gonna be thrown into yer face-array if ya don't stop yer blabberin'. Us dwarves got better things ta do than sit here listenin' to ya mope and whine."

"And you still haven't answered my question, with all due respect! Why do you believe that the orcs are responsible for the murders?" The prince sighed.

"Lord Eliazer and Lord McDuff. May I have a private word with the two of you?" The elf and dwarf followed the prince into a smaller side room, and the prince shut the door behind them.

"There's more to this than meets the eye, isn't there?"

"Of course there is, Lord Eliazer. They stole the Golden Eggs of Gotty Gottya!"

"The *legendary* Golden Eggs of Gotty Gottya!?"

"The very same. Both of them. You are now the only one who still possesses an Egg, Lord Eliazer." A short silence followed.

"This is grim news indeed," muttered Eliazer, his mind teeming with thoughts. "It *must* have been the orcs, then. This could change everything."

"Now you see why this is such a dire situation. If they lay their hands on the third and final Egg, then there will be nothing left to stop them from overrunning my city!"

"You can count on me to protect the final Golden Egg, Prince. I assure you only my closest advisors know where I've hidden it."

"Are you absolutely positive that it's secure, Lord Eliazer? Would you feel better if Victory City safeguarded the Golden Egg for you? Our military is larger and more powerful than that of Elkanshire."

Eliazer grimaced as he returned the prince's gaze.

"Well, I don't think..."

"Ha!" interjected McDuff. "Real funny. Some nice track record you have protectin' em, huh lad?! Ya might as well jus' hand it right over ta the orcs, an' yer brain right along with it! But I still don't see why ya have ta get the dwarves involved in all this hullabaloo."

"One of the Eggs originally belonged to your dwarven clan."

"Well, obviously not anymore! Not since yer blubber-headed nobleman took it from us, thinkin' it was some sort a shiny trinket!"

"Still, it is your responsibility to protect the Golden Eggs! Surely you must remember the Legend of Gotty Gottya!"

"A' course I do. So what?! There are other ways to fight those lily-livered green-skins, ya know. We don't need the stinkin' Egg!"

"Come on, Lord McDuff! Victory City needs your help!"

"I'm sorry 'bout what yer city's goin' through, lad. Really am. But I'll be a scoundrel if ever there was one the day when I have to resort to trekkin' my boys up north just ta have 'em die defendin' someone else's honor. And certainly, *certainly* not fer that blasted Egg! Now if you'll kindly excuse me, lad, out on ya's not gonna walk itself!" McDuff left the room.

"You're making a serious mistake, Lord McDuff!" shouted the prince. "Please reconsider!"

"Come on, lads. Let's get ta' movin'. Have a good evenin', Lucio my lad!" The dwarves grabbed their belongings and walked out of the conference room, visibly annoyed at having been called there in the first place. Prince Lucio groaned as he watched the last of them leave, and then turned his attention to Eliazer.

"We'll help you, Prince Lucio," Eliazer muttered hesitantly. "But only because we understand the seriousness of the greater orc threat. The unification of our armies is the best way to hold the orcs in check and make sure that the remaining Golden Egg is protected."

"I agree, Lord Eliazer. Thank you for your cooperation. But I am disappointed by Lord McDuff's refusal to help."

"Are our combined forces enough for the orcs?" asked General Richmond. "They control an extensive network of caves all throughout the mountains. Perhaps it would be wise to enlist other allies as well."

"You're right as usual, General Richmond. And I know exactly who can replace the dwarves in our little alliance!"

"Who is that, My Lord?"

"Why, Methuselah the fire giant, of course!" laughed the prince. "I'm sure he has some forces to spare. And I have a feeling he'll be in a *very* sharing mood. What time is it, someone? Nightfall yet?"

"Almost, sir," said a soldier who was standing near a window. "The sun is beginning to set."

"All right, then. Perhaps we should disperse for the night."

Just then, the front door swung open with a loud thud.

A familiar figure stood in the doorway.

"No, My Prince! Do not go outside!"

"Yohannis?! You're alive!"

"What's going on, Yohannis?!" shouted the general as he rose out of his chair. Yohannis looked haggard and worn out. Twigs, leaves, and thorns were stuck in his hair and all over his dirty, ripped clothing. He was holding a half-naked, obese orc toddler by the shirt, and, without saying another word, he extended his arm and dropped the toddler onto the table in the center of the room.

"Stwike adddd dddddddddusk!" squealed Orkianu. "Stwike adddd ddddddddddddddddddusk!"

Chapter 7

Night began to fall on Victory City.

"I hunger for human flesh!" growled Tooth-Licker, chieftain of the orc tribe. "I say attack right now!"

"Not yet," warned Angroo. "We don't know if the coast is clear. The scouts should be back any minute."

"You not in charge, white-skin! *I* in charge! I say we attack at dusk! It dusk now! We attack now!" The two of them had been crouching in the bushes at the top of the hill, gazing down at the dark, undefended city walls below them. Hiding in the woods nearby were hundreds of heavily-armed orcish grunts waiting for the signal to charge.

"Hold off a little longer, Chieftain. We don't know if the enemies are preparing an ambush or not."

"I no care! No puny human stand in big Tooth-Licker's way!" Tooth-Licker certainly was big; standing over seven feet tall, he was the tallest orc in the tribe. "Nobody plan ambush while Tooth-Licker here! We attack humans now!" He turned to the other orcs. "Warriors, commence attack right now!"

The orcs began to mobilize. Angroo didn't feel like arguing anymore; he had already spent too much of his energy convincing his bloodthirsty tribesmen not to attack the group of dwarves that had left the city twenty minutes earlier. Angroo knew that the dwarves were furious fighters and that ambushing them would needlessly thin their numbers and possibly blow their cover; it was a stroke of good luck that they had left in the first place. In Angroo's mind, the only reason they were there was to strike the city itself in order to cripple its capacity to strike back, and any other action was unnecessary. But attacking the city at that particular moment wasn't such a bad idea, Angroo finally rationalized. The whole attack had been planned so meticulously by the tribe's leaders that there was no way the humans and elves could possibly have been expecting it. Maybe Tooth-Licker was right for once.

Forty orcs hurried towards the city gate, carrying between them a huge, sharpened log that they were using as a battering ram and gaining momentum as they sped forward into the muggy night. Angroo smiled as he watched from the top of the hill. Everything was going according to plan, and pretty soon the main gate would be in shambles.

The still of night was suddenly broken by the sound of arrows cutting through the thick air; a huge cloud of them had suddenly appeared from out of nowhere like a swarm of hornets and descended upon the heads of the attackers. The arrows found *all* of their targets. Angroo's heart sank in his chest as he watched the battering ram drop from the dead hands of his tribesmen and tumble the rest of the way down the hill, crashing harmlessly on its side into a guard tower.

"Damn it!" cried Angroo. "Damn it! How could they have known?!" He looked around frantically.

"CHARGE!!!" screamed Tooth-Licker. "FIRE THE CATAPULT!!!!" Throngs of orcs poured down the hill from all directions, screaming war cries and waving weapons in the air; many were felled by the archers within seconds. It was amazing how dramatically fortunes had changed in such a short time.

A crudely built catapult launched a massive boulder at the wall, landing a direct hit and punching a ten-foot-wide gap. Tooth-Licker ordered his warriors through the gap, but those who made it past the storm of arrows were immediately repelled by a greeting crew of spear-wielding human soldiers pouring out of the wall. The catapult flung another boulder, this time punching a gap at the base of a corner section connecting a tower to the main wall. The new opening was all the way in the northeast corner of the wall, out of range of most of the archers and poorly defended. Now was their chance to get into the city.

"This way!" shouted Angroo as he rushed down the hill. He and his band of warriors avoided several arrows as they pressed ahead with their heads down, finally arriving at the wall to find a single spear-carrying defender waiting for them with great anticipation.

"Foul orcs!" shouted the defender. "You all deserve death, you filthy scum!" Angroo charged forward and swung his trident like a bat, deflecting the man's spear and then whacking him in the face with the backswing. The man dropped his weapon and stumbled backwards as Angroo slashed him with a blade he had tied to his forearm. He then kicked the man to the ground and pressed his foot against his chest. In the dim light, Angroo could see that his contorted face was drenched with a mix of sweat and blood as he looked up with an unwavering aggressive stare. He couldn't do anything, though; he was unarmed and badly injured. He was already a casualty. Angroo eased up after a moment; there was no reason to finish him off.

"You filthy cur!" spit the man. "You sick, sick monster! Is this how you get your thrills, killing a man while he's down?!"

Angroo reflexively thrust his trident into the man's chest. The man convulsed with pain, vomited blood and rolled awkwardly to his side. Angroo stepped back.

"Ha! You sure show that weakling who boss, white-skin!" laughed one of his warriors.

"Yah! We not let single weak human live!"

"Yah!"

"Enough of this!" shouted Angroo. "Now's our chance to get into their city! Move it!" Almost as soon as he had said that, though, a huge cluster of human soldiers unexpectedly swept in from around the city walls and engaged them from their flank. These soldiers were armed primarily with swords, and they began to surround the orcish warriors. Angroo was forced to abandon his plan; he and several of his fighters rushed through the circle and managed to escape most of the way up the hill, but the remaining orcs were now completely surrounded by a superior number of humans.

"Drop your weapons!" yelled a dark-haired female who seemed to be one of their commanders. The orcs reluctantly did as they were instructed. "We will take these orcs into custody. Bind their arms and march them into the prison at once!"

"We're just gonna let them live?!" shouted one of the soldiers. "You saw what they just did to poor Morris, did you not?! That white one cut him down while he was helpless on the floor, cut him down in cold blood! These creatures don't understand mercy!"

"We're better than them," the commander answered dryly. The orcs were led one by one through the gap in the wall.

Angroo returned to the outskirts of the woods, where most of the surviving orcs had regrouped under the pitch-black shadows of the trees. Over a hundred orcs had already been captured or killed, and fifty more were crippled by injury, but they still outnumbered the defenders by a good margin and it seemed as though they had lost little of their morale.

"We divide now in two groups!" ordered Tooth-Licker. "One group follow me! One group follow white-skin! Leave no weak human or puny elf-man alive!" The battle-crazed warriors roared in approval of this plan and quickly organized for the attack. Angroo's group, by far the smaller of the two but still numbering about seventy-five, began to travel around the hill and towards another side of the city. Tooth-Licker's group attempted another frontal assault, distracting most of the defenders away from Angroo.

By this point, it had become apparent to Angroo that there was no way they could realistically capture the city in one night. Their cover had been blown and the city was too well-protected. The focus now would be to weaken the humans in any way possible and prepare for what would have to be a drawn-out conflict.

After several minutes of travel, the warriors found themselves within sight of the back gate of the city. Angroo couldn't believe his eyes: a brigade of about twenty-five or thirty humans had gathered with their weapons at their feet, apparently oblivious to the possibility that orcs were capable of hitting them on this side of the city, and now they were ripe for the taking. Their young commander was reading a map and shouting instructions to his men, readying them to cut off what he must have believed was an inevitable orc retreat. A nice healthy collection of prisoners would be the perfect tool to undermine Victory City; Angroo had finally caught a break.

The warriors quickly surrounded and surprised the brigade.

"Drop your weapons!" shouted Angroo. The men whipped their heads around to confront the orcs, their faces flush with anguish as they realized that there was no escape; they raised their hands above their heads. "Quickly, warriors! Tie their arms and take them back to the woods!" His orders came too late, though. The orcs had already begun to slaughter the unarmed humans.

"Chief Tooth-Licker say let no weak human live!"

"Stop!" cried Angroo. "Stop it! They're defenseless!" The slaughter continued. "We can use them to bargain with the city! To get our own prisoners back! Stop at once!" By this point, it was no use. The few humans who remained alive picked up their weapons and tried to fight back in vain. All thirty soon lay dead; there were no orc casualties.

"Ha! Humans weak!"

"Why did you do that?!" screamed Angroo as he seethed in rage. "Why?! You barbaric morons! They were defenseless! This was our chance to finally..."

An arrow whizzed past his face. Angroo dove out of the way of another arrow and scrambled up the hill; the sudden barrage drove the orcs in separate directions. Another wave of swordsmen suddenly rushed at them from out of the shadows and cut down those who had ventured too close to the wall. There were way too many of them, but there was no time for Angroo to get a good estimate of their number because he was forced to duck under another arrow salvo. He turned and sprinted back towards the woods, nearly colliding with Tooth-Licker.

"This way, white-skin!" shouted Tooth-Licker as he pulled Angroo back with him.

"There are too many men that way, Chieftain! We can't take them!"

"Too many the other way!" answered Tooth-Licker as he continued to run, goring one of the soldiers with his horned helmet and continuing past the throng of enemies and away from the city. Angroo and a handful of other orcs hurried after him as he entered a stretch of the woods far from where the attack had originally commenced. After a few minutes, when they had distanced themselves enough from the city's defenders, the orcs stopped to catch their breath.

"We're separated from everyone else," muttered Angroo. "We've been driven away. We'll have to find our way through the forest to get back to the others."

"We not going back yet, white one," grumbled Tooth-Licker. "We continue in this direction."

"What do you mean?! The warriors have nobody to lead them!"

"They already run back. They hiding back in the woods. The battle be lost."

"Then why won't we go back to them?"

"Them humans be looking for us," replied the chieftain. "They see us go here. They know we be cut off and they be coming to get us. Shhh. Listen." They stood still and halted their breathing; enemies were talking nearby. It was getting louder and louder. Angroo realized at this point that Tooth-Licker was right; there were too many soldiers on the prowl and only nine of them, so they couldn't get back. He took a deep breath. They would need to keep moving in order to survive.

Chapter 8

Two days had passed since the victory over the orcs. Eliazer, king of the elves, sat in the hall of Prince Lucio with his daughter, Silara. It was late and they were both tired. They thought they were alone.

"There you are, sir. I've been looking all over for you." A man stepped out of the shadows.

"What is this about?" asked Eliazer, looking up at the man. "Who are you?"

"I have a little proposition for you, sir." The man was a little over six feet tall and had a curly red mustache. The image of a gray foot was emblazoned on his black shirt.

"Silara, please leave the room. Daddy has some special business to discuss with this man, tootsie." Silara didn't ask any questions and quickly left.

"Eight-hundred thousand gold pieces for the Egg, Eliazer."

"The Egg is, uh, not for sale."

"Are you sure about that?"

"Yes. I'm very sure." The man paced back and forth.

"Do you have the Egg on you now?"

"Of course not!"

"Where is it?"

"It's, uh, back home. Back in Elkanshire."

"What's going on in here!?" shouted Prince Lucio as he entered the room with three soldiers.

"Oh, Prince Lucio... what a pleasure. King Eliazer and I were just discussing something. It's really none of your concern."

"That symbol!" gasped Prince Lucio as he noticed the foot on the man's shirt. "You must be here for the Golden Egg of Gotty Gottya!"

36

"What makes you so certain?"

"Leave at once, villain! You are not welcome in my court!" The prince's soldiers drew their swords. "Make haste or my men will throw you out!"

"Such big words, sir. Your men couldn't even throw a tantrum."

"RRRRRR!!!!!! I'll show you what my men can do! Sir Rubbington!" One of the soldiers stepped forward. Nothing in his appearance set him apart from the other soldiers. "Sir Rubbington, please demonstrate what will happen to our friend here if he fails to leave at once!"

The soldier nodded his head. He then raised his hands into the air and began to wave them. A glob of dark green, bubbly acid sprung out of his palms and blasted a small statue on the other side of the room, reducing it to a slimy, plastery blob in seconds!

"Oh, a bit of sorcery!" cried the mustached man, holding his pointer finger to his lips for a fleeting second. "Very, very impressive. Now watch this!"

The man snapped his fingers. Three hooded figures simultaneously stepped out of the darkness behind him and lifted their hands above their heads; lightning flashed from their fingertips and struck Rubbington and the other two soldiers! The soldiers wobbled and fell limply to the ground with loud clanks.

"What have you done?!" cried Lucio as he grabbed for his sword. "You've killed them!"

"They're not dead. My helpers here just gave them a little shock to the system, that's all." The soldiers still didn't get up, though.

"You fiends!" cried Eliazer.

"I hope you all enjoyed this little demonstration. Just imagine what we could do if we were really trying." The man looked at Eliazer. "Perhaps you should reconsider my offer, sir. I wouldn't want anything unfortunate to happen to you or *someone you care about*. Now, have a pleasant evening." He and his three men turned and walked back into the darkness.

"Oh no..." mumbled Eliazer as he shook his head in disbelief. "Oh no!"

Chapter 9

"So you were just waiting in the forest for an entire week, Yohannis? What made you decide to do that? You could have escaped with the rest of us."

"*Somebody* had to protect our city. *Somebody* had to keep an eye on the grubby pig-faces. I knew they would be planning something sinister, and I was right."

"What did you do the whole time?" asked the general. "You didn't even have any supplies with you." Yohannis opened his mouth to answer but stumbled on a lava rock and fell before he could say anything, rolling back down the steep, narrow mountain path they had been climbing. He grabbed onto a dead branch and stopped himself before tumbling too far, though, and he climbed back towards the others. He brushed himself off and grunted loudly, more annoyed than embarrassed at having tripped.

"Oh, it was just great. I had to hide the entire freaking time, sitting and doing absolutely nothing! The whole time! And I was forced to eat disgusting insects the whole time also! You hear that? Doing nothing but sitting and doing nothing, with putrid, foul, six-legged, bug-eyed vermin my only sustenance! But it was worth it, of course. If not for me, the savages would have taken us completely by surprise!" As they turned a corner, he stopped talking and looked up at the huge, black, wooden gate that suddenly stood ahead of them. They had finally arrived at their destination. General Richmond walked ahead and pushed a gigantic wooden knocker against the gate, generating a thundering boom that startled the rest of the group. A moment later, the head of a giant rose up from behind the top of the blackened, charred walls.

"Yes? Who is it!?" shouted the giant.

"Representatives from the Court of Victory City," replied

the general. "We have been sent here by our prince to discuss a matter of grave importance with your leader, Lord Methuselah. We request his audience." The giant stared down from his guard post at General Richmond, Yohannis, and the small detachment of men who accompanied them. He had an ugly, greasy face and was completely bald, and his huge ears were festooned with hoop earrings. He had brick red skin and wore a slick, black uniform that fit tightly on his muscular upper body.

"METHUSELAH!!!" shouted the giant, the sonic pulse of his voice rattling the ground. "METHUSELAH!!!!!!! SOMEONE'S HERE TO SEE YOU!!!!!!!"

"Moving like wild fire!" shouted a voice in the distance.

"That means he's hurrying up and almost here," explained the giant. "It's fire giant speak, guess you can say." General Richmond nodded and stepped back slowly. He and his men used this opportunity to finally look around and take in their surreal surroundings: the sky was blood red where it wasn't blanketed in black smoke from volcano eruptions, while massive gray and black stones covered the ground where they stood. Dark mountains dotted the landscape. It was very warm, and the air was dry and smelled smoky. They were high in the fiery mountains of Flamewind, the capital of a region known as the Fire Realm.

"Ah, more little people!" chuckled Methuselah as he peered over the wall. "Why didn't you tell me, Gnarly?"

"Shall I open the gate for them, sire?"

"Of course, Gnarly. We wouldn't want to be rude to the little runts now, would we?" The huge black doors creaked open. "Now what brings you little midgets all the way here?" Methuselah had a long reddish-gray beard and he wore a blacksmith apron and a helmet. He was a little bit bigger and about a foot taller than his henchman. Slung over his shoulder was an enormous, flaming greatsword that looked as though it were made of molten lava. He smiled haughtily as he gazed down at them.

"Enough of your name-calling, hothead!" screamed Yohannis. "Your kind would do well to leave our kind alone, lest we slay you where you stand!"

"Please ignore him, Lord Methuselah," said General Richmond.

"No, no! I enjoy his antics, actually!" chuckled the giant as he kneeled down and playfully flicked Yohannis into the mountain wall.

"The people of Victory City, as well as their allies, the high elves of Elkanshire, are currently engaged in war with the orcs," said General Richmond. "We have been sent by Prince Lucio Pensword to seek the help of the people of the Fire Realm in our war against these savage creatures."
Methuselah stood up.

"Orcs?"

"Yes, Lord Methuselah. The whole tribe is mobilizing against us. The situation is dire."

"Hmm…" Methuselah stroked his long beard. "I assume you speak of the orcs in the mountains west of here. They are savages indeed, General. Rotten scoundrels, all of 'em. But they do not threaten *us.* Why should *we* feel inclined to help *you*?"

"We don't need any help from these overgrown freaks and their fancy, italicized words, General!" screamed Yohannis as he aimed an arrow at Methuselah's head.

"Hold your fire, Yohannis! This is very important! Now is not the time for hostility!" General Richmond turned back to face the fire giants. "Methuselah, I have been told by Prince Lucio that you owe a debt to our city. Is that true?"

"Ha! A debt to you little people?! Preposterous! What

kind of debt?!"

"A *gambling* debt, Lord Methuselah. According to our prince, you are very deep in debt from a gambling binge years ago."

"Hahahahahaha!!!" Methuselah shook the earth with his hearty chuckle.
"Hahahahahahahahahahahahahahahahahaha!!! A gambling debt!? A gambling debt!? Why, never have I heard such silly rubbish!" He looked at Gnarly and shrugged.

"According to this contract that bears your signature…"

"Okay, okay, enough! Enough! Fine! We'll send troops to help! I'll send all of our troops, in fact! Every single last one of them! There, does that settle our stupid debt?!" Gnarly glanced up at him with an agitated expression on his face.

"My Lord, with all due respect, when did you waste all of our kingdom's resources gambling in Victory City?!"

"It was a different time then, Gnarly. I was young, and…"

"But you haven't been young for over nine-hundred years!"

"Look, I'm sorry, okay?" Gnarly shook his head in disgust. An awkward silence followed.

"You're lucky we're letting you help us, overgrown cretins!" hollered Yohannis. "In fact, I seriously doubt we can even trust you to keep your word, being unholy creatures from the fires of Hell as you are! Why, you'll probably end up siding with those filthy, brain-eating orcs! Maybe I should just finish you off right now!" Yohannis reached for his quiver and pulled out five more arrows.

"Yohannis, enough!" shouted General Richmond. "Lord Methuselah, we graciously accept your offer of assistance! When will the reinforcements arrive?"

"Within a few weeks, I'd say," muttered Methuselah as

he paced around with long strides. "It takes time to organize the troops. My fire giant warriors are fickle and are spread far and wide throughout this kingdom; it'll be no small task to round them up and force them to march, though it has been done before."

"A few weeks?! Is there any way you can spare anyone sooner than that? Time is of the essence and we cannot just return to the city empty-handed."

"As I said, it takes time to organize the troops. I just..." Methuselah suddenly held out his hands as he noticed General Richmond reach for the contract again. He winced and slowly rolled his eyes. "All right, all right. I suppose it would be befitting of me to send you with *someone*. My apprentice has been itching to leave here for a while now, and..."

"Bah!" spit Yohannis. "Bah! I'm sickened by the very idea of traveling with your kind!"

"Yohannis!"

"It's okay, General. I'm sure your comrade-in-arms will be happy to know that my apprentice is a little shrimp like all of you."

"Pppppffffffff! A shrimp!? With all due respect, we neither want nor need the assistance of such slimy, slippery sea abominations!"

"No, not an actual shrimp! I meant a pipsqueak, just like all of you. A 'little person,' if you will, and one who you will find quite capable of fighting the orcs at that."

"Oh, a 'little person.' Interesting. Well, I hope your 'apprentice' really is as capable as you say and doesn't end up hiding like some sissy girl at the sight of those grotesque pig-noses." There was no response. "Well where is the sissy now, then!? Is wuwil baby sissy guwl afwaid to tawk to the scawy stwangers?"

"Enough, Yohannis!"

"You know what? Knowing you fiends, you probably really would try to dump some sissy, nagging jezebel on us! You wouldn't hesitate, would you?! It would be some kind of hilarious joke, right?! The last thing we would need is some cheeky she-devil undermining our war efforts by reminding us to tuck in our shirts, comb our hair, and wash our face and hands at every turn! Ha! Where are my buttermilk pancakes, cheeky she-devil?! That's more like it! And then you can finish sewing my socks! And then wash the dishes! *Such hilarity*! So, when do we meet him?"

Chapter 10

It had been nearly a week since Angroo, Tooth-Licker, and the few orcs who followed them into the woods had last seen the rest of their brethren. The Victory City armies that had been combing the land in search of stragglers from the battle had driven them further and further away. But now, *they* were the hunters. For several days now, they had been trailing a small detachment of humans that had left the city on some kind of special mission. They did not know where the men were headed but they followed anyway, waiting for the chance to ambush. They followed them all the way into the Fire Realm, where the humans traveled through a narrow pass in the mountains on their way to the city of Flamewind and were forced to leave their horses behind. The orcs drove off the horses and now waited patiently for the humans to return, in the meantime establishing a temporary base on the side of an inactive volcano where they were able to watch the roads.

Looking through his spyglass, Angroo was the first to notice the returning humans, and he realized that there was now a young woman among their numbers who hadn't originally been part of their group. The woman appeared to be in her early twenties; she had long, brown, wavy hair, soft facial features, high cheekbones, and dark green eyes. Her light leather armor did little to hide the curves of her body. Angroo immediately found himself attracted to her, which greatly disturbed and embarrassed him because he knew she wasn't an orc. But what was she, though? She seemed to possess the features of both a human and an elf. And why was she traveling with them?

"There little weaklings are!" laughed Tooth-Licker. "Prepare ambush now!"

"Remember what we discussed, Chieftain," said

Angroo. "There's a high-ranking officer among their group. We should capture as many of them as possible so that we can use them to gain leverage on the…"

"What I say, then?! Shoot to not kill?!" screamed an angry Tooth-Licker as he loaded a longbow. He motioned for the other orcs, who were positioned in various hiding places around the road, to do the same. Angroo loaded his bow and aimed at one of the soldiers near the front.

It took about a minute for the unsuspecting humans to walk into their range.

"Fire!" shouted Tooth-Licker. The bowstrings twanged, and three soldiers fell; Angroo was secretly relieved that the female was not among the fallen. As soon as the humans realized what was going on, they grouped together and prepared their weapons. The orcs reloaded and fired the next volley of arrows; two more men fell.

"Show yourselves, you cowardly, filth-encrusted bastards!" screamed a blond-haired soldier who starting running by himself towards the volcano. He nearly tripped over an orc that had been hiding in the tall grass, and then he kicked the orc's weapon out of his hand and fired an arrow through his head at point-blank range. Another orc, who had been squatting on a rocky ledge nearby, stood up and prepared to fire at the lone man. The man shot first, though, and hit the orc in the stomach, causing him to lose his balance and fall off the ledge to his death. Several arrows were fired at this soldier, all missing. By this point, the remaining humans had begun to charge towards the orcs' positions, so the orcs got up and ran towards their volcano base. Angroo, Tooth-Licker, and one other orc provided cover fire as the others returned to the safety of the base.

"They have thirteen left, and we have seven," whispered Angroo as he peered at the humans from behind a pile of rocks. "We'll need to be very careful if we want to even the odds."

"Careful? Ha! Humans puny!" laughed Tooth-Licker. "We kill them all, easy peasy!" Tooth-Licker motioned for one of his warriors to run out and attack; as soon as the warrior stepped out from behind the rocky outcropping, though, his body was stuffed with arrows.

"Coast… not clear…" reported the warrior as he fell lifelessly to the ground. Angroo gave Tooth-Licker an angry glare, then turned back to watch the humans. They had begun to climb the volcano in pursuit of the orcs and were now mere feet away from the trap that he had set.

"Onward!" screamed the blond soldier. "The cowards are up here!"

"Now!" whispered Angroo. Two orcs pushed a pile of boulders down a crude slide that had been dug out earlier; the boulders triggered a small landslide that tumbled down and landed at the base of the mountain trail with a thunderous crash, crushing two of the humans to death and cutting off any possible escape for the others. It had worked perfectly! Angroo howled in glee.

"You filthy orcs!" screeched the blond soldier. "I'll kill you all myself!" He began to fire arrows towards the rocky outcropping in a futile attempt to force the orcs to flee further up the mountain.

"Now!" shouted Angroo, this time not caring if the humans could hear him. Another pile of boulders was pushed, starting another chain reaction that led to a landslide blocking off the humans' ascent! The men found themselves stuck on a narrow stretch of the path surrounded by the mountain wall on two sides and huge piles of rocks in the front and back of the path. They were trapped like rats.

Angroo looked down at the panicking humans with a

gleeful smile. They were panicking because of something that *he* had planned and executed perfectly, something that had happened because of what *he* did. The idea that he could have such an effect on others empowered him. He felt invincible as he looked down at their anguished faces, one by one, but this feeling came to a halt when he got up to the female. She didn't seem to be afraid at all; in fact, she was looking around with a smug grin as if *she* were in control, not him. She was concentrating on her surroundings and seemed completely oblivious to her hopeless situation. What a stupid, arrogant fool. Angroo suddenly brimmed with anger; it was time for him to put her in her place.

"Surrender, humans!" he hollered.

"NEVER!!!" screamed the blond soldier.

"Warriors, forward! Push the rocks onto them! Crush them!" Angroo knew that attacking the humans head-on was a bit reckless, but he figured that this was the most direct way to intimidate them into surrendering. All of the orcs rushed down the path, waving their weapons and screaming battle cries.

Suddenly, a huge, dead tree landed behind the orcs with a loud crash of snapping branches. It was completely engulfed in flames! Now, the orcs found themselves clustered in a tiny space between the flaming tree and the very same pile of rocks that they had used to trap the humans!

"Idiot!" snarled Tooth-Licker as he kicked Angroo to the ground. "This why *I* lead charge! *I* say attack, not stupid white-skin weakling!"

"How could this have happened?!" muttered Angroo. Suddenly he realized; the woman must have been some kind of fire sorceress! She had lured the orcs into a trap of her own! It was the only explanation. Her reason for traveling with the humans had finally become clear to Angroo.

The fire suddenly spread down the trunk and flared out

of control!

"Fast! Retreat!" screamed Tooth-Licker as he frantically climbed over the fire, searing his hands and feet. Angroo managed to follow him, but the others couldn't make it out before the flames were too high. Angroo ran as fast as he could but he couldn't escape hearing the horrible, tortured wails of the dying orcs as they burned behind him, wails that would live forever in his memory and would always remind him of his failure.

Chapter 11

The sun was beginning to set. It had taken several hours for the men to dig their way through the rocks, and now they were standing near the charred remains of the fallen tree and of the orcs who had been trapped by the tree.

"Collect our dead," ordered a morose General Richmond. "We will bring them back to the city for proper burial."

"Should we search for those orcs, sir?" asked one of the soldiers. "They couldn't have escaped this mountain."

"Vile, vile creatures," muttered Yohannis as he shook his head back and forth in disgust. "Cowardly, filthy, pig-faced abominations! I'll kill them myself!" He began to walk quickly up the mountain path.

"Yohannis, wait!" shouted the general. "It's too dangerous!"

"I'll go with him, General Fishmond," said the sorceress. "Don't worry."

"It's Richmond."

"Uh, sorry. You'd think I'd remember your name by now." She smiled. "Seriously, though, I think it's best that I go with him. I'm a specialist at this kind of thing."

"Are you sure you want to do it, Firelight?"

"Yeah. It's better if we don't lose any more lives to their traps. I can handle them by myself." Up until that point, the sorceress had not said much.

"Very well, but be careful." Firelight nodded her head and followed Yohannis up the trail, her hair blowing softly in the breeze as she ascended. The general ordered his troops to prepare their weapons in case any orcs attempted to retreat down the mountain, and then it was time to wait.

Fifteen minutes passed without a sound, and the sky

was almost completely dark. The general started to become anxious; he turned to face his men.

"Flopson!"

"Sir, yes sir!"

"Come with me. I can't wait for them any longer. Lead the way."

The soldier nodded his head and ran up the path, with General Richmond following close behind. The two of them traveled up the mountain for a couple of minutes until the general stopped in his tracks.

"Flopson, come here! There's a secret entrance!" The general pushed a boulder away from the mountain wall, revealing a narrow corridor. "You first, Flopson. Be careful."

The tunnel was very quiet and dark, and the rocky walls were warm to the touch. They crept forward slowly. Very slowly.

The corridor widened, but they didn't have the chance to go very far before Flopson unexpectedly collided with someone. The shadowy figure jumped back in surprise, but then plunged forward; it was all over in seconds as Flopson screamed and fell to the ground. The figure stepped forward into a patch of moonlight that radiated in from a crack in the wall; it was the white orc. General Richmond was suddenly gripped with panic as he leapt backwards.

The huge orc took another step closer. He was an imposing sight, armed to the teeth: in addition to his blood-soaked trident, he had long, sharp blades tied to each of his arms, an axe in his belt, and a dagger tied to his shin. He wore thick hide armor, complete with spiked shoulder pads and knee pads. Two long tusks protruded upwards from the sides of his wide lower lip. His facial features were sharp and well-defined for an orcish face, the general thought, but the savage, fire-red glare of his eyes erased any doubt that the creature in front of him was not human.

General Richmond swung his sword at the orc, who stepped back and caught the sword in his trident. The general let go of his sword and quickly grabbed Flopson's, which had been lying on the ground, immediately parrying one of the white orc's trident thrusts. He then jumped out of the way of a second trident attack and knocked the weapon out of the orc's hand with a sudden, fierce kick. The orc tried to stab him with his arm-blade, but the general parried this attack as well.

The orc backed up, and the general rushed forward and swung his sword, cutting into the orc's arm. His next swing was blocked by the orc's blade. The orc smashed the sword out of the general's hand and walked forward, backing him into the wall. He lifted his arm to strike, but the general picked up a rock and bashed the orc's arm out of the way. He kicked the orc to the ground with all his might and then quickly recovered his sword from the ground and held it at the orc's neck. His face was drenched in sweat as he looked down at his frozen foe. He had emerged the victor.

"Don't move a muscle!" shouted General Richmond. "Where is the other orc?! The big one you were with?! Your chief?!" The white orc did not respond. The general heard loud, heavy breathing coming from behind; he turned his head to see the chief orc standing in the corridor entrance directly behind him!

"My, my. Looky what we got here!" laughed the chieftain. He was big and ugly. The general figured that he was well over seven feet tall, and his blood-red eyes stared down with contempt. He smirked and lifted a huge pickaxe over his head, bringing it down with such violent force that the general's sword was flung far off into the darkness with an ear-shattering clang as he tried to block the blow. The general jumped out of the way of a second vicious swing. Now the white orc was free, and the two orcs surrounded the general and forced him into a dark corner.

"We must take him alive, Chief Tooth-Licker!" shouted the white orc. "I'll bind his hands!"

"NO!" roared the chieftain in disgust. "NO, white-skin! I through listening to you!" The chieftain lifted his pickaxe very high above his head. "I the chieftain here! I kill puny human, NOT MAKE NICE!!" But the only thing faster than the pickaxe making its descent towards its helpless target was the white orc's own weapon intercepting it in midair and whacking it away with one swift lateral motion.

Suddenly, an arrow whizzed past and smashed against the wall. General Richmond looked up to see Yohannis and Firelight standing in the corridor entrance. The orc chieftain had no time to react before Yohannis sent an arrow through his neck; he let out one last muted wail that sounded more like a hiss than a scream as he crumpled to the ground in a fountain of blood. The white orc ran towards the exit, but a sudden burst of flame from Firelight's hands forced him backwards. General Richmond smashed him over the head with the butt of his sword, causing him to fall to the ground and drop his weapon. Yohannis held his loaded bow to the orc's head.

"This is for what you and your kind did to the good King Lucius, you murderous freak!"

"No! Don't shoot him!" shouted the general. Yohannis held his fire. "Don't shoot. This orc saved my life. We'll take him back as a prisoner."

"Saved your life?!" sputtered a flabbergasted Yohannis. "This villainous being of filth?! Such foul maggots are incapable of noble deeds!"

"Remove his weapons and armor, and bind his hands. We'll take him with us back to the city for questioning."

Yohannis begrudgingly did as he was told. The orc didn't resist; he had a blank expression on his face as he was led outside and down the mountain trail.

"It sickens me that we are letting this hideous piece of scum live," muttered Yohannis after they had returned to the base of the mountain. "We saw him kill our comrades-in-arms. He deserves to be cut down where he stands!"

"This orc tried to take me alive when I was helpless, Yohannis. He will receive equal treatment."

"You never should have gotten yourself into such a predicament, *Richmond*!" bleated Yohannis. "Why didn't you stay back like you said you would and let me and the half-breed witch take care of the wretched beasts?!"

"I became worried when you didn't return. You were taking a long time."

"Well that's because this idiot mongrel woman, who supposedly came here to 'help' us, led me into a dead end instead!"

"It was too dark! We couldn't see the cave entrance!"

"Oh, then why didn't you light up a torch using your 'magical powers,' half-breed?"

"Enough, Yohannis! We owe her a debt of gratitude for saving our lives earlier today! She outsmarted the orcs!"

"With all due respect, General, a freaking flea-ridden monkey could have outsmarted the freaking pig-noses. Even freaking Orkianu could have outsmarted the freaking pig-noses. We don't need some high-and-mighty 'sorceress' to come here and…"

"Listen!" yelled Firelight as she pointed her finger menacingly at Yohannis's face. "I don't have to take this from you! You should be thanking your lucky stars that someone with my talent is…"

"Your *talent*?" snickered Yohannis. "You have *talent* now? Talent for getting everyone around you killed, maybe!"

"I have more *talent* in my little finger…"

"Oh, so *that's* where you keep all of your talent, is it? Doesn't seem like there's room for much talent in your little finger, though. If you were really trying to impress me you should have said that you keep it in your big, fat…"

"Both of you knock it off!" shouted the general. "Yohannis, get a grip!"

"No! I'm the only one who understands what we're up against, and no one ever listens to what I have to say! These are vicious, stupid, idiotic animals you're trying to befriend! Freaks of nature! They're all a bunch of sniveling idiots!" Yohannis walked over and knelt down next to the orc prisoner, who was sitting on the floor, and stared at him while he tried to look away. "You hear that, whitey? Hey!" He snapped his fingers in the orc's face. "Hey! Hey, you hear that? I'm talking about your family. Mom, dad, bro, sis. Even old grandma pig-face. They're all a bunch of sniveling, snot-nosed morons! That's what I said! They're all freaking morons! Their lives are worth nothing!" There was no response. The orc's expression did not change as he stared at the ground. Yohannis shoved him but was restrained by the general before he could do anything else.

"You need to control your emotions, Yohannis. I know that you're upset about what happened to our comrades today, as we all are. But it's part of war." Yohannis slowly shook his head.

"I'm just so angry that we're so quick to trust this murderous simpleton," he muttered. "He was just trying to kill us a few minutes ago, but now he's practically our best friend. Orcs can never be trusted. They're just *different*."

"We should give him a chance. He showed character. We should just give him a chance." Yohannis spit at the dirt but didn't say anything else. The general turned to the rest of the group. "Men, we'll rest here for the night. Set up camp. We'll depart tomorrow at dawn."

Chapter 12

It was a gloomy day in Victory City. It was very hot and humid outside, but it was also somewhat dark because the sky was filled with clouds. A young man lay on a bed inside of the castle, covered nearly from head to toe in bandages. He stared blankly out the window.

"Are you recovering well, Sir Rubbington?" asked a woman. The man was startled; he hadn't noticed her arrival.

"As well as can be expected," he responded weakly. He looked up at the woman standing at his bedside; she was quite a beauty. Her gray eyes and silky skin contrasted strongly with her reddish, earthy hair. She was wearing a dull white outfit that appeared to be very tight on her, especially in the chest area. He was mesmerized.

"Do you know who is responsible for your condition?"

"Three wizards. I don't know anything else about them, Crista. They were wearing hoods. I don't think they were especially powerful, though, whoever they were."

"That's a funny thing to say considering you have burns all over your body from their lightning spell."

"In my years of training, I've seen more powerful magic. The lightning itself wasn't nearly as strong as it could have been." He sighed. "Just a little shock. The reason I'm so badly burned is because I was wearing full plate armor at the time, so my skin was covered in metal." Crista nodded her head.

"I don't think I've ever seen you wearing so much armor."

"I'm the court wizard, Crista. I'm not supposed to be dressed up like a common soldier. However, the prince insisted that I come fully armored." Crista paced around the small room.

"Did the prince seem to think an attack was imminent,

Sir Rubbington?"

"Uh… yes, yes he did. He wanted us to dress in full armor because he thought there was somebody in his halls who didn't belong. He thought it would turn into a fight."

"That seems to make sense, then. I suppose he wanted to disguise you as a normal soldier, to give him an element of surprise if he needed it. Consistent with his way of thinking, I'd say." She looked out the window. "Do you know how he knew there were enemies in his castle?"

"No, he said nothing about that. He just told me to equip myself with heavy armor and follow him."

"Interesting."

"Madam! No visitors allowed at this time!" Crista turned quickly to see a tall man wearing a blue outfit. His face was almost completely covered by a large surgical mask; the only parts of it she could see were his eyes staring belligerently down at her. The man's hand came down on her shoulder but she pushed it off.

"Anyway, I'd better be off. Get well soon, Sir Rubbington." She left the room as quietly as she had entered.

Chapter 13

They had been traveling with the white orc for two days already, and he still hadn't said a word. General Richmond finally tried to initiate a conversation with the captive, whose arms were tied and who was being held by two soldiers as he walked.

"Do you have a name, orc?" asked the general. No response. The orc just stared.

"You can't expect meaningful dialog from these savages, General Richmond," explained Yohannis. "Their purpose in life is to be cut down like animals. They know nothing of civility."

"Angroo," muttered the orc. "My name is Angroo." The general and his men were somewhat taken aback by the orc's sudden willingness to talk.

"I'm glad you've finally decided to speak, Angroo. My name is Charles Richmond and this is Yoha..."

"I know who you are."

They arrived at a fork in the road and stopped. The general took out a map and examined it for several minutes without reaching a definite conclusion about which way to go. However, the fact that the trail on the left led into a forested area led him to believe that the trail on the right would be the safest route. He ordered the others to head to the right.

"Move left!" the orc suddenly shouted. Yohannis swung around.

"Don't even think about listening to this scum, General Richmond! There's surely quicksand or some other peril awaiting us if we venture into the woods on the left!"

"Perhaps we should listen," answered the general. "Are you sure about this, Angroo?"

"Yes."

"Angroo probably knows this area better than we do. He appears to be trustworthy. I suppose we…"

"General, no!"

"Yohannis may have a point," said Firelight. "I don't think we should be so quick to trust the prisoner."

"All right, all right," conceded the general. "Safety first, I suppose. Anyway, I think we came from the right on the way here because I do not recall going through such dense wood at this location. Men, to the right!" The party turned right and walked for several paces.

"I'm disgusted that we even considered letting the lying bastard guide us!" snarled Yohannis as he looked up at the sky. "Who knows what manner of hidden trap might have awaited us had we traveled the way he sug…"

"Shh! Quiet!" whispered Firelight. "Something's wrong." Several men dressed in black and armed with swords suddenly leapt from the bushes! Firelight reacted quickly and drew her own sword, slashing one of the ruffians with it and then throwing a fireball at the others in the same fluid motion. Another man tried to rush her from behind, but she leapt out of the way and his blow never landed. Yohannis grabbed that man by the arm and flung him into the side of a tree, and then he loaded his bow and sent an arrow through the man's brain. Mere seconds after the ambush had begun, all four attackers lay dead along the trail.

"Bandits," mumbled the general. "Common highway thugs. They could have killed us." Everyone turned to look at the white orc.

"Human bandits frequent this road," muttered the orc. "Caravans avoid the woods just like you did and become easy pickings for the bandits."

"I suppose we should have listened to you, then, Angroo."

60

"Listen to a pig-face, General Richmond?! Did I just hear you correctly?! A freaking pig-face?! That's the most ridiculous thing I've ever heard in my entire life! The filthy cur obviously made an arrangement with those bandits to hide there simply so that he could tell us not to go right, and then once we didn't take his advice and went right anyway the bandits could jump out and attack us! All just so that we would think that we could trust him!"

They turned back and went left at the fork instead of right.

"So you know this area well?" asked the general. The orc nodded. Nobody said anything else for a couple of minutes.

"What do you orcs even want, Angroo?" asked Firelight. "Why are you attacking on such a large scale? I don't understand." The orc stared at her and didn't answer.

"Stop trying to communicate with the beast. Everything he says is a lie!"

"Angroo, why are the orcs attacking?" asked the general. The orc simply stared.

"Look into his eyes!" screamed Yohannis, startling everyone. "His cold, glaring eyes! He's calculating his next move, the sick animal! He's deciding how he will lie to us next, what kinds of foul tricks he will pull next! Can anyone else see this?!"

"Yohannis, let me remind you that even though he was an enemy, Angroo saved my life back there on the volcano. He didn't have to do what he did."

"I don't know what this pig-face tricked you into believing, but I've fought orcs for years and years! They have no moral understanding! They know only lying, killing, thievery and torture!"

"Well this orc might be different, Yohannis. Orcs are

often brutal savages, I agree. But *nothing* applies to everyone. Maybe you should try to understand that."

"*Nothing applies to everyone*! *Nothing applies to everyone*! Bah!" Yohannis shook his head in frustration. "Mere words, General! I've seen so many men killed by these foul creatures. So many good men. Have you forgotten what happened to King Lucius? He was ruthlessly murdered by the kin of this filthy creature! They cut his head open and ate his brain!"

"Ate his brain?"

"What, you think they just kept it as a souvenir?! Of course they ate his brain! They eat anything, the dogs! They ate Sir Milkbone's brain as well! Did these men of such high stature deserve such a gruesome fate?!"

"Yohannis…"

"I'm through listening to your pedantic reasoning, General!" screamed Yohannis as he stormed over to the white orc. He stared the orc directly in the eyes. "You remorseless insect! Mark my words: one day, I *will* kill you. I'll send an arrow right through your damn head, you swine-faced, brain-eating pig-nose!" Yohannis pointed his finger at the orc's forehead. Then he turned around and walked ahead of the others.

"Save your anger, Yohannis." said the general "Nothing applies to everyone. You know that." Nobody said anything else as they continued down the trail. Night began to set in.

Chapter 14

"You wanted to see me, Prince Lucio?"

"Yes, Lord Eliazer. Please come in and close the door behind you." Eliazer did as he was told. He was now alone in a small room with the prince, and the two of them sat down at a table.

"Has the general returned with word from Flamewind, Prince?"

"No, not yet. I'm becoming a little concerned, but I'll give it another day or so before I send out a search party for them." The prince looked around. "Now, Lord Eliazer, have *you* sent back for reinforcements? I think we underestimated the number of forces that we would need to fend off the orcish onslaught and the fire giants of Flamewind may not be enough. That is, if the giants ever show up."

"But Prince Lucio, we've already defeated the orcs in battle once. Decisively, if I remember. You think they still can muster enough strength to pose a serious threat to your city?"

"Of course, Lord Eliazer. Of course. They infest the mountains and forests. They've been planning this attack for years and they have unknown powers at their disposal. It would be foolish to give the battle anything less than the total combined strength of our two kingdoms."

"Well, I *have* sent for reinforcements. They should be arriving from Elkanshire in five or six days."

"Good, good. I just wanted to make sure about that. That will be all, Lord Eliazer." The elf king did not get up from his seat.

"Prince Lucio, who were those people who threatened me the other day?"

"You saw the symbol emblazoned on their shirts," the prince responded grimly.

"A dark foot. Yes, I know. Can it really be that they are part of the Order of the Filthy Foot?"

"I hope not, Lord Eliazer. I *pray* not."

"They must be loyal to Lord Footmol!"

"Must you say that cursed name in my halls, Lord Eliazer?! The mere sound of it makes me cringe!" He shook his head. "But yes, I believe it is the only possibility. They must be working for that villain."

"Dinther Footmol is a formidable enemy indeed, Prince Lucio."

"That is a serious understatement, Lord Eliazer. Please promise me that you will not let the remaining Golden Egg of Gotty Gottya fall into that miscreant's hands!"

"I'll do everything I can. But I am curious, though: why would Dinther Footmol collaborate so closely with the orcs? What motivation would he have?"

"I don't know, but who are we to try to decipher the wicked mind? Although, it is certainly possible that they each want the remaining Golden Egg for their own reasons and that they aren't working together at all." Eliazer scratched his chin.

"I think that's the case here, Prince. Footmol probably wants the Eggs for his own purposes. I quiver at the idea of any of them gaining control of the Eggs."

A faint, melodious sound suddenly intruded on their conversation. It was singing coming from another room.

"Is that your daughter, Lord Eliazer?"

"Yes. My beautiful Silara." The singing grew louder. It was accompanied by harp playing. A slight smile appeared on Prince Lucio's face.

"Princess Silara has a beautiful voice, Lord Eliazer. And she plays her instrument beautifully as well. You must be very proud of your daughter."

"Of course I am. She's a serious student of music,

Prince Lucio."

"I can tell. She must come to court and sing for us more often." They stopped talking for a moment to listen to the harmonious elven tune. It sounded kind of like Twinkle Twinkle Little Star.

"I love hearing that music. It makes me happy every time I hear it." A tear dripped down Eliazer's face. "Her mother would have been so proud of her, just as I am. I only wish she were still alive to hear her daughter's beautiful voice."

"What of her mother, Lord Eliazer? What ever became of your wife?" Eliazer's eyes welled up with tears.

"I'm sorry, but it pains me too much to say. There has been great sadness in our family."

"I understand," replied the prince. "I'm afraid I can relate to the situation. I never knew what happened to my mother because my father never told me anything about it. I was too young to remember her." Neither of them spoke for a minute as the singing in the other room continued. After a while, Eliazer pushed his chair back and stood up slowly. He nodded at the prince, who nodded back, and then left the room.

"Silara! Enough of your singing! You'll wake up everyone in the castle!" Silara stopped suddenly as her father entered the room. Her big, bright eyes avoided Eliazer's stern gaze.

"Daddy!"

"Silara, sweetie. We're in a foreign land. Prince Lucio was hospitable enough to let us stay here in his castle, and we simply can't keep everyone awake with loud noise. It wouldn't be fair."

"Noise?! But you said you love my singing!"

"Of course, pumpkin. But you're still young, and let's

just say that your voice needs to develop a little before everyone else will recognize your talent. You know that, dear." Silara nodded her head dejectedly. Her blond hair fell in front of her face as she looked down at the floor.

Suddenly, fierce growling interrupted the silence. A tiny yellow poodle ran out from under the bed and frantically yapped at Eliazer.

"Shhh! Quiet, Furlin! Don't you recognize Daddy?" The dog suddenly recognized Eliazer and it jumped up on its hind legs, its tail wagging like crazy.

"Make sure you keep the dog quiet, Silara. I'm regretting bringing him here already." Eliazer walked over and sat down next to his daughter on the bed. "And make sure *you* keep quiet as well."

"But Daddy…"

"Look. We don't know who could be listening to you. There are some strange people around here, and you don't have to draw any unneeded attention to yourself." He kissed Silara on the cheek and then got up and walked towards the door. "Now go to bed, sugar. It will all be better soon." He left the room.

Silara petted the puppy for a while. She began to think about what had just happened. Why did her father say those things? She knew she was a good singer and harp player, yet her father always seemed to hold her back. She was fifteen years old, not a little kid anymore. But her father seemed even more worried than usual this time. There wasn't really anything to be afraid of here in Victory City, was there? She didn't think there was, at least nothing that should force her to stop singing.

"Goodnight, Furlin," she said in her sweet, melodic voice. She stretched out her arms and yawned. "I'll see you in the morning, poodle puppy." She lay down on the bed and closed her eyes, completely unaware that she was being watched by someone hiding in the closet.

Chapter 15

It was late at night. Angroo's skin burned as painfully as it ever had, but the rope binding his hands to a pole left him unable to scratch his arms and legs. He suffered in silence as he brooded alone inside of a thick-walled tent; the humans had set up camp for the night and had left him by himself. The only source of light was a red glow that illuminated one side of the tent. Angroo watched the dark silhouettes of his captors as they sat around the campfire outside, laughing and joking about the day's events. It reminded him of nights he used to spend with the other warriors after successful hunting trips, but he figured those times were long gone.

The tent wall rippled slightly as the woman entered and walked over to where Angroo was sitting. She stood in front of him and looked down.

"Sorry if I'm intruding on your private thoughts. I wanted to apologize for doubting you earlier about the directions you gave us."

Angroo easily saw through her lies. He was an orc, and *nobody* trusted orcs. For good reason, in fact. She would have had to have been an idiot to trust him, especially after he had tried to kill all of them during the battle. Therefore, he didn't care at all that she didn't trust him earlier, and he knew that she knew he didn't care. She was too smart not to know that it wasn't something worth apologizing about.

"It's okay," he grumbled.

She kneeled down in front of him. He had a hard time maintaining his stern composure because his skin burned like never before.

"It seems like you're lonely in here. Seems like you want some company."

Angroo didn't answer as he braced for more sweet talk.

He knew he had to stay alert and try his best not to be pulled under by any of her interrogative methods.

"I know you're supposed to be our prisoner and all, but that doesn't mean we have to treat you like a complete outcast. I'm sure you've already suffered enough from being an outcast in your own tribe. I mean, your skin really sets you apart. You must have gone through a lot of hardship at the hands of your peers." Angroo winced at hearing this; what she said really hit home. Images of the brutality he had endured as a youth sprang to his mind even as he tried to repress them. This conversation was already taking a turn for the worse. He had no idea what kind of devious tricks the woman was trying to play with his mind, but he knew that he must do everything he could to resist; Molar-Licker had taught him not to trust anyone.

"Why are you saying this?"

"I feel sorry for you, Angroo, and I can relate to your struggles. My mother was an elf and my father was human. Because of my mixed blood, I've always been a little bit of an outcast myself; I've never felt truly accepted anywhere. Humans see my elven side, while elves see my human side. I'm always an outsider everywhere I go."

"You cannot relate to my struggles, woman. You have no idea what I've had to go through because of my appearance."

"You're right that I don't know what you've had to go through, but that doesn't mean I can't relate. We're both outsiders, and in a way that makes us the same." She paused. "But doesn't it kind of make everyone else the same as us, too? Isn't *everyone* an outsider? I mean, we only know about the world around us through our own senses and our own thoughts; all of the world exists outside of ourselves. Can we ever really be a part of it?"

"You cannot understand what I've been through."

"Can anyone really understand what anyone's been through, though? Maybe I don't know what I'm talking about here. But I just think it's good to try and put things in perspective, you know? You're not as different from the rest of us as the world makes you seem."

"Why are you talking like this? Why are you... being nice to me?" The woman didn't respond right away. She walked back and forth for several seconds, and then slowly turned and looked him directly in the eyes.

"General Richmond told me that you have a strong sense of honor. I just wanted to get to know you a little bit better so that I could judge for myself."

"You're wasting your time, then."

"Angroo, the way I was raised, I was always taught to have an open mind and to give everyone a chance. The fact that we happen to find ourselves on opposite sides in this war doesn't mean I have to hate you. Haven't I made that clear already?" Angroo simply stared up at her. Something about her seemed so fragile and delicate when compared to the other captors. Angroo's body began to quiver.

"You shouldn't..."

"General Richmond is a good man. He'll make sure that nothing bad happens to you when we arrive at the city because he sees something more in you than a bloodthirsty savage. He'll make sure that you're given the same respect you gave him back at the volcano, so just relax. Don't worry about it, okay?" She slowly turned and walked off. Angroo thought that she had a beautiful body. Fertile-looking body. Maybe these non-orcs weren't so bad after all.

Chapter 16

"What is it, Furlin? What's wrong?!" Silara jumped out of bed as her toy poodle growled at something in the corner of the room. The poodle was obviously very nervous as it stumbled backwards and stared, its growling mounting in intensity. Silara squinted; it looked like there was some kind of dark object in the corner. She walked over to it very, very slowly.

"It's just my harp, silly puppy! See?!" The dog cautiously approached the harp and sniffed it carefully. After thoroughly investigating the object, he began to wag his tail, clearly relieved at the harmlessness of the dark form. "Go back to sleep, puppy. It's way past your bedtime."

She began navigating back towards her bed. As she walked past the door, she was startled by a loud knock that rattled the entire wall and shattered the peaceful silence. Who could it be? Silara nervously opened the door and stepped back quickly as a tall, brutish man walked into the room without saying anything. In the dim light she was able to see his curly red mustache, and she immediately recognized him as the man her father had been talking to a few days earlier. She was petrified with fear.

"Princess Silara, sweetheart. Your father heard a racket coming from your room and asked me to check if everything is all right." He stepped closer. Furlin ran to attack but the man used his foot to sweep the tiny dog into the wall.

"That's unlike Daddy. Certainly he would have checked on me himself if he thought…"

"Your father is a very busy man. He is currently discussing matters of great importance with the good prince."

"Everything's okay here, mister. I'll just be going back to bed…" The man grabbed her arm before she could pull it away. He was much stronger than she was, and his tight grip paralyzed her.

"Please come with me, young one. Your father requested that I bring you somewhere safer."

The man suddenly released his grip and lurched forward – somebody had jumped onto his back and was holding something against his mouth! He struggled futilely for a couple of seconds and then fell on his face with a thud. He was still breathing but was otherwise motionless.

"That should keep him out for a while," whispered Crista. "Grab whatever you'll need for the next few days and come with me. Your life is in immediate danger."

Silara wasn't sure if she could trust this woman or where she had even come from, but she decided that it wasn't worth waiting for the man to get back up. She quickly changed into a thin white dress and followed the woman out of the room. She shut the door behind her and locked it; her dog had already left to find a hiding place as far away as possible, so now only the mustached man remained inside of the locked room.

They walked quickly through a dark hallway. When they arrived at a window near the end of the hallway, there was already a rope hanging from it and leading to the ground three stories below. It was obvious that the whole escape had already been planned out.

Crista quickly climbed down the rope and waited on the ground. Silara began to climb down slowly, but she lost her grip about halfway down and fell; luckily, Crista caught her before she landed. They hurried through the empty streets and towards the gates of the city wall. The two guards who were supposed to be guarding the gate were tied up and unconscious, rags stuffed in their mouths. Silara became very nervous.

"Why did you do this?" she gasped.

"Keep your voice down!" whispered Crista in a harsh tone. "I had no other choice. We cannot make a scene and we cannot trust anyone." She led Silara through the gate and out into the gray, starlit fields surrounding the city.

"You can trust my daddy."

"Obviously, your father wouldn't try to harm you. But I'm afraid that he wouldn't know who to trust himself. It's not safe to tell anybody what's going on until the time is right."

"But…"

"Listen to me carefully, Princess Silara. I've hired a ranger to lead you back to Elkanshire. He's an experienced traveler and he will keep you safe until your arrival. I hope you understand the severity of the situation."

"But I *don't* understand. What's going on? Who's trying to hurt me?!" Crista looked around so that she could be extra sure nobody was watching them.

"Your father holds a very valuable artifact that some people are trying to get their hands on. Evil people. They want to kidnap you so that they can demand the artifact as ransom for your release, and they will stop at nothing."

"What?! For a valuable artifact?"

"Yes. You have no idea how much it's worth to them. The villains will go through great measures to obtain it, and I don't want you to get hurt." Tears began rolling down Silara's cheeks.

"But, won't Daddy think I've been kidnapped now? Won't the evil men be able to pretend that they've kidnapped me?"

"I'll tell your father everything once there's time. Don't worry. But the important thing now is that we get you as far away as possible." They traveled for several minutes more towards the outskirts of the forest. Once they found good cover in the woods, they paused for a minute to catch their breath.

"Who is this ranger that you hired? Can I trust him?"

"I don't know him well, but he's an outsider. He has no way of knowing what's going on here. He'll just do his job without asking any questions, so you can trust him. I paid him well."

"But, I'm scared! I don't want to leave yet! Can't we go back and at least get my puppy?" They stopped and stood still when they heard some leaves rustle nearby.

"Grrrrrrrrrrrrrrrrrrrr!!!"

"Furlin!? You followed me all the way here!?"

"That's not your dog, Princess." They suddenly found themselves completely surrounded by wolves! Crista drew a short sword and held it towards the wolves as Silara hid behind her back. One of the beasts suddenly rushed forward; Crista swung her weapon in an arc and made hard contact with the wolf's snout, sending it to the ground with a yelp of pain. She wouldn't be as lucky the next time, though. A different wolf sprang from the side and shoved Crista to the ground, and several more pounced on her as she lay helpless on the cold forest floor.

"Help!!!" screamed Silara. "Somebody help!!!" She heard somebody rushing though the forest. A wolf approached Silara but the dark shape of a man sprung out of the brush and tackled the wolf to the ground! Another wolf tried to bite the man but Silara saw the gleam of a sword in the moonlight as the animal yelped and then fell backwards with a dull thud. The man leapt up and charged at the other wolves, driving them all away. He then walked slowly towards Silara. He was very big and brawny, but Silara couldn't make out what his face looked like in the darkness.

"What… who are you?!" screamed the elf princess as

she cowered on the ground.

"Name's Brack. Ranger fr' around these parts. Been hired to take y' back to your home, and I take m' business ver' seriously." He extended his hand to help her up, and she stood up slowly.

"Is she okay?" asked Silara as she gazed at Crista's motionless body. She was lying on her side, completely covered in shadows. Silara reached down to touch Crista's leg and felt nothing but cold, wet blood; she immediately pulled her hand away in horror.

"Leave her!" the man uttered gruffly. "She did what sh' could to protect you. Nowt's my turn. Let's go." Silara began to sob uncontrollably. What was happening? Would she ever see her family again? It was all so surreal. She couldn't control her hysterical crying and the ranger practically had to drag her off into the forest.

"Silara, dear?!" yelled Eliazer. "Silara, your dog ran into my room! Is everything all right?!" He arrived at his daughter's bedroom. The door was smashed open and nobody was inside. Eliazer's face turned pale.

Chapter 17

It was morning. Even though she had left the Fire Realm several days ago, the intense heat made Firelight feel like she hadn't gone anywhere. She continued to wonder about why she had been sent alone to help the people of Victory City as she lagged several yards behind the rest of the group; she wanted to put what she had spent all those years learning to good use somehow, but this wasn't exactly what she had in mind.

Maybe it wouldn't turn out so bad, though, she figured. After all, there might be some cute guys for her to meet in Victory City. That's where Yohannis was from, right? The place was probably crawling with blond-haired, muscular Adonises like him. Yohannis the Adonis. She started laughing out loud, but soon quieted herself and awkwardly covered her face with her hand to avoid detection. No others looked her way, though; they were consumed in their own silent misery as they continued forward under the bleary sun. Why was she on this trip again? She at least had to admit that spending all her time hanging out with giants, lizards, and other creatures of the volcano for the past few years had been getting pretty tiresome.

The orc prisoner, his hands still bound, walked ahead of her with two soldiers escorting him by the arms, and the rest of the group was several paces ahead of them. All of them were visibly fatigued from the heat as they trudged onward. The orc began to move his head. He spent a few seconds looking around, perhaps making sure Yohannis wasn't nearby, and then turned back towards the general.

"What will happen to me, Commander?" he muttered, breaking the silence that had persisted for at least a half hour. General Richmond turned his head to face the orc but continued to walk at the same speed.

"We're going to take you to the castle at Victory City, where we will ask you some questions."

"It's no use. I won't be able to tell you anything you don't already know." The general raised his hands into the air and called for everyone to gather. Once they were stopped, he walked up to the orc and faced him.

"Can you tell me why the orcs have decided to attack?"

"You attacked us first, Commander." The orc pointed to Yohannis. "He attacked us first. I saw everything."

"Lies!" howled an outraged Yohannis as he ripped an arrow from his quiver. "Nothing but lies! They murdered our king! I can hardly think of a more blatant way to start a war!"

"We still don't know for sure who murdered King Lucius," responded the general. "Yohannis, did you attack the orc camp before they attacked you? Were you the one who fired the first shot? You were, weren't you?"

"No! Of course not! Of all the despicable accusations... actually, I *did* attack first. But the filthy scoundrels were already camping outside of our walls, waiting for the opportunity to strike! Their intention was crystal clear!" General Richmond looked the orc in the eyes.

"Why were the orcs camping outside of the city walls, Angroo? Were they planning on attacking us?" The orc frowned and averted the general's gaze.

"I'll be honest, human. I don't think it was supposed to be such a widespread assault. It wasn't my idea, but my superiors wanted to raid your city for supplies."

"Yeah, supplies. Like the king's brain!"

"Yohannis, silence! Continue, Angroo."

"We prepared camps around your city because we wanted to be in position to cripple your forces if you attempted to attack us. We were afraid that Victory City was preparing to kill us all off." General Richmond scratched his beard.

"I was aware of no such plans. I will say, though, that the people of Victory City are very wary of orcs and that they were not prepared to tolerate the presence of orcs so close to their city walls. Your kind has been a threat to our city for a long time, and many of us fear you."

"It's okay," replied the orc. "I understand." Yohannis shook his head in disgust but didn't say anything. General Richmond crossed his arms.

"So the primary reason your tribe is attacking us is to prevent us from attacking your tribe?"

The orc nodded.

"Then it sounds to me like this war accomplishes little for either side and doesn't need to go on any longer. Angroo, if you and your warriors agree to leave the area around Victory City's walls and promise not to attack our city or our trade routes anymore, I will see to it that we leave you alone as well. There's no reason we can't coexist, is there? Would you agree to this truce?" A smile lit up the orc's face despite his apparent efforts to hide it. "Would you agree to a truce?"

"Of course I would."

"Outrageous!" screamed Yohannis as he jumped into the air. "You're saying you'll let these murderers off the hook for killing our king?"

"No, no," replied the general as he turned back to face the orc. "Angroo, are you certain that the orcs are not responsible for the assassination of King Lucius?" The orc shook his head.

"I don't think it was one of us, but there's no way for me to be sure. It wasn't discussed by our leadership. I suppose it's possible, though, that there's a renegade among us who would commit such a crime for his own causes." The orc paused for a minute. "But if we agree to a truce, I can assure you that we'll do everything in our power to help you search for the killer, even if it means handing over one of our own. I cannot think of something more dishonorable than murdering another land's leader during a time of peace, and whoever did it is a criminal and that's all there is to it."

"I'm glad to hear you feel that way. Are you sure you can promise what you say, though?"

"The king's death hurt our cause as well as your own. We do not want the assassin among our ranks."

"That's ridiculous!" shouted Yohannis. "It was right in line with their cause! Any orc would have gladly jumped at the chance to murder our poor, defenseless King Lucius!"

"Enough, Yohannis. So you would be willing to help us work out a truce with your people, Angroo?"

"If you promise never to attack us, we'll promise never to attack you. Never. Can humans keep that promise forever?"

"If the orcs can, we can as well."

"Are you absolutely sure?"

"It's going to take some shaking up, but I will see to it that a permanent truce is worked out. We'll work out all of the details later." The general turned back around and started walking. "It's about time our people coexisted peacefully with the orcs. A long time coming. Now let's move! Yohannis, lead the way!" He looked back. "Oh, and thank you for your cooperation, Angroo. We'll move forward immediately with the peace plan upon our arrival."

The group continued down the path at an almost imperceptibly faster pace than before as the sun climbed higher into the sky. Firelight made eye contact with the orc for a second; his face was brighter and more smiley than she had ever seen it, yet she couldn't help but think that, deep down, the white orc was still extremely distrustful of the humans. There was no way she thought he could be so certain Victory

City would keep its end of the deal. Was he trying to delude himself? At that moment, something in the orc's face somehow reminded her of Yohannis's angry scowl; the two were a few strides away from each other and had reacted in opposite extremes of delight and disgust at the general's truce offer, yet there was some kind of common thread connecting their facial expressions. Disappointment, maybe? Something didn't seem right.

Chapter 18

The prince stood at his balcony, watching the town bustle beneath him. Although it was still fairly early in the morning, it seemed like it should have been later to him because he had been awake for many hours. The night's events were still swirling in his head.

King Eliazer stood next to him. His face was stained with tears, and he was beside himself with grief. He stared blankly at the wall and didn't flinch when somebody walked up to them from behind.

"P...P...Prince Lucio!" The prince turned around to see a big, portly man with dark, curly hair and red freckles all over his face. He appeared to be in his early twenties.

"Ah, Lieutenant Erikhome. Thank you for coming. I want you to do something for me."

"Why m...me, My Lord?"

"General Richmond is away, and most of your superiors are busy organizing patrols and establishing our defenses in anticipation of another orcish attack. I need somebody whom I can trust to embark on a special mission for me, and I believe you're perfect for it. Do you think you're up to the task?"

"Of... uh, of course! Anything you... you want, P...Prince Lucio!"

"I expected no less. Now listen to me carefully. Last night, Lord Eliazer's daughter, Princess Silara, was kidnapped. Isn't that right?" Eliazer stared at the wall and didn't respond.

"Kidnapped!?" gasped the man. "Was... was it the wo...wo...work of the or... orcs, s...sir?" The prince walked back and forth.

"I can't be certain, Erikhome, but I don't think so. I believe the Order of the Filthy Foot was responsible."

"You mean… the m…minions of Din… Din… Dinther Footmol?! I th… thought he was only the st… stuff of leg…ends!"

"He is very real, Lieutenant. And I think his men have established a hideout somewhere inside of the city. I want you to search every suspicious-looking house, shop, or whatever else somebody could possibly hide in within the city's walls. Can I trust you to carry out this task?"

"Of… of c…course, Prince Lucio! You can count… can count… count on m… me!"

"Excellent. You are to report back at once as soon as you see any sign of the Order of the Filthy Foot. Oh, and Lieutenant. If you succeed in finding those villains, I will see to it that a little promotion is in order. How does *Captain* Chazwick Phinneas Erikhome sound to you?"

"It… it sounds just f…fine, sir!"

"Very well, then. You are dismissed."

"F…for the glory of V…V…V…V…Victory Cit…City!" exclaimed Erikhome as he marched out of the room. Prince Lucio turned to Eliazer.

"We will begin the search for your daughter at once, Lord Eliazer. I can assure you that we will find her in short order and return her safely." Eliazer's tears began to stream down his face again. The prince looked him directly in the eyes. "Listen to me, Lord Eliazer. Do not submit to the demands of the Order of the Filthy Foot or anybody else who may be responsible for your unfortunate situation. You know that they're only trying to steal the Golden Egg of Gotty Gottya away from you. You simply can't let that happen."

"I… I know, Prince Lucio. But I would give anything to see my beautiful baby again, safe and sound. I don't know if I'm strong enough to resist the offer."

"Think of the big picture, Lord Eliazer!"

"I *am* thinking about the big picture. But… I just don't know…" Eliazer slowly shook his head from side to side. The prince stepped closer to him.

"You should go back to your room and take a few minutes to ponder this, Lord Eliazer. Remember that many lives may be at stake. We'll do everything we can to get her back without forcing you to give up the Golden Egg. Do not worry about it." The elf king began to stumble off. "And remember that we still do not know who is behind this. It could be an inside job. Be watchful at all times."

Eliazer soon found himself walking slowly down the hallway to his room. He was consumed by his misery and needed all the strength he could muster to simply open his bedroom door. He stumbled forward in a daze.

"Lord Eliazer... I have something very important to discuss with you in private." Eliazer suddenly stood up straight. Somebody was in his room! His grief was replaced with nervousness as he hastily closed the door behind him and rushed forward. The prince's female attendant was lying on the floor near the window, staring up at him with bloodshot eyes. Her clothes were mostly in shambles and she was covered in dried blood, with numerous bite marks around her body. She looked even weaker than he did and she panted heavily.

"Crista? What are you doing here?"

"I have something important to tell you about your daughter."

"What about Silara?!"

"She's safe. Last night, I sent her back to Elkanshire with a ranger. She's on her way to safety." This was the last thing that Eliazer expected to hear. The spark of hope ignited a fire inside him and he sprung back to life.

"But why was her door busted open? Why didn't anyone tell me what was going on?!"

"She was being attacked. There was no time."

"The gentleman with the red mustache?" Crista nodded weakly.

"You cannot tell anyone about this, King Eliazer. Trust no…"

"HEY!!!" screamed an ecstatic Eliazer as he threw open the door. "HEY EVERYONE!!!!!! SILARA'S SAFE!!!!!! SHE'S SAFE!!!!!!!!!! A RANGER IS ACCOMPANYING HER BACK TO ELKANSHIRE EVEN AS I'M SAYING THIS!!!!!!!!"

Crista began crawling towards the window as quickly as she could.

"I told you not to…"

"Where do you think you're going, missy? You need urgent medical attention!"

"No! Not now!"

"Nonsense, young lady. Nonsense! I'll have none of it! I'll make sure you receive the best care. It's the least I can do for you."

"No… no…" muttered Crista as she made one last attempt to crawl to the window. There was already a rope hanging down to the ground from the windowsill, but Eliazer pulled it away before she got to it and slammed the window shut. His joy and excitement prevented him from realizing the seriousness of the mistake he had just made.

Chapter 19

Another long day of travel was coming to a close. The sky was becoming darker, and the humans decided to retire for the night. Angroo sat alone on a log; his skin was burning and his arms were very sore from having his hands tied behind his back for such a long period of time.

"How many more days until we reach Victory City, sir?" a soldier asked the human commander.

"Probably three. Two if we make good time." The men were beginning to set up camp. Angroo was led to his tent, the only one that had already been set up, and he was left alone while the humans gathered wood for a campfire.

After a few minutes, a shadow appeared on the floor in front of him and he looked up to see the half-elf woman entering the tent. Something told Angroo that she would come.

"It doesn't seem fair for you to be alone in here while everyone else is out there doing stuff," she uttered. Angroo couldn't concentrate on what she was saying, though. The woman was obviously dressed for bed; she was wearing a long red shirt that went about a quarter of the way down her legs. Apparently, she wasn't wearing anything else, or at least nothing that could be seen. The milky white of her bare legs was brought forward by the dark tent wall she was standing in front of. Her thighs grew wider as Angroo's eyes followed them up from her knees, but they were soon obscured by the red shirt. She must have at least been wearing underwear, though. Angroo just couldn't see it because the shirt was in the way. Of course she was.

"I'm happy you could join me, Firelight."

"Sure, no problem. I was just getting ready to go to bed and I thought I'd stop by to talk." What if she wasn't wearing anything under there? A ridiculous idea. Completely ridiculous.

Angroo began to sweat. What was she doing in here half-naked with him?

"I have nothing to talk about."

"I don't believe that. You must have something interesting to say. I'm sure you have some war stories at least, right? I have nothing else to do." She stepped closer.

"No. No. Please." She stepped closer again.

"You seem like the quiet, humble type, but I know you're a skilled fighter. You remind me a little of my old friend Yoshimito. He was the same way."

"Yeah. Okay."

"I don't know too much about orcs. What kinds of things do you usually talk about with the other orcs?"

"Nothing."

"So you never talk about anything?"

"No."

"Never?"

"SIR!!!" blasted a voice from outside. "Orc sighting at one o'clock!" The woman quickly turned towards the entrance of the tent, her shirt lifting up slightly as she turned her torso. She was wearing shorts.

"How many of them?!"

"Two, sir. They've already been apprehended."

Angroo stood up. He and the woman both watched from inside the tent as two orcs walked forward, surrounded by men holding spears at them. They were dressed in animal skins and straw hats, and Angroo did not recognize either of them.

"What business do you have in this part of the wilderness?" asked the human commander.

"We's just out fishing. We mean no harm to puny humans."

"Yah. What he say."

"Pffff! Baloney!" quipped the blond soldier, who was now standing next to the commander. "The disgusting animals are obviously here to spy on us!" Angroo hated the blond soldier.

"Honest! We just fishing!" The orc scratched his back.

"Then where are your fishing rods?"

"We left it back by river."

"Yah."

"Did whitey over here tell you to use that alibi, pig-face?" asked the blond soldier. The orcs looked confused. "Oh, playing dumb are you? I'll bet our damn pig-nose prisoner's been sending you and your ilk secret messages the whole time!" He turned to the human commander. "Sir! Requesting permission to execute the prisoner immediately!"

"Permission denied."

Angroo finally stepped out of the tent. The orcs turned towards him and stared.

"Return to where you came from, brothers! I am Angroo, a commander in your army! Go back and tell the shaman Molar-Licker that I'm safe and that I'm negotiating a deal for peace!" The two orcs looked at each other.

"Oh, come on!" whined the blond soldier. "We can't let these villains go for free!"

"They've done nothing wrong!" howled Angroo. "Let them go!" He had finally gathered the courage to put the blond soldier in his place.

"I won't even dignify you with a response, you overgrown gorilla. General Richmond, surely you agree that we can't let these filth-ball pig-faces off the hook, right?! They may not have committed any crimes that we're aware of, but we both know they'd kill all of us if they had the chance! They'd rip your brain right out of your skull, General! Your freaking skull!" He turned back towards the orcs and reached for his quiver. "Say the word and I'll kill them both right now!"

"Don't move from your spots, orcs!" shouted the commander. "Men, bind their arms!"

"But…"

"We are in a time of war, Angroo. They will receive fair treatment from us and will be released in time." The commander raised his sword. Soldiers stepped forward and tied the orcs' hands together. The orcs simply looked at the floor.

"We might as well slaughter these monsters and save ourselves the trouble of guarding them."

"It's okay, Yohannis. Send them to the tent, men." Angroo and the other orcs were led into Angroo's tent, tied down, and left alone.

They sat around in near darkness for nearly twenty minutes in the annoyingly hot tent without saying anything, sweating as they listened to their captors walking around outside. Finally, one of the orcs started whistling an old orcish tribal song, a song Angroo knew from when he was much younger.

"I haven't heard 'Kill Them and Eat Them' in ages. It brings back lots of memories."

"Yah. Me has it stuck in my head."

"Yah. Me too."

"So, where are you guys from?"

"We from same place as you, white-skin."

"How do you know?"

"We were sent by Molar-Licker to find you. He already find Tooth-Licker's body and declare himself new chieftain. He want us to find you also."

"You were sent to look for me? So you weren't really here because you were fishing?"

"No. No fishing."

"Yah. No." A short silence followed.

"It wasn't a good idea for you to lie about it." The orcs seemed like they were offended by this last comment. They stared confrontationally at Angroo.

"What you talk about? Humans no need to know what we doing!"

"Yah!"

"Our goal is to make peace with the humans. We do not need to lie to them without good reason."

"Our goal is to kill puny humans! You sympathize with pink-skins?"

"Yah?"

"No!"

"You lying to yourself, white-skin. You do not want to help humans. It's not good."

"I'm not trying to help the humans. I'm trying to help *us*! It's a peace deal!"

"No peace! Peace means humans win!"

"You have no idea what these humans are capable of doing!" shouted Angroo as he stomped his foot. "Listen to me! They can kill us all if they wanted to! If we keep attacking them, they won't hesitate!" The two orcs looked at each other. "You don't understand. They have the ability to kill all of us! Every single one of us! They have an artifact that they can use to do it!" The orcs shook their heads.

"Silly humans cannot do that. They too stupid and puny."

"Yah! Puny!"

"You have no idea what they can do!"

"You think about your loyalties now, white-skin. Who you want to help? Your fellow orc? Puny human? It not right to help puny human. If they have magic artifact to kill all orcs, they can use it whenever they feel. They can threaten orcs forever, use them as pawns forever. You think about it and make right decision."

"Yah..."

Angroo thought long and hard about what the orc had said. As much as he didn't want to admit it, the orc did have a point. Maybe this was really all just a big scheme for the humans to bully the orcs into doing what they wanted the orcs to do. Maybe the human commander had lied when he said that the humans would seek everlasting peace. The commander didn't seem like a liar, though. Angroo reevaluated his situation as total darkness fell. He remained awake and silent for another hour. There were no longer any sounds outside save a few cricket chirps, so he figured that most of the humans were already asleep. Apparently the other orcs came to the same conclusion because they suddenly struggled to their feet.

"Help us escape, fellow orc. We promise to leave immediately and deliver your message."

"Yah. Help us."

"You won't hurt anybody on your way out?"

"Yah." Angroo groaned and pulled a small knife out of his clothing; he had been hiding it within finger's reach in case he ever felt the need to escape.

"Here, take this..." he said as he gave the knife to one of the orcs, who slowly cut through his bonds and then helped the other escape. They began to cut Angroo free as well, but he stopped them. "Now go. Leave immediately and do not touch anything or anyone."

"Yah, okay."

"And be very quiet and fast. There will be two guards stationed outside of the tent, and you'll need to be careful sneaking past them. And make sure you tell Molar-Licker about the peace agreement. Got it?" The two orcs nodded and left the tent as Angroo lay down on the floor.

There was no sound for a few minutes as even the cricket chirps seemed to abate. Complete silence.

"Help!" screamed one of the soldiers. "Help! The orcs! Arrggghhh!!!" Angroo tore off what remained of the ropes and rushed out of his tent to find the dead bodies of two human soldiers in a heap next to what was left of the smoldering campfire. The orcs, carrying blood-drenched swords they had stolen from the humans, emerged from one of the tents and ran towards a different one. Angroo sprinted after them, but as he approached one of the orcs suddenly turned around and viciously shoved the sword hilt into his forehead! He fell to the ground stunned and in a great amount of pain, tasting blood in his mouth.

"Don't move!" shouted the woman, who had left her tent seconds earlier and was now standing next to the campfire. The orcs turned around smiled. They started walking slowly towards her.

"Well, if it isn't a little girly. Very pretty." The orc began chuckling and he elbowed his buddy. "Forgot to wear pants today, little girly?"

"Yah! Hehehehehehe!"

"Leave her alone, you brutes!" screamed Angroo from his helpless state on the ground. The two orcs ignored him and suddenly charged at the woman. One of them got too close and jumped away after a flame leapt out of the woman's hands. The other circled behind her, so now the orcs were surrounding her on either side and were only a few feet away.

"You play nice now, girly!" muttered one of the orcs as they continued to circle around. Finally, they simultaneously ran forward. One orc was immediately engulfed in flames and tumbled lifelessly to the ground, but the other grabbed the woman's hands from behind and held them together so that she couldn't repeat the magic trick on him. The woman struggled uselessly against her much stronger attacker, who forced her to fall onto her knees.

The orc suddenly released his grip and backed off. An arrow was lodged in the side of his head. He tried to move towards the woman again but he fell backwards as another arrow appeared in his shoulder and another in his arm. He finally fell to the ground when a fourth arrow nailed him in the chest. A fifth arrow penetrated through his eye. He was finally dead.

"Damn it!" screamed the blond soldier. "Damn these treacherous bastards! I told you all that they couldn't be trusted, but nobody believed me!" He felt the two soldiers by the campfire for pulses, but he found none. "These bloodthirsty animals! Why wouldn't anyone believe me?!" He walked over to where Angroo was lying and kicked him. "Look at what your friends have done, you lying, murderous traitor!"

The full moon was hidden behind a cloud. Angroo growled in frustration and buried his face in the mud; he felt as terrible as he ever had. It wasn't fair. Why did the orcs do that? Were there any others of his kind out there who weren't cold-blooded psychopaths? He was starting to seriously doubt it. Maybe that blond-haired bastard was right the whole time. Either way, everyone would certainly think he was now. Why did this have to happen? Angroo finally let himself succumb to the intense pain of his head wound, slipping into unconsciousness as the campfire finally burned out.

Chapter 20

It was late at night. Even though several candles were lit, the room was still cold and dark. Someone sat alone in a large chair, completely obscured in darkness, while the man with the curly red mustache stood in front of him.

"Men have been dispatched along the northern border of Victory City," muttered the figure in the chair. "No sign of Eliazer's girl has been found. Nothing." The man with the mustache shivered slightly. It was as if a dark shadow had been talking to him. A shadow with a voice.

"No sign, sir?"

"No."

"What do you think happened to her, then?"

"Somebody else must be after her. That's the only possible explanation."

"Somebody else? Who?"

"I'm sure you can answer that question for yourself. Or do you not remember what you saw with your own two eyes the night of the assassination?" The man looked down at the floor.

"What would you have me do, then?"

"We'll have to proceed with our secondary plan for now. You should lay low for a while."

"Agreed." The man nodded his head and began to turn towards the exit.

"Wait."

"Yes, sir?"

"I hope you do not think that I'm letting you off the hook so easily. That child was yours for the taking and you failed to obtain her. For your failure, you will be disciplined."

"No! I'll do better! I promise!"

"I believe you will. But I think a quick 'session' will serve to remind you not to fail me again, just in case you forget." A gloved hand extended out of the shadow and pointed towards a strange-looking metal contraption in the corner of the room. The man with the mustache shivered with fear as he walked slowly towards the torture device.

Chapter 21

The men hadn't said much since the brutal attack they had endured the night before. Three of them had been slain by the escaped orc prisoners, and the survivors added the bodies of these soldiers to the others that they had been carrying back from the fight at the volcano. As a result, the group was forced to advance more slowly than before. General Richmond himself guarded the remaining prisoner while most of the others walked ahead. It was another hot, humid day, and the sweltering sun beat down on the weary soldiers as they lumbered forward.

"Looks like we've got company," uttered Firelight. "There's someone hiding in the bush all the way over there." The general squinted. He thought he saw something move.

"Yohannis. Investigate those bushes over there."

"With pleasure, General," answered a smiling Yohannis. He loaded his bow and crept towards the bush while everyone else stopped walking and watched. He was getting closer.

"Hold y'r fire," muttered a voice. A burly man in dark clothing stood up very slowly as Yohannis approached, clutching his sword and holding it in front of him. His rough face was covered by a graying beard, and he seemed to be snickering.

"Drop the sword, ruffian!" screamed Yohannis as he aimed his arrow at the man's face. The man reluctantly dropped his sword and lifted his hands above his head. "What are you doing here, spying on our company?"

"Just a tr'vler 'round these parts, m' good sir. Not spying on y'."

"Then who's that?!" He turned his bow to aim it at a different bush, but before he could do anything else the man brought his arms down quickly and knocked the bow out of Yohannis's hand! He then punched Yohannis in the face and sent him sprawling backwards.

"Cut it out!" hollered General Richmond. He and two of the soldiers were now aiming their own bows at the man. After lifting his arms above his head again, the man quickly turned and tried to run away. Yohannis tackled him and pinned him to the ground.

"Stop it!" shouted a feminine voice that none of them had expected to hear. "Stop fighting!" A blond elf girl, who was wearing a mud-encrusted dress and was barefoot, jumped up from behind a bush and ran over to separate the two.

"Wait! Get away from them!" shouted the general as he ran over. The girl stopped moving and looked up at him. "Aren't you King Eliazer's little girl? Silara, was it?" The girl nodded.

"And you're General Richmond."

"Yes, we've already met." The general looked around. "What are you doing all the way out here?"

"Nothing. Me and ol' mister Brack here were just picking flowers."

"Bah!" spit Yohannis as he continued to hold down the struggling man. "Picking flowers, General?! Surely you're not swayed by this child's make-believe stories!"

"Tell the truth, Princess," said the general as he took another step closer. "You're so far away from the city. Where was this man really leading you?" The girl looked at the white orc, who quickly averted his gaze. The soldiers began to follow the general, stepping toward her almost in unison. She took a step back.

"Don't hurt Brack, please! He was just leading me back home because somebody at Victory City's coming after me!"

"Somebody's after you? Does your father know you

left?" The girl shook her head and looked down.

"It was all a secret, but this lady was supposed to go back and tell my daddy the whole thing afterwards. She didn't quite make it, though."

"Wait. A lady was supposed to tell your father you were leaving?"

"Yes."

"Why didn't she?"

"She was… she was killed by wolves. She was so, so brave. I just never had the opportunity to thank her for getting me away from that horrible man who attacked me in the night."

"So now nobody knows that you left?"

"No. They probably all think that I've been kidnapped." A tear rolled down the girl's cheek. "My daddy's probably worried sick. I wish I could tell him I'm all right." General Richmond scratched his chin.

"You were going back to Elkanshire in the north? Then why was the ranger taking you east?"

"He didn't seem like he knew how to get..."

"Let m' answer that question, Genr'," muttered the man on the floor, interrupting the princess. He breathed in through his nose. "No way north. Too m'ny orcs blocking the path."

"That's strange. Most of the orcs are east of the city, closer to where we are now."

"Those orcs 'r a tricky bunch. Tr'ky fellows. Never know where th'r gonna be hiding."

General Richmond looked at Firelight, who returned his gaze but didn't say anything. Then he turned back to the man.

"We'll be guiding the princess for now. Princess Silara, please come with us. We will keep you safe." The princess slowly stepped forward and continued to weep silently. The ranger suddenly jumped up.

"I was given an import'n job to do, and you can' stop

me from doing m' job!"

"Then perhaps my arrow will have better luck stopping you!" cried Yohannis as he aimed his bow at Brack's head from inches away. Brack finally stopped snickering and he kicked the dirt in frustration.

"I said I w' giv' an import…"

"And *I* said I'm going to kill you if you take another step, woodland filth!" The man turned and stared loathingly at Yohannis.

"All right, a' right. Leave m' be."

"It was nice meeting you, sir," said the general. "Yohannis, let him leave." Yohannis continued to aim his bow as the man backed off into the forest. Once he was no longer in sight, Yohannis turned back towards the others.

"Who was that guy?" asked Firelight.

"His name was Brack, but that's all I know," answered Silara. "I've been traveling with him for more than a day and I still don't know much about him. He seemed okay, but he was *so* distant."

"You should be careful about whom you trust," said General Richmond. "That man acted very suspiciously."

"He acted suspiciously?" asked an astonished Silara. "Really? How?"

"For one, he was taking you out of the way of your destination. And his accent is foreign. Despite what he claimed, he's definitely not from around these parts." Silara looked down.

"He was nice to me, though. He didn't say much, but he was being pretty nice when he did talk. I guess."

"That's not reason enough to give your blind trust to a stranger."

"Crista told me to trust him, though." The general's eyes suddenly widened.

"Crista?! The prince's assistant?! She's the one who helped you escape?!"

"Yeah. Poor, poor lady." The general paced back and forth quickly.

"What did Crista tell you, Princess? Try to remember. This is very important."

"She said that I couldn't trust anyone. She said that not even Daddy knew who to trust."

"What else did she say, now?"

"She said that some evil people were after some sort of valuable object that my daddy owns. She said that they want to kidnap me to use me to get my daddy to hand over the valuable object!"

"I knew it!" shouted the general as he raised his pointer finger in the air. "This makes things much more complicated. Did Prince Lucio know anything about what went on? Was he the one who sent Crista?!"

"I… I don't know. She said not to trust anyone, so I assumed…"

"Okay. I'll have to think about this. Men, we'll stop here for lunch." He crossed his arms. "This makes things very complicated indeed."

Chapter 22

"Why are we so far away from the rest of the group?" asked Firelight. General Richmond had told her to follow him as he walked off into the woods, and now they were alone among the trees.

"Listen, Firelight. Extreme measures need to be taken. The princess of the elves is our responsibility now."

"What does that mean?"

"The princess's father, King Eliazer, holds a very powerful artifact known as the Golden Egg of Gotty Gottya."

"The Golden Egg of what? Am I really supposed to take it seriously if it has a name like that?"

"Its name is not important. Somebody wants it, but nobody except Eliazer knows where it's hidden. Eliazer is known to be extremely protective of his daughter, so I assume whoever is after the Egg is trying to capture his daughter and hold her for ransom." Firelight twirled her long hair.

"Are you sure?"

"As sure as possible. I suspected that this would happen all along, and I thought that the ranger was in the process of kidnapping her. The princess appears to be very naïve, so I just assumed that she was fooled into traveling with that man. However, things aren't that simple, since Crista was the one who sent her with the man and I know Crista would look out for her best interest."

"Crista?"

"Yes. She was the prince's personal agent. A very skillful thief and spy, but also a genuine human being I trusted completely. If she really is dead then it's a terrible shame."

"I'm sorry about what happened, but are you really sure you can trust her? I don't know what to think about all this." The general looked around and then hushed his voice.

"After years and years of service in the military, I've seen people who would watch your back just like a brother. I've also seen too many who would be on your side one minute and then turn on you the next as soon as a better offer came along. Now, I can tell what I need to know about most people simply by looking into their eyes. Crista was sly and crafty but a genuinely good-hearted woman. Same as you. That's why I'm telling you and nobody else."

Firelight smiled and blushed slightly.

"Awww."

"I mean it, but that's not the point. Listen closely. The princess's homeland is not the best place for her to go. Whoever is after her could get to her even if she were locked in the most secure castle in all of Elkanshire, and many lives would be lost in the process as well. We're dealing with forces that we can't easily comprehend."

"What about the Dwarven Mountain Clan?" she asked. "McDuff and his dwarves won't fall prey so easily to whoever is after the princess."

"That might be a slightly better option, but I still don't trust them to protect her, either. You have no idea who we're up against." Firelight suddenly gasped as she thought of something. Then she rolled her eyes.

"Don't tell me Sootfoot's behind this one also!"

"Sootfoot?"

"You know, Dinther Football or whatever his real name is? That guy was pretty relentless."

"Footmol. Yes, you may be right. He and his Order of the Filthy Foot might be the ones behind all this; suspected agents of the Order have been spotted near the castle in recent weeks." Firelight looked down.

"We have to hide her, then. Nobody can stop Sootfoot; he can teleport through walls, for crying out loud! And he can easily overpower anyone in his way with that *huge* axe of his. But he can't get to her if she remains hidden and he doesn't know where she is."

"That's exactly what I was thinking, Firelight. We have to find a good place for her to hide for a long time. At least until things settle out."

"*If* things settle out," muttered Firelight. "Well, wherever she goes, she'll need protection. We can't *just* hide her somewhere; some wolves or bandits might get to her simply by bad luck. Not to mention orcs…"

"You told me that you're well-traveled. Do you know anywhere she can hide *and* be protected at the same time?"

Firelight thought about it for a few seconds.

"I think so. I had a friend several years back, an elf who was a powerful water sorceress and healer. Her name was Winterfrost. She's living by herself along the coast now, and I think she'll do the trick just perfectly."

"*You're* a powerful sorceress, though. Wouldn't you be able to protect her?"

"Yeah, sure, and then when two orcs attack us we'll be finished! You saw what happened last night, right? I was double-teamed by two orcs and I couldn't handle both of them at once! I was almost killed!"

"It's all right. That's over with."

"And plus, I'm not even that much older than Princess Silara. I'm not good enough to take care of myself, and definitely not somebody else. Winterfrost *is* good enough, though. I've never seen anyone like her. She just points her finger at you and, boom, you're dead. She'll fire an icicle right through your head. It's incredible. And she's skilled at healing wounds, too. She uses healing magic."

"Are you sure she'll do it?"

"Yes. She definitely would. She takes responsibility

very seriously." The general thought about it for a moment.

"Along the coast, you said? That will take another several days of travel at least."

"Yeah, probably."

"You know exactly where she lives?"

"She lives somewhere near Frog Village. I'm sure we could ask around once we get there; I mean, how many elven sorceresses really live in that area, anyway?"

"That's probably almost a week of travel from here. Not all of us should go, obviously, because a group of fewer people is less likely to be detected."

"I agree. Only one or two should go with her."

"Are you willing to go, Firelight?"

"Sure. It makes sense that I would go, anyway, because I'm the only one who knows Winterfrost. Better than doing nothing in a stuffy castle, anyway."

"Do you know the way, though? Would you feel comfortable traveling there?" Firelight shook her head. "Yohannis knows the terrain pretty well from his years of serving as a scout. I guess he could go with you, although I have a feeling he'll do something stupid on the way there."

"Gee, what makes you think that?"

"There's got to be a better way. I don't know if Yohannis is the right person for the job."

"Of course I'm the right person for the job!"

"Yohannis?!"

"Give me any job, and I'll do it!!" screamed Yohannis like a madman. "Tell me what the job is!"

"Are you sure you want the job?"

"Yes!"

"Positive?"

"YES!!!"

"All right, but you might not like it. You see, we've been

conducting a study on the food preferences of different wildlife species in this region, and we were just deciding who should be sent off into the woods to collect animal stool samples for our study. I figured that you've already been through enough the last couple of days, but Firelight just continued to insist that you would be the best man for the job."

"Oh, did she now? The mutt decided that it should be my job to dig around for animal crap? All right, I'll help you with your little 'study,' but we had better be talking about some serious positive implications for the long-term preservation of the ecosystem here. And when I say serious, I mean serious!" Yohannis stomped his foot and stormed off into the woods.

"Let me think about this a little more, Firelight. In the meantime, let's rejoin the others." Firelight could only nod her head in approval as both of them turned back towards the rest of the group.

Yohannis never returned, and the group was forced to spend the remainder of the day searching through the woods for him. Darkness finally fell with no sign of him anywhere. He had completely disappeared.

Chapter 23

Angroo sat alone in the tent again. It was already completely dark, and he tried unsuccessfully to fall asleep. He lay awake listening to the sounds of crickets chirping, his arms and legs burning as they usually did. Also, his head still throbbed from being smashed with a sword hilt the night before.

The tent walls rippled. Was the woman coming in again? Angroo didn't think she would after what had happened last night; she knew he was the one who allowed the murderous prisoners to escape. It couldn't be her, but who else would it be? He turned to make out the dark shape of a female; it was the elf girl they had discovered earlier that day.

"Are you still awake, An...groo was it?" Angroo sat up but didn't say anything. "Sorry if I'm waking you up. I just couldn't sleep and I thought I heard you rustling around as well. I'm really sorry if I'm keeping you up."

She heard him rustling around? He had hardly moved. Angroo thought that she was lying until he remembered that elves have excellent hearing, and thus it was conceivable that she knew he was awake after all and wasn't just trying to wake him up to get on his bad side.

"It's okay. I'm awake," he muttered.

"You know, I've never seen a real orc before. You look so much different than I always imagined. I didn't know orcs had white skin!"

"No, orcs don't have white skin. Only me."

"So, wait. Let me get this straight. Are you saying that you're not really an orc, then?" This elf girl was so much stupider than the woman. Just a little, stupid kid. Angroo didn't have the patience for this.

"I am an orc," he responded tersely.

"Oh, I'm sorry if I'm annoying you, mister! I really don't know much about orcs at all, or any other kinds of people for that matter. I've lived a very sheltered life, you see."

"That's okay."

"The one thing that I always hear is that orcs are mean and nasty. But I don't see that in you. You really seem like a good person to me."

Angroo had no response.

"You're like a big, tough guy, but nice inside. You know, like a big, friendly rhinoceros."

The girl looked at the tent wall, her eyes following the winding shadow patterns created by the trees against the dim moonlight. She stretched her arms.

"I don't know why we're fighting each other, Angroo. We don't have to fight. Why does everyone always have to fight?"

"I don't know."

"Why can't we have peace? It doesn't seem right to keep fighting like this." She caressed his arm as if she were petting a dog. Angroo felt the burning sensation go away for second.

"Sometimes you just have to fight for something."

"Don't tell me that. I know you want peace."

"What?"

"I know you want peace because everyone wants peace. Everyone." She continued to massage his arm.

"Everyone?"

"Yeah. Why not? You're not alone!"

"Uh…"

"Come on, you know that everyone just wants peace. Nobody wants to keep fighting!" The girl was a little bit on the whiney side. Also, she annunciated her words a little bit too much. The woman, on the other hand, spoke more clearly.

Yes, definitely.

"I hope you're right, Princess Silara."

"Oh, you remembered my name! Heh! I'm so... wait, did you hear something?"

"What?"

"Somebody's coming!" Angroo jumped up. He heard it now also: footsteps approaching from all sides. All sides at once. He immediately knew what was going on.

"Quick, hide!" he whispered as he frantically looked around the tent for a hiding place for her. There was none. He pushed her onto the ground and stood in front of her. Seconds later, the side of the tent ripped apart as it was slashed open with a machete. Four orcs climbed in through the tear, their torch casting an eerie red glow around the inside of the tent.

"There you are, white-skin. We been looking for you." Angroo recognized all of them as acquaintances from his tribe. The speaker was a short, especially ugly orc named Borkoo whose muscular body was almost completely covered in dark war paint. Drool hung from his chin.

"Good to see you, warriors."

"Untie him." An orc stepped forward and slashed the ropes binding Angroo's hands together. He was now able to freely move his arms around for the first time in a while, but they were very weak and sore.

"Thank you for freeing me, but I have business to settle with these humans and I wish to speak with them before we leave."

"Speak with them? You *real* funny, white-skin."

"Yah! We no speak with puny humans. We kill puny humans!"

"No. We will not harm these humans. The safety of our entire tribe depends on it!"

"You killing me, you so funny!" shot Borkoo as he licked

his lips. Suddenly, his eyes widened and a big, toothy grin appeared on his face. He continued to lick his lips. "Looks like you brought some company, white-skin. Very, very nice." Damn, the stupid idiot saw her!

"What are you talking about?"

"Who you hiding behind your back?"

Angroo became sick to his stomach.

"Leave the child alone. Leave right now and do not try anything." The orcs simultaneously stepped forward. Borkoo held out his machete pointed towards the elf girl with his right hand and held the torch in his left hand while the other three drew small axes from their belts. The elf girl was startled by the sudden appearance of these weapons, quickly backing into the corner. Her eyes were wide with fear as she looked up at the drooling orc warriors.

"I don't know what got into you, white-skin, but you get out of our way now or we be forced to cut you down!" Borkoo took another step forward. Angroo clenched his fists. He heard the girl crying softly behind him.

"Don't even think about touching her!"

"Oh, don't worry. We won't touch her, won't hurt her. No. We just want to bring her back for questioning, right boys?" The orcs chuckled. Angroo just kept thinking about the two orcs from the night before and what they had tried to do to the woman. The two orcs who persuaded him to help them escape. Were all of his kind really that bad? He wasn't ready to find out.

"You're lying! I'll kill you all with my bare hands if you take one more step!"

The orcs stopped and stood still. Angroo was bigger and stronger than any of them, but they knew that he would have no chance taking on all four at once without a weapon.

Borkoo snickered and took another step.

Angroo accepted the dare. He lunged forward, whacking the torch out of Borkoo's hand and then sending a fist into his nose. Borkoo reeled backwards but then slashed with the machete, striking Angroo's shoulder and causing him to yelp in pain. A different orc kicked Angroo onto the ground. The girl screamed but didn't move.

"Won't you tell little girlfriend to leave? Your house is on fire!" He was right; the far wall of the tent was now ablaze as a result of the fallen torch. Angroo leapt to his feet.

"Run, Silara! Get out of here!" The girl finally got up and sprang out of the tent. An orc tried to follow her but Angroo grabbed his arm and flung him towards the other orcs. He then turned and darted out of the flaming tent with the orcs in close pursuit.

Angroo looked around the campsite: all of the tents were ablaze! The flaming body of a human soldier lay next to one of the tents, and there was also an orc body nearby. An entire ambush was going on. Angroo must not have noticed what was happening outside because of his own predicament. But where was everybody else?

"Help!" screamed the frantic elf girl. Her arm was being held by another orc who had been waiting outside. Angroo let instincts take over as he leapt towards the orc and grabbed his elbow, forcing him to release his grip and then punching him in the face and shoving him face-first onto the ground. He looked and saw that he and the girl were now surrounded on all sides by the four orcs who had originally broken into his tent. Borkoo stepped forward.

"We don't want to hurt little girl, Angroo," he muttered. "Really. But we forced to hurt *you* now." He slashed at Angroo again with his machete but missed. The four orcs stepped forward and the fifth one got up from the ground.

"You won't hurt her?!" screamed Angroo as he charged

at them. "You won't hurt her?! You're liars!" As he rushed forward, he felt one of the orcs' axes come down and slice into his thigh, and before he had time to react a second orc kicked him in the stomach and knocked the wind out of him. Angroo stumbled backwards and fell onto his back as the girl screamed. Borkoo stepped forward and planted the heel of his foot on Angroo's chest, raising his machete above his head as he prepared to deliver the coup de grace.

Sudden, unexpected footsteps were heard nearby, and as soon as Borkoo turned to look he was grabbed by the waist and shoved hard into the ground.

"Back off and put away your weapons!" shouted the human commander. "Angroo and I are working out a peace deal with your kind. I have no desire to hurt any of you, so if you back off now, I'll allow you to leave with your lives."

The orcs laughed.

"I said back off."

He was ignored. The orcs rushed forward, but the commander was ready with his sword and, with one stroke after another, it was only a matter of seconds before all five of them were cut down. The ones who weren't immediately killed groaned and gasped helplessly as they bled to death on the dirty, muddy ground. The girl screamed again. After taking a few seconds to catch his breath, the commander turned to Angroo.

"Take these. Wrap up your wounds." He gave Angroo some cloth bandages and helped him wrap them around his shoulder and leg. Angroo sat down.

"There will be more coming, General Richmond. They know where we are."

"They've already come. Fortunately, most of our party escaped from them unscathed. The others are on their way back to Victory City as we speak, but the orcs are hot on their trail and I'll have to hurry to catch up with them at an arranged rendezvous spot. This can't take long."

"What can't take long?"

"Listen very closely, Angroo. I have an extremely important task for you and I don't want you to tell anybody about it. Do you know where Frog Village is?"

"Yes."

"Princess Silara's life is in danger. I want you to guide her to Frog Village, where an elven sorceress named Winterfrost will look after her the rest of the time. Just tell the sorceress that Firelight sent you. She knows Firelight."

"She's in Frog Village?"

"She doesn't actually live there. She lives somewhere in the area. And she has black hair, if that helps you identify her."

Angroo looked him in the eyes.

"Why are you telling me this? Who's coming? Is…isn't Firelight coming also?"

"No. Firelight and the others are being chased by the orcs right now, so I don't know what's going to happen to them. Nobody will be coming with you; you need to go by yourself. I know you're familiar with the countryside and right now you are our best bet for getting the princess there safely. Do you accept this responsibility?"

Angroo looked down at the girl. Her face was lit up by the light from the burning tents, and he could see the tears streaming down as she gazed at the bodies of the dead orcs. He looked back towards the human commander and nodded his head.

"Are you sure you'll be able to make it back to the others?"

"I don't know, but I can handle myself. Victory City is only about a day's travel from here, so I think I can at least make it there. Don't waste your energy worrying about me." The commander put his hand on Angroo's shoulder. "I'm trusting you, Angroo, and I do not place trust lightly. I… oh… give me just one second."

Angroo watched as the commander turned and hurried off towards one of the burning tents nearby. He searched around on the ground for a couple of seconds before picking up something and coming back. It was Angroo's trident.

"And here, I saved this for you. Now please get moving immediately, and do not attract any unnecessary attention on your trip. In the meantime I'll discuss peace plans with my superiors as soon as I return to the city. Good luck."

"You're very brave for trusting me like this, General Richmond." The commander nodded as he hurriedly tossed Angroo the trident and rushed off into the darkness. Angroo was finally reunited with his trusty weapon, but this wasn't exactly a time to get excited. His work was far from over.

He was left alone now with the elf girl. He turned to look at her, reaching out his free hand and holding hers with a loose, gentle grip.

"Everything will be okay, little one. Come with me." The girl remained still for a few seconds, and then she looked up and nodded quietly. She allowed him to walk her slowly towards the forest as the light from the burning tents began to fade. Her puffy lips looked kind of cute in the dim firelight, he thought.

It was soon almost completely dark. Angroo and the girl found a huge oak tree that cast a large, wavy shadow over the surrounding terrain, and the two of them sat down beside it to rest. The girl stayed up for a while but finally succumbed to sleep, resting her head on his lap, while Angroo remained awake and vigilant; this was no time for him to doze off. He was given an important task, and he would not rest until he saw the little girl to safety. She was his responsibility now whether he liked it or not.

Chapter 24

A day had come and gone since General Richmond and what remained of his entourage had returned to Victory City with news of the new alliance with the fire giants. Prince Lucio still had not seen the general since his return, and he dispatched one of his messengers to request an audience with him in the main meeting room of the castle. The prince was sitting at the head of the table in the room, examining a map, when the messenger finally reported back to him.

"Is the general ready to speak with me?"

"Yes."

"Very well. Send him in." The messenger nodded and left, and a minute later General Richmond entered. He was dressed in a brown cloak and had trimmed his beard slightly since the prince had last seen him.

"Good to see you, My Prince."

"Likewise, General. How are your wounds?"

"Oh, they're nothing. Just a couple of scratches. My men endured much worse than I did on our trip."

"Yes, well, I'm glad that you and your men made it back in one piece. Or, at least some of your men came back. Before you arrived yesterday afternoon I was almost certain that we'd never see any of you again."

"Our horses were driven off, Prince. We were forced to walk all the way back, traveling rather slowly to avoid mishaps."

"Yes, of course. The orcs are rather relentless out there. Excellent work in slaying their chieftain, although I have no doubt he will be quickly replaced."

"You were told of that, Prince?"

"I was. Your soldiers have briefed me on the happenings of your trip. I'm glad that Methuselah agreed to send his forces, although I'm slightly disappointed that we'll be forced to wait for them. Regardless, we shall press on with our attack."

"So my men told you everything that happened already?"

"I was told about your encounters with the fire giants and with the orcs." The general nodded his head.

"That's right."

"And your men also reported that you found a girl on your way back, or something like that."

"Uh, yeah well..."

"She's some sort of fire wizard, I hear?"

"Oh yes! Lord Methuselah sent her along with us. She proved invaluable in fighting the orcs."

"That's good. We can use all the help we can get." General Richmond was certain now that the prince knew nothing about his run-in with Princess Silara. He had thought for a long time about whether or not he would tell the prince or even King Eliazer about it, and he decided not to tell anyone, just as Crista had instructed before her apparent demise. But he had not considered the possibility that one of his men would blow his cover; the prince certainly would not be happy to find out that his most trusted general had been deliberately hiding such an important piece of information. The prince was not a fool. General Richmond decided to change the subject before he could risk catching himself in a lie.

"I wanted to talk with you about something important, Prince Lucio. My men and I encountered one orc who was different from the others. He had white skin."

"Oh, yes. Your men told me about that, too. I almost forgot about it."

"They did? Yes, well, his name is Angroo and he's one of their leaders..."

"Andrew?"

"*Ang*-groo"

"Angroo? What kind of name is that?"

"An orc name, obviously!"

"What of your tone, General?! You suddenly sound as if you've become quite *angroo* with me!" The prince began to laugh.

"This is very serious, Prince."

"Sorry, sorry. I'll stop. I know how sensitive you are about what those savages have done; you're probably raring to get back at them as much as anyone!"

"That's what I wanted to talk to you about, Prince Lucio. The orc and I have been discussing a peace deal."

"A peace deal?"

"Yes. For permanent peace."

"A *peace* deal?"

"Yes."

The prince stood up and slowly began to pace back and forth.

"Do you have reason to believe that what he told you is anything more than a collection of lies?"

"The orcs do not want full-scale war, either. They fear us as much as we fear them."

"What has gotten into you, General?! You're saying that these orcs, who cut down our citizens like cattle, who laugh and sing as they murder our people, do not want to continue the war? Are you suggesting that these savages *wouldn't* stop at nothing to hack every single one of us to pieces?!"

"With all respect, Prince, that's exactly what I'm suggesting." The general watched as Prince Lucio continued to walk back and forth.

"What kind of peace deal?"

"We call off our troops, they call off their troops, and

that's it. No more fighting. We aren't setting up diplomatic ties or anything like that, just a permanent cease-fire. Isn't peace the goal here?"

"Of course. But a simple peace deal is unrealistic. They've been warring on and off with us for years and years; we simply cannot trust them to hold up their end of the peace bargain." The prince leaned closer. "And what about the Golden Egg? As soon as we let down our guard that murderous orc will step forward and steal it."

"I thought the elves are keeping it."

"It doesn't matter who is keeping it, Charles. Don't you understand who we're up against? We have to continue to put pressure on the orcs; it's the only way." He placed his hand on the general's shoulder.

"We need to keep trying because these orcs want peace, too. They said they would hand over whoever was responsible for the murders."

"Really?"

"Yes. That's what Angroo told me."

"Are you sure?" The prince tapped his fingers on the table.

"Yes."

"Listen, General Richmond. I don't know who this Angroo character is, but if you can catch my father's killer and show me definitive proof that it's him, I don't see why we wouldn't be able to open negotiations with the orcs – assuming the orcs are even willing to negotiate, that is."

"What if the killer isn't one of the orcs, though?"

"He *is* an orc. But this doesn't matter; it is simply too risky to attempt to talk to the orcs until the killer is dealt with, regardless of who he may be. The city's safety is my chief concern, and I must do everything I can to make sure that the remaining Golden Egg of Gotty Gottya is protected. Do you understand?"

"Yes, My Prince." The general nodded. He then stood up from his seat and turned towards the door with a sigh. He decided he would have to take what he could get.

"Oh and General, one more thing before you go."

"Yes?"

"Be careful. The killer may have some sort of supernatural power that you cannot comprehend, so stay on your toes."

"Supernatural power?"

"Just be careful, General Richmond. That is all."

Chapter 25

It didn't take more than a full day for Firelight to become bored of hanging around the castle. She found herself spending a lot of her time lying on the bed and looking out the window, watching a small, unusual-looking black cat lounging on a tree branch and otherwise doing nothing. The cat had a long, bulky body and a relatively short head, with a somewhat elongated snout and enlarged jaw; it appeared to possess the proportions of a much larger animal. It didn't seem like it had a care in the world. Firelight admired its independence and its calm demeanor as it sat around and wasted the day away.

She wasn't about to waste her entire day away, though. There had to be something else to keep her occupied somewhere in the city. After lying down with her face in a pillow for a few minutes, she got up and walked down the hallway, eventually leaving the castle and wandering down the street in search of something to do.

It was pretty quiet outside. Unusually quiet. Very few others roamed the streets; it seemed that most of the city's residents were either away serving in the military or hiding in their houses, apparently afraid that the king's killer might come after them if they did so much as step outside. All of the shops seemed to be closed. After walking for a while, Firelight was just about to head back towards the castle when she finally found a shop that was still open.

She peered in through the open window at the small, dimly lit room. Glass vials containing liquids of different colors cluttered the shelves, and the only person in the store was a man who sat behind the counter reading a scroll. He was wearing a blue hood that completely concealed his face and he didn't flinch as Firelight entered.

"Excuse me, sir. I'm new to this area, and I was just

wondering what kinds of things you sell here." The man looked up, but Firelight still could not make out his face.

"Magical potions."

"Magical potions?" Firelight walked around. "You mean, like healing potions? Exploding potions? Potions that transform people into pigs?"

"You're a very educated customer."

"I was just making those things up off the top of my head."

"I know an educated customer when I see one." He suddenly got up out of his seat.

"Don't be ridiculous. What else is a magical potion going to do?"

"This!" screamed the man as he hurled a small vial directly at Firelight's face! She quickly ducked, and the potion went right over her head and through the window. The pop of shattering glass could be heard outside. Firelight reached for her sword but then remembered that she had left it in the castle.

"Just try that again, scum!" she screamed as she leapt to her feet. "I'll turn you into ashes before you can even..."

"Easy, Firelight! Easy! It's me, Rurik! Remember me?" He pulled his hood off to reveal a handsome face with brown hair and a mustache. "It's been a long time."

"Rurik!? It *is* you!" She gave him a quick, friendly hug. "How's everything been? What are you... why did you just throw that at me?"

"Oh, I had my reasons. Turn around..."

"That mustache looks horrible. You have to get rid of it."

"Gee, good to see you too. Don't worry because I was just about to shave it off."

"Seriously, shave it. Sorry if I'm being a little too honest here."

120

"No, no. I don't mind at all. By the way, your new long-hair look isn't exactly a real turn-on, either. You looked a lot better with shorter hair."

"What are you talking about? My hair looks fine! I just brushed it for like a half hour."

"Yeah, whatever. I was just joking, anyway. Are you going to turn around now and see what just happened?" Firelight turned and looked: outside the window and across the street was a big fat man frozen in a block of ice!

"That was a freezing potion? You got him with a freezing potion just now?"

"Sure did. He was spying on us."

"Are you sure?"

"Yes. He was just standing there watching for a while. He seems to walk by every day and peek in, and I was starting to get sick of it."

"You have no idea who he is. You might get in trouble for doing this."

"Of course I will. We should move him so that nobody sees him."

"It looks like he's stuck against the wall of that store across the street, though."

"All right, let's just get out of here quickly before anyone notices him. Follow me." As they walked past the frozen man, Firelight got a closer look at the very surprised expression on his chubby face. She giggled slightly.

"Aww, he's just adorable, isn't he?"

"Yes. Adorable."

"So what are you doing in Victory City, Rurik?"

"Well, it's actually a long story, but the basic gist is that I needed some money and I decided to sell some of my extra potions. Business was much too slow down in Redcloud, so I ended up traveling up here to look for a profit. It's all temporary."

They walked down an alley.

"You know, you're not going to make a very good profit if all of your potions are stolen right now."

"Oh, don't worry. Those bottles are filled with colored water. I always keep the real potions on me at all times."

"You always were clever like that. I can't stand that mustache."

"So what are you doing here, anyway? I thought you were in the Fire Realm studying."

"I was until I was sent here. It's a long story and I'll tell it to you later." She leaned on the wall. "What kind of business do you get in your shop, anyway? Who buys your potions?"

"Mostly mischievous kids from down the street who want to play practical jokes. And recently the healing potions have become pretty popular, too."

"Oh, really?"

"Uh huh. There's some gruff-looking guy who buys them in bulk on a fairly regular basis. He doesn't say why he needs them, but I've watched him travel to and from the castle. I can only assume that he's part of the medical staff there."

"That's weird that he would buy his supplies from some shifty guy who wears a hood and has an ugly, twirly mustache that looks like it's fake. I would think that the official castle medical staff would have a more legitimate place to buy healing supplies."

"Thank you for your ringing endorsement. But yes, you're right about all that. I wouldn't worry about it too much, though; the guy probably has some perfectly justifiable reason to avoid as much human contact as possible and sneak out here every week to obtain his supplies."

Firelight thought about it for a minute.

"Yeah, I'm sure. A perfectly justifiable reason. Well, it was good to see you, Rurik. I have to go check on something important." Firelight began to walk off, but Rurik grabbed her arm.

"Wait. Can you thaw the frozen guy? Let's deal with this now because I want to return to my shop without having everyone who goes by stopping to ask questions."

"Yeah, all right. As long as you agree to shave your mustache." They walked over to the frozen man, and Firelight used her magic to carefully melt the ice.

The man collapsed to the ground in a half-conscious stupor. He was shivering and soaking wet, and his skin was red from the cold. Rurik stood over him.

"Why were you spying on me, sir?" he asked. The man looked up at him, and then looked at Firelight. He coughed and rubbed his wet forehead.

"I... I was... just..."

"What's your name?"

"My... na... name? Erik... Erik..."

"I think I hear your mother calling. You had better run home, Erik. Home!" Firelight came over and helped him up, and he stumbled off as quickly as he could. Rurik turned back towards Firelight. "He was probably just some young kid who was curious about what the potions could do. He wasn't a threat. I hope I satisfied his curiosity."

"I guess that's one way to do it." She looked around. "Anyway, Rurik, I have to get going now. I'll see you again soon."

"Don't get yourself into too much trouble. Be careful." Firelight nodded at Rurik and then hurried back towards the castle. She smiled because she had finally found something that would keep her occupied.

Rurik removed his fake mustache and threw it in the

garbage.

Chapter 26

It was noon of another warm day, although the temperature was somewhat more pleasant than it had been for the past few weeks. It was sunny and not too humid, but the air was filled with pollen. Angroo and the elf girl finally exited the deep woods that they had been traveling through for a little over two days and came upon a grassy field, startling some rabbits that had been gathering near the edge of the woods and causing them to scramble in different directions.

"Looks like *nobody* likes you!" chuckled the girl. She seemed to be in a better mood than she had been the previous two days.

Angroo didn't answer her. She looked up at him.

"Come on! You know I'm just kidding around!" Angroo nodded and continued walking forward, his expression unchanging. "You know, you never told me about yourself. What is your family like?"

"I don't have a family."

"Don't be silly. Everyone has a family!"

"My family abandoned me when I was a little child. I was raised by a shaman."

"Your family abandoned you!? That's horrible!" She shook her head. "I can't even imagine how horrible that must be, but you must be thankful that the shaman found it in his heart to raise you into the person you are today."

"You don't know anything about me."

"You're too negative all the time, Angroo. Always negative about everything. Surely you at least had some close friends who you used to hang out with when you were younger, right?"

"No."

"No?"

"No."

"Well at least..."

"Shut up! I don't have to stand here and entertain you with stories now! I have one job to do and that's to get you to your destination, so shut up and leave me alone."

"But..."

"Listen carefully, you little brat. I could easily kill you if I wanted to and rip you to ribbons, but you're very lucky that I'm letting you live. Any other orc would kill you in half a second. Leave me alone." The girl didn't respond. Neither of them said anything for several minutes as they trudged ahead through the tall grass. A gentle breeze began to sweep in.

"It's a nice day today, Angroo. It's much too nice outside for that kind of talk, and I don't want to hear it anymore." He didn't respond. The girl suddenly stopped walking and looked up at him.

"Why did you stop?"

"You know, Angroo, not all orcs are like that; they're not all out to kill innocent people and you know it. Stop lying to yourself!" She stared into his eyes.

"You..."

"You've been living with the orcs for your entire life and you know what they're like. They're not all merciless killers, and neither are you! You think you're only hurting me with those kinds of words, but you're hurting yourself much more."

Angroo put his hand over his face.

"Apologize to me, Angroo. Apologize right now!"

"All right. I'm sorry, Princess Silara. I'm really sorry for what I said."

The girl nodded.

"So anyway, I couldn't help but notice... weren't those bunnies sooooooo cute?"

126

Chapter 27

It was the late afternoon. General Richmond was strolling through the hallway of the castle and sipping tea while talking with several of his officers.

"General! Can I speak with you in private for a minute?" The general stopped and looked up. In front of him stood Firelight, whom he had not noticed hurrying down the hallway towards him. She was wearing a dark, wrinkly shirt that wasn't tucked in and her hair was completely in disarray. The general looked towards the officers.

"You can go on ahead. Let me talk to her for a moment." The men nodded and continued walking, leaving Firelight alone with the general.

"Something very suspicious is going on in the medical ward of this castle, General Richmond. Something that may be related to the king's murder."

"Something suspicious in the medical ward? What makes you think that?"

"Have you ever been there? There's only one guy working there, and none of the patients even know his name. Some big guy who wears a surgical mask that covers most of his face."

"It *is* highly unusual that only one man would care for all of the patients, but that by itself does not seem to be of any significance to the murder case. He may just be an immensely skilled doctor, for all I know."

"But he's not a doctor. He's been using healing potions that he's bought from a street vendor and then arbitrarily wrapping his patients in bandages."

"Healing potions?"

"Yeah, yeah. Anyone can drink a healing potion to heal cuts, broken bones, burns, or stuff like that. It does very little for *sick* patients, though, except make them think that they're cured by temporarily alleviating some of their physical symptoms. I've taken the potions plenty of times before."

"Are you sure that this man's only been using healing potions, though?"

"As sure as can be. I've been looking into it the entire night and all day, and every one of the patients I talked to told me the same thing. He's been treating everyone with potions and bandages."

"So what are you trying to say?"

"What am I trying to say? I'm trying to say that the castle's head medical doctor doesn't know a thing about medicine, doesn't have a name, wears a mask all the time so that nobody can recognize him, and is in a position that allows him to manipulate everything that's going on inside of the castle. It sounds like the perfect situation for someone with rotten intentions, don't you think?" The general looked stunned.

"Follow me, Firelight. Let's take this investigation a little further."

"What do you mean no visitors are allowed!!?" sputtered Eliazer. He nearly dropped his bouquet of flowers onto the floor.

"Sorry, sir. No visitors are allowed at this time," responded the masked doctor.

"But I must see the woman who saved my daughter's life! I must know how she's doing! She was hurt badly!"

"I am not allowed to comment on the condition of any patient, sir. You'd best be leaving at once."

"What is your name, Doctor? I'd like to report you to the prince!"

"Please leave right now, sir." The doctor and Eliazer both turned and looked as General Richmond and Firelight approached them from the hallway.

"Excuse me, Doctor. I have a few questions for you."

"You might as well not even ask him, General Richmond! There's no reasoning with this man! All I wanted to do was visit a dear friend who was seriously injured in a wolf attack several days ago, and he wouldn't even let me talk to her or see her at all! Of all the indecency!" Eliazer shook his head and walked off in disgust.

"Wolf attack?" murmured the general as he turned back towards the masked doctor. "As I was saying, I need to ask you a few things."

"I am not permitted to answer any questions right now..."

"I don't think you know who I am, Doctor. I'm General Charles Richmond of the Victory City Armed Forces."

"I said I will not answer any questions. Please leave at once, sir." General Richmond took several steps forward, backing the masked man into the wall.

"Can I see your medical certifications, Doctor? I have been given direct orders by the prince..."

"What's going on here?" asked Prince Lucio as he suddenly appeared behind them. "I do not believe that I approved of any such searches, good general. You must be mistaken." The prince was accompanied by four armed guards.

"We have reason to believe that this man is not a licensed doctor as he claims, Prince Lucio."

"We?"

"Firelight and I."

"You're Firelight? Oh, you must be the sorceress I've heard about. It's a pleasure to meet you for the first time; you know, you're quite lovely."

"Thank you very much." She bowed slightly. "You're not so bad yourself. I mean, uh, it's an honor to make your acquaintance, Your Highness."

"Flattering. Well, as grateful as I am for your service to our fine city, I'm afraid I cannot so readily take the word of a stranger. What evidence do you have of your claim?"

"*Our* claim…" the general butted in.

"Yes, of course. What evidence you two have, though? Dr. Gorman Rugby has maintained a sterling record as a physician."

"Your Highness, I know that this man's been buying magical potions from a street vendor and using them to treat his patients. I got a firsthand account from several patients who were recently released."

"He's been buying potions from a street vendor?"

"Yep."

"Would this vendor you speak of be able to back up your claims if we were to ask him in person, by any chance?"

"Yeah, definitely." The prince looked the doctor in the eye. Suddenly, he turned around when somebody tapped him on the shoulder.

"Lieutenant Erikhome? What are you doing here?"

"P...P...Prince Lucio! Don't talk…talk to that…that g…girl!" The fat, freckled man pointed at Firelight, whose eyes went wide as she immediately recognized him. She backed into the wall.

"What? Why?"

"She's coll...uding with a m…man on the street. They att…attack…attacked…d me yesterd…day evening!"

"Really? A man on the street?"

"Y…yuh…yes sir. A p…p…potion…p…potion seller with a hood and a mus…mustache. I've b…been watching h…him for a f… a few… a few days n…now, v…v…very suspici…ous."

"A potion seller attacked you? A *magical* potion seller, someone who might sell potions of healing? That's funny, we were just speaking about such a man." The prince turned back towards Firelight. "Is this true, what he says?"

"No!"

"Yuh…yuh huh! They f…fr…fr…fr…froze m…me s…olid in a b… a b…block of ice!"

"This is crazy, Prince Lucio!" shouted General Richmond. "Don't believe any of it. Why are you making up such ridiculous stories, Lieutenant?"

"I'm n…not m…m…making… making this up! Hon…est!"

"We'll have to find out for ourselves, then," said the prince. "Lieutenant Erikhome, lead us to this potion vendor that you speak of. All of you come along."

"I cannot leave the patients, sir. Some of them are very sick." The prince turned back towards the doctor.

"Very well, Doctor, but you're not off the hook yet. I'll have to have one of my guards keep an eye on you while we investigate this street vendor."

"I can't let anyone near the patients, sir. They are highly vulnerable to infection from outside sources, so it is imperative that you leave me alone with the patients."

"He'll kill all of them now that he knows we're onto him!" screamed Firelight. "Don't leave him alone with them!"

"I believe such wild accusations are quite uncalled for, Firelight. The good doctor has worked here for years and has a first-rate reputation. You, on the other hand, have shown me nothing to assuage my suspicions of your own character and you will have a lot of explaining to do once we locate that street vendor." He turned back to the doctor. "That being said,

I'm afraid you must be watched until we can get this whole thing cleared up. Give my guards sanitary surgical masks if you're afraid for the health of your patients."

"But sir…"

"That's an order, Dr. Rugby. Erikhome, lead us to this street vendor you spoke of."

"R…r…right…right a…way!" Two guards stayed behind to watch the doctor while everyone else traveled through the hallway. The other two guards walked on either side of Firelight to make sure she didn't try anything, although they were not actually touching her. Firelight was clearly uncomfortable. She continued to look back at the doctor only to see him standing in the same spot and returning her gaze with stone eyes.

They exited the castle and traveled through the streets for several minutes, braving heavy rain. They finally arrived soaking wet at Rurik's shop and, just as Firelight expected, Rurik was sitting in the same chair she had found him in the day before. His hood completely concealed his face, but he wasn't immersed in his reading this time and was instead sitting up as if he had been expecting their visit.

"Prince Lucio? My, what a lovely surprise. You have no idea what a tremendous honor it is to see you in my humble little shop."

"Well met, good shopkeeper. I'm here today on very important business, so listen carefully." Rurik nodded and folded his arms behind his head as the prince continued. "I've been told that you've been selling potions of healing to the castle's head medical doctor. Is this true?"

"I have been selling many potions of healing to one man in particular, yes. I may have seen him enter the castle once or twice, so I *guess* he could be head medical doctor." The sound of the rain beating the roof above their heads intensified.

"What did this man look like, good shopkeeper?"

"He was well-built, pretty tall. I don't remember all the details."

"He… he might be l…ly…ly…lying, Prince!"

"That brings up one other order of business that I must take care of while I'm here." The prince pointed to Erikhome. "Have you ever seen this man before, Shopkeeper?"

"Nope. Never."

"You…you lie!"

"He claims that you've been acting suspiciously lately, perhaps plotting against the royal family. He also claims that you attacked him with a freezing potion of some sort. Does any of that ring a bell?"

"Absolutely not."

"Are you quite certain, Shopkeeper? Assaulting an officer of the Victory City Armed Forces is a grievous offense, punishable by years of…"

"Hey, wait a minute!" interjected Firelight. "Wait! Didn't the lieutenant say that the shopkeeper had a mustache?"

"Yuh… yuh huh! I sure d…did say th…at." Rurik removed his hood to reveal that he did not actually have a mustache.

"That's quite peculiar," muttered the prince as he rubbed his chin. "Are you thinking of someone else perhaps, Lieutenant Erikhome?"

"He… he must…must've sh…shaved…"

"Oh, speaking of mustache, that's another thing I forgot to mention about the potion buyer."

"Yes, Shopkeeper?"

"He had a curly red mustache. Very distinctive-looking."

General Richmond had secretly separated from the group at the first opportunity he could find and hurried back into the castle. He crept back to the door of the medical ward and pulled it open to find the two guards lying on the floor, breathing heavily but otherwise motionless. They were both wearing large surgical masks; the doctor must have coated the inside of the masks with chloroform or some other knockout drug, the general thought. What was going on? He rushed forward and shoved open the door to the next room.

The doctor quickly turned his head back; he was so surprised by the general's sudden intrusion that he dropped his scalpel onto the floor. The general ran forward and kicked the sharp tool to the other side of the room. Then he grabbed the doctor by the arm and shoved him into the wall.

"What are you doing!?" screamed the doctor. "Unhand me at once!" The general tightened his grip.

"What have you done to Crista?!"

"I have no idea what you're talking about! This is madness!"

"Where is she?!" The general suddenly noticed what appeared to be a female body completely wrapped up in bandages in the other side of the room. The body was lying perfectly still on the floor and looked like a mummy, with the bandages wrapped very, very tightly. This must have been the patient that the doctor was about to begin 'working' on, the general figured. He released his grip and approached the body.

"You're not allowed near the patients!" the doctor shrieked in vain. General Richmond began to unwind the bandages on the face, immediately revealing wide-open eyes with eyeballs rolled back into the head! He stumbled backwards, sick to his stomach.

Suddenly, the doctor's hand reached around from

behind him and stuffed a rag into his mouth! The general began to feel woozy from the knockout gas that laced the rag, but he decided that he wouldn't be beaten that easily. He shoved the doctor backwards and then ripped the rag out with his hand. He turned around to see the doctor holding his scalpel.

"Easy now, sir..." the doctor mumbled. "Easy now..." He was no longer wearing his mask, as it had fallen off during the struggle. General Richmond backed into the corner. He could feel his body succumbing to the knockout gas that remained in his system. His knees suddenly gave way; he clumsily fell forward as he watched the blurry image of the doctor coming closer.

"Drop it, Rugby!" cried Prince Lucio. The doctor turned quickly to see the prince and one of his guards standing in the doorway, dripping wet from the rain storm outside; their weapons were drawn. The prince immediately recognized the doctor as the man who had confronted Eliazer in the hall a little over a week before.

"Wait! I can explain!"

The guard stepped forward to apprehend the doctor, who wasted no time in tripping the guard and pushing him into the wall. The doctor then barreled past the prince and shoved a second guard out of the way, soon running off down the hallway in a full sprint.

"After him! Get him!" howled the prince. The few guards within earshot began to scramble down the hallway after him. Firelight, Rurik, and Erikhome finally arrived on the scene, but they were too late to be of any assistance; the prince and his two guards had separated from the others during their frantic run back to the castle and had taken a shortcut that the others didn't know about. The prince stomped on the ground in frustration.

"Wh…who was th…at?"

The prince looked at Erikhome and grimaced. He clenched the hilt of his sword as the anger built up inside of him.

"The Filthy Foot…" he muttered in disgust. "The Filthy Foot!"

Chapter 28

"Your feet are filthy!" laughed the elf girl after Angroo stepped in a puddle. "Oh no, you're leaving footprints! Brack's gonna be hot on our trail now!" Angroo grinned. He and the girl had been joking about Brack coming after them for the past half hour.

"You b'r watch out, 'r he's g'nna getcha, little g'r." His voice sounded nothing like Brack's, but that didn't stop the girl from cracking up like a six year old. Angroo laughed a little bit, too; he was beginning to get used to the girl's company.

"You know, you never did tell me much about your past, Angroo. Are you ever gonna tell me?"

"I don't think..."

"Just tell me about it already!"

"I don't know. It's painful for me to talk about it, Princess Silara, but..."

"Oh, please stop calling me that. Just call me Silly. That's my nickname."

"Princess Silly?"

"Just Silly."

"That's a 'Silly' name."

"Very funny, you big ape. Now tell me more about yourself."

"I don't know. It's hard to talk about." He shook his head.

"It can't be that bad, can it?"

"It's pretty bad. As a kid I was always beat up by the others because I looked different. Beaten like a rag doll."

"Don't say that!"

"It's over now, though..."

"That's terrible," she muttered. "Beaten like a rag doll? And by the way, why do you keep scratching your arms?"

Angroo didn't even realize he was scratching; it had become so automatic.

"I don't know," he muttered, shaking his head. "I've always had a painful skin condition ever since I could remember. It's why my skin looks like this; the pigmentation is completely gone."

"That's why your skin's white, you mean?"

"Yeah. I think so."

"Is there anything you can do about it?"

"I drank a magical potion a few weeks ago that was supposed to stop the burning, but it hasn't worked at all. In fact, I'm pretty sure it's made it worse."

"Maybe you need to drink more of it."

"Molar-Licker said that only one sip was necessary. He was very insistent that I only take one sip."

"Molar-Licker? What kind of name is that?"

"Yes, it is a 'Silly' name, isn't it?" The girl frowned. "He's the shaman who raised me, and he is now the chieftain of the tribe."

"Wow! Your foster father is now the leader of the entire tribe?! That's pretty impressive." Angroo laughed at the girl's naivety, but at the same time he was struck by how she had referred to Molar-Licker as his foster father. He had never really considered the shaman to be much of a father figure; he was really more of an associate or a friend to Angroo. A peer, even, although Molar-Licker was actually a good twenty years older. He figured that Molar-Licker was about as close to a real father figure as he had ever had, though, so maybe the girl was somewhat justified in saying that.

"What about you?" he asked. "You haven't told me much about your life, Silly. Silly Billy."

"All right, fine. Don't call me Silly. It's a stupid nickname anyway."

"I'm sorry…"

"And there's nothing to say about my life anyway. You know, I just lived in the castle with my father, nothing else to say. Very boring. Don't even ask." Angroo nodded as they continued forward.

"I'm sure your life wasn't *that* boring."

"No, it was. I would talk about my life story now except that I don't want to put you to sleep. My stories aren't nearly as exciting as your stories must be; my life is just too boring.

"I don't know. I think I would at least like the security of living in a castle surrounded by people who care about me and pamper me, even if it were a little uninteresting at times." There was no response from the girl, so Angroo decided to change the subject. "We should arrive at the Frog Village in another day or so. It won't be much longer, so don't worry."

"I don't know," mumbled the girl as she slowly shook her head. "I don't know if I'm looking forward to this, Angroo. I mean, who is this Winterfrost lady anyway? I'd rather be safe and snug at home. You're making me a little homesick."

"These are dangerous times. You don't have a choice…"

"You know what? Part of me wants to be safe at home." She looked into Angroo's eyes. "Part of me wants to be here in the wilderness with you, though. In a way it's liberating. Why can't *you* just protect me? Why do I need some fancy sorceress?"

"This woman is supposed to be very powerful. I'm sure that…"

"I don't know, Angroo. I think I want to stay out here with you. I kind of like being with you." She rubbed Angroo's arm, and the burning disappeared for a fleeting moment. Angroo began to feel a little strange inside.

"I cannot protect you."

"Yes you can! You can protect me from anyone; remember those people who attacked me in our tent the other day? You sure showed them!"

"You need someone else to protect you because I'm not strong enough by myself." He patted her on the back. "Now let's keep moving. You'll be safe soon." They walked off as darkness began to descend.

Chapter 29

It was late at night. The door opened, and light entered the room for a brief second. The man with the red mustache entered and closed the door behind him, plunging the room back into pitch blackness. There were no candles this time.

"You have failed me again, Rugby!" boomed the dark voice.

"Sir, I..."

"You were buying magical potions from some street vendor all along?! How *careless* of you!"

"What else could I do? You know that I'm not that kind of doctor..."

"You've made me very angry. I cannot believe your cover was blown so easily."

"It was that sorceress..."

"Don't try to blame anyone else! Now, because of your clumsiness, things have become much more complicated." There was a short pause. "But you're right, of course. The nosy half-elf sorceress should be eliminated as soon as possible. She's a little too dangerous for my liking. She'll be an afterthought once the plan is in full effect, obviously, but it's better to get her out of the way right now."

"I'll see what I can do, sir..."

"What about Crista? It's a shame that you were unable to finish her off before you were forced to retreat."

"She isn't a threat right now, sir. She's in a deep coma."

"A coma? All right. All right, good. She can wait, then. Leave her alone for now and do not touch her; we have much more important matters to take care of."

"I agree, sir."

"Good."

"In the meantime, though, what is to be done about

King Eliazer's daughter?"

"I can only assume that the orcs have her. She was not seen again after her little rendezvous with Richmond's party and the subsequent orcish raid, so the white orc must have kidnapped her and taken her back to his lair. We'll have to suspend the search for her."

"So what should we…"

"We must initiate the second part of the plan, Doctor. The Golden Egg of Gotty Gottya is not the only thing that we're after, of course. You know that better than I."

"Yes, of course."

"That's enough. I will initiate Part Two of the master plan. In the meantime, you and your lackeys will hunt down and slay the meddlesome half-elf sorceress. Do I make myself clear, Dr. Rugby?"

"Crystal, sir."

Chapter 30

"So you're telling me that there's no sign of Dr. Rugby anywhere?"

"No, My Prince. We've searched the entire city."

"He'll show up, I hope." The prince shook his head in disappointment. "That was foolish of me to confront him like that. I should have waited until more of us were in position to halt his flight." He was surrounded by several of his men.

"Don't doubt yourself, Prince Lucio," said General Richmond. "If you had come any later, that man may have killed me."

"He may have killed Crista as well. Dear, dear little Crista. What is her condition?"

"She's currently in a deep coma. Rugby must have administered some sort of poison."

"She'll pull through. Erikhome, what are the weather conditions for the next few days?"

"P…partly cloudy, ch…chance of sh…showers…"

"I have no time for games, Lieutenant!"

"But, how…how am I supp…osed to tell the w…eather?"

"All right, we'll have to make do without the forecast. General Noosants, are the troops prepared to strike?"

"Aye."

"Very well. Now listen closely everyone. Men, as you all know, the orcs have stepped up their raids significantly in the past few days. Many good soldiers have already perished defending our borders from their incessant attacks, and we must see to it that these attacks finally come to an end. As far as I'm concerned, though, I can see only one reasonable way to accomplish this task. I now will tell you why I have gathered you all here: the time has come for a full-on assault of the orc territory."A murmur erupted among the assembled officers.

"A full-on assault, Prince Lucio?!" gasped General Richmond. "Did I just hear you correctly? Haven't we already established that Gorman Rugby..."

"As you are no doubt well aware, General, there were two players in the death of my father. The Order of the Filthy Foot was just one."

"But we have no evidence that the orcs..."

"The orcs were involved somehow. I am quite sure of it."

"But what about our agreement?"

"General, I remember our agreement well and I intend to uphold it. But there is simply too much at stake for us to stand here and do nothing! Shall we wait around for the orcs to strike us again?!"

"We won't need to worry about an orcish attack if we are successful in working out a peace agreement!" Prince Lucio shook his head as he paced back and forth.

"I can see there's no convincing you, General. I do not want to do this, but I'm afraid I cannot allow you to lead our forces in their main strike. Our commander must have his heart in the battle. General Noosants, you will take command of the primary assault force."

"Aye!"

"As for you, General Richmond: if you can somehow produce evidence as to the identity of the killer, we may be forced to alter our strategy. I will consider peace negotiations only once the killer has been identified. Oh, and Lieutenant Erikhome, I want you to take charge of the search for Gorman Rugby."

"O...kay..."

"But Prince Lucio, how am I supposed to obtain this proof?"

"I don't know, General. But until you do, or until you come to your senses and realize the severity of the orcish threat, you are your own man. Is that understood?"

General Richmond opened his mouth to answer, but no words came out.

"We will further discuss the assault in one hour's time. For now, we proceed with battle preparations. Officers dismissed!"

Chapter 31

For the first time in months, it was actually a little bit on the chilly side. The girl insisted upon stopping so that she could find something to wrap around her bare feet, and Angroo soon found himself helping her collect leaves, grass, vines, and twigs from the forest floor. After the materials were gathered, Silara somehow managed to stitch together functional and surprisingly sturdy moccasins for herself in a matter of minutes.

"I guess you *are* good at something," Angroo joked. Or at least he meant it as a joke.

"I'm good at singing also!" she replied. "*And* I play the harp. You should listen to me sometime."

"Well, I don't see any harp anywhere. I guess we have to keep moving, Silly."

"Did you have any songs that you used to sing when you were younger?"

"Not really."

"No songs?"

"No."

"Oh, come on. I'm sure that the other orc children used to sing songs all the time! Children love singing!"

"You don't understand. I didn't get along with any other children because they were too busy beating the crap out of me."

"No…"

"It was brutal. They would gang up on me and punch me and kick me and stab me without warning. They'd fight me until I was barely alive."

"Don't say such horrible things!"

"Luckily I was good at finding places to hide, or else I might not be standing here today."

"Are you making this up?"

"I am not making any of this up. I had a horrible childhood, but you know what? It made me stronger. Every time I took a punch, I got a little bit tougher and a little bit smarter. Eventually, when I was older, I made the others pay for what they had done. I beat them so good that they never challenged me again. I beat every single one of the bullies to a pulp."

"That's a horrible story! How did you continue to live with these people?"

"I don't know. I guess you get more mature as you get older. Even the most savage orc children mature to some extent." The girl had a stunned look on her face. "I finally earned the respect of the others after years and years. I was the best fighter around and all the others knew it, and they stopped judging me by my skin and became friendlier. They became tolerant. Sometimes things just take a little bit of time to settle out."

"Wow, I'm sure glad I'm not an orc! I wouldn't survive two seconds!"

"I don't know about that. You're one of the toughest people I've ever met."

"Really?"

"Of course. You were whisked away from everything you knew and thrown out into the wilderness to fend for yourself, and yet you're still in high spirits. You would fit right in with even the toughest orcs."

"You're just saying that."

"No, I'm not." They continued walking through the forest for a few minutes. A cool breeze set in.

"You look a little bit cold, Angroo. Would you like me to make you leaf moccasins as well?"

"No. I'm good."

"Are you sure? You might get sick."

"Yes, I'm sure. Don't make me any leaf moccasins."

"All right." She folded her arms and tilted her head to the side slightly as they continued to walk. "You know what? I don't *have* to play the harp to sing. I can sing without it."

"Okay."

"Would you like me to sing for you now?"

"You don't have to." She ignored him and started to sing an elven melody. Her voice sounded a little bit whiney at first, but it strengthened as the song progressed. Angroo thought the tune was actually kind of catchy. He stopped walking.

"How did you like it?"

"It was very… nice. Pretty good. Not bad."

"Thanks."

"What song was that anyway? It sounded kind of like The Farmer in the Dell."

"It was an old elven tune."

"Well it sounded very nice. You have a nice voice."

"You really think so?! You mean it?!"

"Yes, of course."

"My father doesn't like my singing anymore. He always tells me not to sing in public."

"I don't know what your father's talking about, Silly. You sound great."

"Oh, thank you!" She gave him a small hug, and he responded by patting her on the back and smiling. He felt warm inside.

"You don't have to worry about anything because I'm here to take care of you. I'll protect you. I'll always be here to protect you."

"Thank you, Angroo. That makes me so happy why, I could even sing another song! How would you like that?!"

148

"I'd like nothing better." She began to sing a song that reminded him a little of Pop Goes the Weasel. "You know, maybe you should keep it down a bit. We don't want to be too loud."

"But…"

"We don't want anyone else to hear us, so just keep it down just a little. Continue."

"Okay, okay. Here goes: *All around the mulberry bush…*" The singing continued in a hush whisper as they walked on through the forest. It was too late, though; the damage was done. Someone else *had* heard the song, and that person wasn't very amused. Not very amused at all.

Chapter 32

The sun was high in the sky as Firelight made her way through the royal gardens. She came upon someone she didn't recognize: a skinny man wearing a huge straw farmer's hat. The man definitely didn't look like a normal farmer – he had the shiny white skin, golden eyes, and very sharp facial features of a prince or king – and he seemed to be trimming some plants with shears. He looked up from his work as she approached.

"Oh, hello there my dear! Well met!"

"Hi." A breeze suddenly came in and carried off the man's hat as he unsuccessfully attempted to keep it on with his hand. His golden, flowing hair and pointed ears came into view, and Firelight immediately realized that he must have been the king of the elves. She picked up his hat and gave it to him.

"Thank you so very much!" He put the hat back on his head.

"Your Majesty, it's an honor to meet you. My name is Firelight..."

"Oh, please. You flatter me with all that 'Your Majesty' mumbo jumbo, but it's rather unnecessary. Please just call me Eliazer."

"All right..."

"You must be the sorceress I've heard all about. It's nice to finally meet you in person."

"Thanks."

"You know what? Hehehehehe, I just got a silly idea! Don't call me Eliazer. Why don't you call me Elly instead? That was my nickname back when I was your age!"

"All right, *Elly*. If you don't mind me asking, though, why are you out here doing yard work? I thought you were an honored guest."

"Oh, it's not work at all. I just love gardening. Look at these beautiful flowers I've planted."

"Those are certainly very nice fl…"

"OKAY!!! Okay, I'll admit it! I've been so nervous these last couple of days. So very nervous, Firelight. I've had to keep myself busy because otherwise I'd be overwhelmed with fear for my little girl. I mean, I know she's in safe hands, but still I pray for her safety every day. She's out in the wilderness somewhere. I'm sure there's nothing to worry about but, oh, I just hope no harm befalls her."

"Yeah she seemed… I mean, I hope she's okay." Firelight had to catch herself; General Richmond had strictly instructed her not to tell *anybody* that Angroo was escorting the princess to Winterfrost's house. In fact, she was pretty certain that she and the general were the only ones who knew about it, and she was supposed to keep it that way for the princess's safety.

"Oh, what I wouldn't give to see my little girl safe again. Or just for the knowledge that she is safe. I…"

"GrrrrrrrrrrrrrrrrrRRRRRRRRRRRRRRRRRRRRRRRRRR!!!!!!!!!!!!! !!!!!!" A tiny flash of yellow zipped past Eliazer's feet and nearly knocked him off his balance.

"Not aga…"

"Raf! Raf! Raf! Raf! Raf! Raf! Raf! Raf! Raf! Raf! Raf! Raf! Raf! Raf! Raf! Raf! Raf! Raf! Raf! Raf! Raf! Raf! Raf! Raf! Raf! Raf! Raf! Raf! Raf! Raf! Raf! Raf! Raf! Raf! Raf! Raf! Raf! Raf! Raf! Raf! Raf! Raf! Raf! Raf! Raf! Raf! Raf! Raf! Raf! Raf! Raf! Raf! Raf! Raf! Raf! Raf! Raf! Raf! Raf! Raf! Raf! Raf! Raf! Raf! Raf! Raf! Raf! Raf! Raf! Raf! Raf! Raf! Raf! Raf!"

"Furlin! You little idiot! Furlin!" Firelight laughed at the tiny yellow poodle that was now up against the chain-link fence barking like mad.

"Raf! Raf! Raf! Raf! Raf! Raf! Raf! Raf!" What was it even barking at?

"Excuse me one moment, Firelight." Eliazer ran over towards the tiny dog. "Furlin! Bad boy! Bad boy!" The dog suddenly stopped and cowered as Eliazer got close, allowing him to pick it up and carry it off, but it turned its head back towards the fence and growled as it was being taken away. It had been yapping at the black cat Firelight had seen a couple of days earlier; the cat had been sitting peacefully on the other side of the fence and completely ignoring the dog the whole time.

"That's such a cute little doggy. His name's Merlin?"

"No, no. Of course not. His name's Furlin and he happens to be quite a little bundle of joy!" Eliazer nudged Firelight and rolled his eyes. "Yeah, right! More like a little nightmare! His racket will surely annoy the neighbors." He put the dog down.

"Is he fully grown?"

"Hard to believe, isn't it? He's actually pretty big for a toy poodle, you know; his twin sister Velma's only three pounds!"

"I wish I had time to take care of a pet. They're just so cute!"

"Oh, it's a lot of responsibility. My daughter loves taking care of this dog, though. It's worth it to her. "

"You know, you and your daughter look a lot alike now that I think about it."

"What?! You've seen my daughter?!"

"Shit."

"When!? When have you..."

"Raf! Raf! Raf! Raf! Raf! Raf! Raf! Raf! Raf! Raf! Raf! Raf! Raf! Raf! Raf! Raf! Raf! Raf! Raf! Raf! Raf! Raf! Raf! Raf!"

"When did you..."

152

"Raf! Raf! Raf! Raf! Raf! Raf! Raf! Raf! Raf! Raf! Raf! Raf!"

"When…"

"Raf! Raf! Raf! Raf! Raf! Raf! Raf! Raf! Raf! Raf! Raf! Raf! Raf! Raf! Raf! Raf! Raf! Raf! Raf! Raf! Raf! Raf! Raf! Raf! Raf! Raf! Raf! Raf! Raf! Raf! Raf! Raf! Raf! Raf! Raf! Raf! Raf! Raf! Raf! Raf!"

"Stupid dog! Wait just one second, Firelight…"

"Raf! Raf! Raf! Raf! Raf! Raf!"

"You know, maybe I should be going…"

"No! Wait! What do you know about my…"

"Raf! Raf! Raf! Raf! Raf! Raf! Raf! Raf! Raf! Raf! Raf! Raf! Raf! Raf! Raf!"

"I really have to…"

"Wait!"

"Raf! Raf! Raf! Raf! Raf! Raf! Raf! Raf!" Eliazer was standing halfway between her and the barking dog, who had rushed back to the fence to bark at the cat again. Firelight had been inching away, but Eliazer inched towards her at the same pace; he was conflicted about whether to get the dog or to prevent her from leaving. Firelight realized the right thing to do.

"All right, get Furlin!" she shouted above the dog's nonstop yapping. "I'll wait!" Eliazer nodded then quickly ran back to grab the dog. He carried off the growling animal to one of the castle's back doors and threw it inside. Then he hurried back towards Firelight.

"I just know that dog is going to get onto the kitchen table," he mumbled to himself as he looked up. "Now please tell me everything! Please!"

"All right, I'll tell you what I know. Five days ago we found your daughter traveling with a ranger who was acting very suspiciously."

"He acted suspiciously!? But he was leading her to the safety of her kingdom!"

"We didn't think so. We thought that he had other motives, so we scared him off." Firelight looked around to make sure nobody else was listening in on her. "And we didn't think that Elkanshire was the safest place for her, anyway. We figured that the enemies would get her there."

"Her own kingdom is not the safest place for her!? Are you crazy?"

"We sent her away to a safer place. We sent her to be watched by…"

"You *sent* her?! With whom?!"

"This orc, and…"

"AN ORC!?!?!?!? You sent my daughter into the wilderness alone with AN ORC!?!?!?!?!?!?!"

"Raf! Raf! Raf! Raf! Raf! Raf! Raf! Raf! Raf! Raf! Raf! Raf! Raf! Raf! Raf! Raf! Raf! Raf! Raf! Raf! Raf! Raf! Raf! Raf! Raf! Raf! Raf!" Apparently, the back door had been left slightly open.

"Let me explain!" cried Firelight. Eliazer grabbed his shears and walked slowly towards her.

"AN ORC?!?!?!?!"

"Raf! Raf! Raf! Raf! Raf! Raf! Raf! Raf! Raf! Raf! Raf! Raf! Raf! Raf! Raf! Raf! Raf! Raf! Raf! Raf! Raf! Raf! Raf! Raf!"

"Just let me explain!" He swung the shears at her but missed. She backed away.

"Raf! Raf! Raf! Raf! Raf! Raf! Raf! Raf! Raf! Raf! Raf! Raf! Raf! Raf!"

"How could you do that to my daughter!?" Firelight had to increase her speed so that Eliazer wouldn't catch up with her, and soon she was running as fast as she could.

"Raf! Raf! Raf! Raf! Raf! Raf! Raf! Raf!"

"Listen to me!!!"

"How could you hand her over to the orcs!?"

"Raf! Raf! Raf! Raf! Raf! Raf! Raf! Raf! Raf! Raf! Raf!"

"No! Listen to me!"

"Raf! Raf! Raf! Raf! Raf! Raf! Raf! Raf! Raf! Raf! Raf! Raf! Raf! Raf! Raf! Raf! Raf! Raf! Raf! Raf! Raf! Raf! Raf! Raf! Raf! Raf! Raf! Raf!"

"Get out of my sight!" shrieked Eliazer. "Out of my sight, you careless buffoon! Do you have any idea what you've done!?"

"Raf! Raf! Raf! Raf! Raf! Raf! Raf! Raf! Raf! Raf! Raf! Raf! Raf! Raf! Raf! Raf! Raf! Raf! Raf! Raf! Raf! Raf! Raf! Raf! Raf! Raf! Raf! Raf! Raf! Raf! Raf! Raf! Raf! Raf! Raf! Raf! Raf!"

"Listen!" Her cries were of no use. Eliazer continued to chase her, so she ran off around the castle until she was finally out of sight. It began to drizzle. Eliazer knelt on the ground and put his hands over his face.

"No…" he moaned as he broke out into tears. "No! No!" He dropped the shears and rolled onto the ground, sobbing uncontrollably. "Please… don't let anyone hurt… my baby!"

"Raf! Raf! Raf! Raf! Raf! Raf! Raf! Raf!"

Chapter 33

"I'm a little tired, Angroo. Can we stop for a nap?"

"We're almost there. Another hour or so before we reach Frog Village."

"It's starting to get dark, though."

"No it isn't. It's the middle of the day. Just try to stay up a little longer."

"All right." They trudged ahead through the forest. "When we get there, are you gonna just leave right away or can you stay a little bit?"

"I'll stay. Don't worry."

"Good, good." She gave him a hug. "I don't want you to leave me."

"Wait. Someone's following us."

The girl turned quickly but didn't see anyone. They stood perfectly still for a few seconds.

"I don't hear anything, Angroo," she whispered. "Are you sure someone's following us?"

"I can sense it. Just keep moving and keep your eyes open." She nodded. Both of them began to walk at a quicker pace.

"Do you think it's Brack?"

"I don't know. Keep your voice down." They hurried ahead.

"Brack wouldn't really do something like this, would he?"

"Just keep moving. I don't know *who* it is."

"I'm scared. Hold me."

"Just keep moving."

"Hold me." They arrived at a patch of mud.

"All right, I'll carry you." He picked her up and cradled her in his arms as he tried to hurry across the mud.

"I just heard someone, Angroo! Go faster!" He tried to go faster but he couldn't. The mud was slowing him down, and he didn't want to risk slipping by being reckless. He plodded forward.

"I can't go any faster!"

"Go faster! Someone's right behind us!"

"I'm trying!" How much more mud was there?

"Faster!"

An arrow ripped through the sky and plunged into Angroo's back. He yelped in pain and fell forward, throwing the girl out of the way so that he wouldn't crush her underneath his weight and then plunking hard onto the muddy ground. The girl screamed as she rolled away.

"How dare you!" shrieked the blond soldier. Angroo tried to get up but he slipped and fell forward. The blond soldier loaded another arrow into his bow and rushed towards him. "How *dare* you!"

Angroo reached for his trident, but it wasn't on his back where he had strapped it as it had fallen off when he fell into the mud. He didn't have time to dig around for it, though; instead he jumped up and grabbed a big chunk of wood nearby to use as a club. The girl continued to scream as the blond soldier charged forward.

"I said I would kill you one day, pig-face, and today's that day!" He launched another arrow as he ran, missing by a wide margin. Angroo rushed forward with the club over his head and swung with all of his strength, but the blond soldier dashed to the left and got out of the way.

"Leave us alone!" squealed the girl. "Stop it! Angroo did nothing wrong!"

"The swine did nothing wrong!? Everything he's ever done has been wrong! Don't you understand?!" The soldier let another arrow fly, but Angroo leapt out of the way just as it would have hit him. "He sinned just by being born!"

"Stop fighting!"

Angroo swung his club again, but the blond soldier jumped backwards and launched an arrow right into his chest. Angroo's eyes widened and he spit blood out of his mouth.

"NO!!! ANGROO!!!!"

"Sil..." He stumbled forward, clutching the arrow that was lodged in his chest and breathing heavily. His face was contorted with extreme pain as he tried to regain his footing, struggling pointlessly as he melted to the ground. He couldn't do it. He fell onto his side and landed in the soft mud as everything went black. He had failed to protect her.

Chapter 34

It was midday, but the streets of Victory City were eerily quiet; it might as well have been midnight. The lack of activity was peaceful in a way, Firelight thought, but it was also a little bit nerve-wracking in that it seemed so unusual for the streets of such a large city to be so empty at this time of day. Even more empty than usual. She hoped that she wouldn't have to stay in the city much longer, but she figured that she might as well make the most of her time there by paying her old friend Rurik another visit. She wandered into his store.

"So how are things going with you?" asked Rurik.

"Not so good," replied Firelight. "I said something really stupid to King Eliazer yesterday. *Really* stupid."

"Stupid enough to ruin your whole day?"

"Completely." She shook her head. "Poor man. I should really go talk to him again about that."

"Things haven't been so great for me either."

"You lost most of your business after we ran good ol' Dr. Rugby out of town?"

"Yep."

"Yeah. Sorry about that." They both laughed, but Firelight knew Rurik really was just a little bit disappointed about losing his best customer. He always had a business-first mentality.

"So what are you doing the rest of the day?"

"I got a letter from the prince inviting me to a meeting in the war room today. Actually, it's coming up, so I'd better leave soon."

"Are you sure it's really from the prince?"

"I assume… it is…"

"I'd be careful. It might have been forged. Just be very cautious and alert when you go to that meeting."

"You think it could have been forged? You think someone is planning something bad?"

"I can't say for certain. But it seems likely that the doctor wasn't the only insider, Firelight. There are probably others in high-up places who may be involved in the plot."

"I was thinking that also, actually."

"The king's assassination must have taken much more planning and coordination than one man can accomplish alone. It's almost inconceivable that Dr. Rugby acted by himself."

"So you really think that whoever else is behind this might be after me?" Rurik quickly nodded.

"They see you as a threat. Even if the doctor were the only person behind the king's murder, he's still at large and if he's planning anything else, you'll probably be one of his first targets. I don't know. I mean, I don't know any of this for sure; I might be completely wrong about it. But just be careful, okay? You always seem to find ways to get yourself into trouble and it doesn't hurt to be careful."

"All right. I'll be careful, so don't worry about me."

Firelight arrived at the entrance to the war room, but there was no sign of anyone else and she didn't hear anyone talking inside. Was it a private meeting? Was it a trap? Firelight slowly opened the door and found that the room was empty and mostly dark. There were no tables or chairs in the room. Something wasn't right.

She stepped forward, and the door suddenly slammed behind her! The floor began to creak. Firelight wasn't caught off guard, though; she immediately jumped up and grabbed the chandelier as the entire floor opened up underneath her!

"RRRRRRRR!!!" As she dangled from the chandelier,

Firelight made out the dark form of some large creature circling underneath her feet on the lower level. It seemed hungry.

"Nice, doggy!" she said in her most soothing voice, but it was to no avail. The animal suddenly sprang up, and Firelight pulled her legs away just in time as its jaws clanged shut. She quickly hoisted herself up so that her entire body was on top of the chandelier.

"RRRRRRRRRRRRRRR!!!" With one hand gripping the wobbly chandelier, she used her other hand to throw a small fireball at the beast. A direct hit! The creature's face was lit up for an instant, and Firelight saw that it looked like some sort of huge, ugly pit bull. But what was it still doing alive? The beast shrugged off another fireball just like it had done for the first one. It continued to circle around.

Firelight was quickly becoming exhausted from creating the fireballs. Her grip began to loosen ever so slightly. What kind of creature was this?

"RRRRRRRRRRRRRRRRRRRRRRRRRRRRR!!!!!!!!!!!"

This couldn't continue. She had to find a way out, but how? She locked her legs tightly around the chandelier and, using both of her hands, launched a big fireball at the door; it burned right up to her great delight, but the creature beat her to the exit! It had leapt up through the gap as soon as it opened. Apparently she wasn't the only one who was itching to get out of there.

The beast ran around the hallway but was unable to find any prey to satisfy its voracious appetite. It bounded out the window with a loud crash of shattering glass and fell three stories, landing hard on the concrete below and denting it. Some guards who had been patrolling the area shouted and ran towards it, charging and piercing the beast's skin with their spears. The beast backed away from the guards and ran further away from the castle.

The black cat was standing alone in the middle of the lawn, minding its own business, when the beast finally noticed it and began to chase it. The cat panicked and darted away as quickly as it could, but the beast was rapidly gaining on it and there was nowhere to escape! It was no use; the creature was locked in. The cat turned around at the last second to try to fend off its attacker, but the beast was much bigger and it leapt forward for the kill.

"Yaaaaaa!!!" screamed Firelight as she dove onto the beast, jumping onto its back and grabbing its face with her hands. "Take this!" She tried to burn the creature's face, but her own hands were burnt instead as the creature's skin resisted the fire. She yelped with pain as she was flung across the grass.

The creature doubled back and began to run towards her at full speed. Firelight drew her short sword and shoved it between the creature's eyes as it lunged towards her, generating a loud, jarring, clinking sound as the metal made contact with the creature's skull and splattering blood all over the place! The creature tumbled to its side with a thud; it was finally dead. Firelight fell backwards with exhaustion.

"My hands..." she mumbled to herself. "I shouldn't have been so reckless." Her hands were red and scalded from the severe burn she had sustained from her own fire. She rolled over in pain as the shaken black cat ran off towards the woods.

"Firelight? Is that you?" She turned and looked up: it was General Richmond. "My God, what happened?! You're covered in blood!"

"It's not my blood," she murmured, pointing towards the fallen beast in the middle of the lawn. "I was attacked by that... dog thing. It was all a trap."

"Are you injured?"

"A little, but I think I'll be all right. Luckily Rurik gave me one of these…" She took a small vial out her pocket and drank from it. The burns on her hands were healed nearly instantly.

"I'm leaving the city," uttered the general. "I've talked it over with my wife, and she agrees that it's what I must do. I think you should come with me."

She looked him in the eyes from her position on the ground. He was a little bit rough and unkempt, and it looked like he hadn't shaved for a couple of days; it was a far cry from his normal prim and proper image. He was crude. It was almost as though he had become a completely different person since she had last seen him. Almost.

She got up slowly as a cool breeze set in.

"All right, I'll come with you. There's no way I'm staying in this deathtrap of a city another minute!"

"Gather your belongings and follow me, then. We have a long trip ahead of us."

Chapter 35

"Get up, you bat-eared little brat! Get up!"

"No!" Silara was sprawled out on the dirty forest floor, grasping a small tree stump and holding on with all her strength. Tears enveloped her face. "I'm not coming with you!"

"Let go of that!" screamed Yohannis. He had been dragging her for nearly an hour now, and she was finally putting up a spirited resistance. He had to admit that he admired that a little.

"I'll never let go!" He wrenched her hand off of the tree stump and then dragged her away as she clawed at the dirt.

"Stop resisting, you insolent imp! You don't understand what's good for you!"

"*You* don't understand! Angroo was taking me to safety!"

"Oh, was he now? It sickens me that he was able to brainwash you so easily."

"Brainwash me? No!"

"Of course he brainwashed you. Orcs always brainwash their prey right before they slice open their heads and devour their brains! They... prefer clean food." He chuckled to himself.

"He was taking me to safety and you killed him!" she cried. He continued to laugh without the slightest regard for her feelings.

"Kill is such a harsh word. I prefer the word *end*. I *ended* him."

"Let go of me, you murderer!" Her crying intensified.

"Oh, there there little girl. You seem sad. Why don't you sing a little song to make yourself happy? Wouldn't that make everything better?! *All around the mulberry...*"

"Shut up!" she screamed. "Just shut up!"

"I should slap you for speaking to me like that!" She tried to grab a tree branch but Yohannis pulled her hand away. He was now holding onto both of her hands as he lugged her along.

"Let go of me!"

"And you know what? For the record, I do not find your songs very amusing. Not very amusing at all."

"Let her go!" blasted a strange, garbled voice. Yohannis let his gut reaction take over: he dropped the princess and whipped out his bow, crouching into a battle stance. Silara got up and began to run away as quickly as she could, but she bumped into someone and fell backwards.

"Who goes there!?" screamed Yohannis, but he was soon sorry he asked. A huge, hulking man with green skin and the head of a frog emerged from the darkness!

"My name is Frufur von FroggenMcHopper, and I believe you and your little girl are trespassing in my lady's territory."

"She isn't *my* little girl, thank goodness!" retorted Yohannis as he took a step forward. "But *you* will not lay a finger on her if you want to prolong your unholy existence any further!" The frog-man touched Silara's shoulder simply to draw the crazed archer's response; he then easily avoided the incoming arrow with a high leap, kicking Yohannis on his descent and sending him crashing into a moldy, dead tree.

"Come," uttered Frufur von FroggenMcHopper as he extended his hand out to Silara, but she stood still and shivered with fright. The frog-man grabbed her and picked her up, hopping away into the woods as she screamed and struggled in vain.

"Damn it!" cried Yohannis as he climbed to his feet. "Damn it! I'll get you yet, you amphibious toad-face!"

Princess Silara found herself dropped off on the ground in front of a small, wooden, moss-covered house that was built into the gnarled trees of the surrounding swamp. The house's dull colors and soft edges caused it to blend seamlessly with the trees; it appeared as much a part of nature to her as anything else in view. The sound of a cool breeze blowing softly against her skin was all that she could hear above the eerie silence. A heavy white mist saturated the air and made it difficult to see anything far away. Where was she?

"You've finally made it, Princess Silara," said a deep female voice. Silara looked up to see an elf woman standing in the doorway and staring down at her with a piercing, chilling gaze. The woman's long black hair came down in front of one of her severe eyes, and she wore a simple green shirt and pants. She reached out a hand to help Silara to her feet.

"Who... are you?"

"My name is Winterfrost. I believe you are here to see me."

"Winterfrost!? Oh, thank goodness!"

"Who sent you here?"

"I'm so happy to see you, Winterfrost! We were looking all over for you!" She tried to give the woman a hug, but the woman quickly stepped away.

"You have the mannerisms of a child. Who sent you?"

"Firelight..."

"Come inside. You'll catch a cold out here in that soaking wet dress." Winterfrost turned and walked back into the house. Silara looked around before slowly following her inside.

"Thank you for..."

"You have a scrape. Let me take care of that for you." Silara hadn't even noticed the gash on her left leg, but it didn't matter because it was healed completely as soon as the woman put her hand upon it.

"Oh, thank y…"

"Drink this," said Winterfrost as she handed Silara a steaming wooden cup. "It's green tea."

"My daddy said I'm not allowed to drink tea because the caffeine will keep me up all night."

"Don't be ridiculous. Drink the tea." Silara was a little intimidated; she did as she was told and didn't complain even though the tea was a little too hot and it tasted rather bitter. Even still, she had to admit that it was a nice change of pace from the rain water she had been drinking for the last several days. In fact, she even began to enjoy the tea after a few sips. It was different from what she was used to and flavorful in its own way.

"How did you already know that I was here to see you, Lady Winterfrost?"

"Please, just Winterfrost is fine."

"But the frog called you his lady."

"Frufur, you mean? I'm his master. I raised him since he was young."

"Since he was a tadpole?"

"Werefrogs are *never* tadpoles. They retain their frog-like humanoid appearance from birth."

"Sorry, Lady Win… I mean, just Winterfrost. But he's such a fascinating creature. I've never heard of a werefrog before!"

"Let's not get off topic here. You asked why I knew you were here to see me. I knew this because I overheard you and your orcish traveling companion speaking about it earlier today. You appear to be in some kind of predicament."

"Uh… yeah. You overheard us, though? That's impossible! We didn't notice…"

"I have many ears and eyes in this forest. I know *everything* that goes on in this area." Silence followed. Winterfrost turned and left the room, returning moments later with a large roll and handing it to the weary princess, who quickly gobbled it up.

"Thank you! I'm so grateful for your hospita…"

"You're welcome."

Silara just stood and looked at her host for a minute, unsure of what to say next. She wanted to take her mind off what happened to Angroo, so she decided that it might be a good idea to bring up a different, more cheerful topic. Why not talk about music? She was a little apprehensive to bring up the subject, though. Winterfrost would probably just think she was acting childish for even mentioning music and would look down on her even more. But Silara definitely didn't want to continue the awkward silence for any longer, so she decided to take the chance. Why not?

"So, do you have any favorite kinds of music that you like to listen…"

"If Firelight sent you, there must be an important reason. You must be in serious danger, especially since she resorted to sending you with an orc."

"Hey! Nobody *resorted* to sending me with an orc! I went with him because I knew that I could trust him with my life. It was *my* decision. Firelight just recommended that we travel here to meet you. Yeah, that's right."

"Is Firelight safe?"

"The last time I saw her she was okay. She's probably in Victory City now." Winterfrost paced back and forth.

"Why did Firelight choose some orc to accompany you on your trip? Victory City is at war with the orcs."

"He wasn't just *some* orc, all right? He was a great person who showed the greatest amount of courage and compassion that I've ever seen. He was kindhearted, brave, and plus he knew how to get here. I'm hurt by what you have to say about..."

"You do know that orcs are savage monsters who cannot be trusted, right? Why should this orc be any different from the others of his kind?" Silara fumed with anger.

"What about Frufur von FroggenMcHopper then, huh? He's not an elf like you. He's just some dirty creature from the swamp, a werefrog that you found one day. Why are you blindly handing your trust over to some savage werefrog? Tell me that, *Winterfrost*!" Winterfrost stared deeply into her eyes and tapped her fingers on the table.

"I raised Frufur since he was very young. *I* raised him, and I've been raising him for the last three years. He's..."

"Well you know what? Firelight raised Angroo from a very young age, too. She raised him since he was a little baby. You trust Firelight, right? Wouldn't you trust her to raise a fine, upstanding individual, regardless of what he looks like? Why would he be any different from Frufur, then?"

"You don't understand, *Princess*," spit Winterfrost through clenched teeth. Her stare practically burnt a hole in Silara's face. "Orcs are *killers*. It's in their blood. You *can't* take it away from them. You simply don't understand."

"Angroo was different! Firelight trained him to be different!"

"You naïve little girl! Orcs are killers! All of them should be put to death at once!"

"No!"

"They should be rounded up and slaughtered! Each and every one of them!"

"Take that back!!!"

"All right, all right. You can put an end to your little tapestry of lies now, Princess. You had me quite entertained for a while."

"What?" Silara was surprised; Winterfrost's angry, stern face was suddenly replaced by a much softer, gentler one.

"Just about everything you just told me was a lie. *Firelight* raised an orc? Please. But your heart remained true, and that's what's important." Silara was flabbergasted. "You are wise beyond your years, Princess Silara. When you gazed upon Angroo's face for the first time, did you see a bloodthirsty orc, born and bred of filth? You did not, although many would have. Instead, you saw deeper; you saw a noble soul devoted to your protection at any cost. You judged this orc entirely on his character. You have passed my little test and you have shown yourself worthy of my respect."

"It was all a test? You mean, you don't actually hate orcs?"

"No, no. Not everyone is as intolerant as your friend Yohannis out there. Orcs can have good hearts, just like Angroo does."

"Yes." Silara shook her head and looked at the ground. "Poor, poor Angroo. He was… killed, though. He's dead now."

"No, he's not dead. He's still alive."

"What!? Really?!"

"Yes. I watched the whole fight play out from a distance, and then I came in and used my magic to mend his wounds as soon as you had left. He made a complete recovery."

"Oh, thank you!" A huge smile exploded on Silara's face as she rushed forward to embrace Winterfrost, who allowed herself to be hugged this time. "Thank you so much!" Winterfrost couldn't help but smile as well.

"I'll take good care of you," she whispered. "You're safe here."

Chapter 36

It was a cold autumn night, and Angroo wandered the forest in a daze. What had just happened to him? He thought he had been dying at the hands of the blond soldier. The pain had felt so real. But the arrow that pierced his chest was not there anymore, and neither was the one that was buried in his upper back. In fact, there were no physical signs that the arrows had ever even touched him at all. And why did he wake up in a pile of leaves? He distinctly remembered landing in mud before he blacked out.

Why was his mind playing tricks on him? Lately, it seemed like his mind was always playing tricks on him; he couldn't even trust himself. There were too many conflicting thoughts, too many paradoxes. Even the thought of his mind playing tricks on him gave Angroo alternating urges to dismiss the idea as ridiculous and embrace it as the only possible explanation. Somewhere, his mind must have been lying to him about something. But what was the truth and what was the lie?

He concluded that the fight with the blond soldier must have really occurred; that was the truth. Even though his wounds were gone, he found a key piece of evidence once he had returned to the spot where he believed that the fight had taken place: it was his trusty trident, half-buried in the mud in the exact spot where he remembered dropping it. There was no other explanation for why the trident was there.

For a few minutes, Angroo even began to question whether or not the elf girl was real as well. She seemed too good to be real. But she *was* real, and she was currently in the company of the sorceress they had been sent here to find. He knew this because, in his wandering, he chanced upon their location; he overheard the girl's angelic voice conversing with another voice inside a wooden house that he had been walking past in his dazed state. He cringed as he recalled what had happened: the voice had told the girl that all orcs should be put to death. They should be rounded up and slaughtered, the voice had said. At that point, he couldn't listen to the voice anymore; he got up and left, wandering back off into the woods. *This* was supposed to be the girl's guardian? An orc-hater? Was *everyone* an orc-hater? Maybe the orcs brought this hatred upon themselves, though. Were all orcs really evil? His skin burned more intensely than ever before.

The girl wasn't an orc-hater. Definitely not. And she had told him that orcs aren't all evil, so what she said must have been true. Had he ever met others who tolerated his kind, though? Were there any others? It wasn't worth thinking about; it was too far in the past anyway, and he couldn't trust himself to remember such distant events with any meaningful accuracy in his delirious mental state. The only thing that was real to him at that moment was the teenage girl he had promised to protect.

She didn't need him to protect her, though. She already had a *better* protector. The sorceress could protect the girl much better than he could, right? Angroo felt his chest tighten with angst, and a putrid taste materialized in the back of his throat. He began to shiver and sweat. Things couldn't go on like this, but what could he do? He couldn't leave her with that stupid jerk of a sorceress whose name sounded like some kind of chewing gum. No way. He *hated* the sorceress even though he had never even seen her. In fact, he realized then that he had always hated her ever since the night he and the girl first left on their trip, and his hate had intensified with every waking hour. The inevitable had finally occurred: this woman had finally taken everything he cared about away from him.

172

His fists clenched with rage. He wanted to murder her in cold blood, to tear her limbs off one by one with his bare hands. That would show her.

How could he think such horrible things? Was it his mind playing tricks on him again? He didn't believe so, but either way it was no excuse for such appalling, despicable thoughts. He had to calm himself down somehow. He sat down at the base of a tree and clasped his face with both of his hands. Everything was fine. Relax. The girl was safe now because he had successfully accomplished his job of guiding her through the wilderness. Everything was all right. Wasn't he supposed to help negotiate a peace treaty now on behalf of his tribe, or something like that? It was such a distant memory now, but it was his next challenge and he had to tackle it. Tomorrow would be a fresh new day. But still, he couldn't just *leave* her with that sorceress, could he?

Chapter 37

"What news do you have for me this time, Dr. Rugby?"

"The half-elf got away."

"What?! How could you let her get away?!"

"She killed our best dog and escaped from the city."

"Damn it! I thought you fed the damn dog some kind of heat-resistance concoction!"

"I did, sir."

"Then how did she kill it?! Its skin was impervious to fire!"

"She killed it with a sword."

"Damn."

"Don't worry about her, sir; I've sent my men after her with instructions to kill her and collect her body as proof of their deed. My men are closing in on her even as we speak, and they have never let me down before."

"You sent your three magicians after her, huh? I guess she'll be in for a little bit of a *shock*, then, right?! Ha ha ha."

"Yes. Very humorous sir."

"Now in the meantime, Dr. Rugby, I have a new task for you. Listen very, very carefully to what I'm about to say. It appears that Lord Eliazer has somehow discovered the truth about his daughter; he knows that she was captured by the orcs. I want you to keep an eye on him and make sure he doesn't do anything foolish. He is a weak man, and it is only a matter of time before he acquiesces to their demands and gives up the remaining Golden Egg of Gotty Gottya. You must stay alert and be ready to act if he reveals the location of the Egg; you must be swift and obtain it before the orcs do. This is your most important task yet, and failure will not be tolerated."

"I understand completely, sir. I would not have it any other way."

"Failure will *not* be tolerated. Do not fail me again, Rugby!"

"I will not fail, sir."

"You will not fail!"

"I will not fail!"

"See to it that you don't. You are dismissed."

Chapter 38

A full day had passed since Silara had arrived at Winterfrost's house, but she didn't feel very at-home yet. Winterfrost seemed like a pretty nice person inside, but there was no denying that she had a stern temperament, to say the least. She maintained a very strict set of rules, and the princess was starting to feel a little bit uncomfortable hanging around her and was starting to become anxious. When was Angroo going to finally show up and get some of the fun started, anyway?

Silara was wearing a green cloth shirt and green pants that she had borrowed from Winterfrost; she preferred dresses to pants but had to admit that this outfit was very comfortable and also looked pretty good on her. She fixed her hair in the mirror and then walked into the main room of the house to find her host sitting at a table and reading a book. Winterfrost motioned for her to sit down next to her at the table, so she slowly nodded her head and walked over. She had secretly been hoping to avoid talking to Winterfrost because she wasn't really in the mood to talk, but whatever. Her father had taught her that, whenever she was a guest at someone's house, it was important for her to show gratitude in any way she could, and maybe allowing herself to be dragged into a stale conversation was the best way to do that in this case. She hurriedly tried to think of something to talk about so that she wouldn't sound bored.

"I was wondering, Princess Silara...

"I was wondering about something too, Winterfrost. Why would you name your pet werefrog Frufur von FroggenMcHopper, anyway? What did he do to deserve that? Don't you want him to live a normal life without worrying about everyone making fun of his name?"

"I didn't raise Frufur. I befriended him a couple of years back. You weren't the only one who was lying during that conversation. Oh, and they actually do begin life as tadpoles, by the way."

"Oh."

"Frufur doesn't really fit in well with the other werefrogs around here but he's proven himself to be a reliable friend for me."

"Uh huh."

"Anyway, Princess, I was going to ask you: do you possess any magical abilities?"

"Magical abilities? No..."

"I don't know about that. I can sense something about you that makes me think otherwise; you know, elves sometimes have innate magical talent without realizing it. You just have to look inside yourself and find it." Silara smiled.

"That would be neat if I really did have some sort of magical power, wouldn't it? How would I know, though? How do I look inside of myself?"

"Try focusing all of your energy into your hands, and twist your fingers a little bit in this shape. I want to see something." The princess shrugged and did as she was told, focusing her energy and copying Winterfrost's finger positions. Winterfrost felt her hand.

"I think you have something. Continue focusing the energy. Strain."

"Okay."

"Okay, very good. Now see this cut on my hand?"

"It's bleeding! How'd that cut get there?!"

"I just cut myself with my fingernail on purpose."

"Why?"

"Touch the cut."

"Ewwww! No!"

"Just put your hand over it!"

"Okay, fine. There. It's just a regular cut."

"What is?"

"What do you mean what is? The... hey, it's gone!"

"Just as I suspected. You are a healer, Princess Silara. Just like me." Silara was shocked by this sudden revelation. She looked at her hands.

"Wow!"

"Do not be overconfident, though. Your magic is weak right now, and the only way it can become stronger is through practice. One day, if you continue to work at it, you can become a great healer."

"Okay, okay! Cut yourself again, then! I need more practice!" A wide grin brightened up her face. "I have to tell Daddy about this!"

"That reminds me, Princess. I also meant to ask you why you are separated from your father. Why isn't *he* protecting you from these men that attack you?"

"I... was told that you should protect me."

"I *will* protect you, but allow me to obtain a better understanding of this whole situation. You told me yesterday that strange men are after you and you were sent here because you want to be in a place where nobody can find you, right?"

"Yep. Pretty much."

"Why are they going after *you* in particular?"

"I don't know, but I think it has something to do with a powerful object that my daddy owns. They want to hold me for ransom or something like that. I don't really want to talk about it, though; the very thought of that awful man who broke into my room that night gives me the shivers."

"Somebody must really want that object, then, if you need *my* protection. Somebody must be very desperate."

Silara nodded. She then rested her head on her hands and gazed out the window.

"Where do you think Angroo went? I have to tell him about my new healing powers. Do you think he's ever gonna come and visit us?"

"I cannot say, but the possibility remains that he left and went back to wherever he comes from. As much as the two of you may have shared a bond during your travels, you must come to realize that he has things that he needs to do as well. His life needs to go on. He cannot always spend his time looking after you."

"He said he would stay here with me, though. He definitely said that. Do you think he's hurt?"

"No. I haven't received recent word of his whereabouts, so he must have left the area."

"I don't believe it. He wouldn't just abandon me like this."

"Angroo has gone his separate way. You must learn to accept loss. Who knows: you may yet see him again one day."

"I don't want to see him *again one day*, though! I want to see him *now*!" She turned to face the window. "ANGROO!!! WHERE ARE Y…"

Winterfrost dropped her book and lunged forward, wrestling Silara to the ground and holding her hand over her mouth.

"What are you doing?! Don't shout like that, you foolish girl! Your voice carries here!"

"I just wanted to see if Angroo could hear me." The princess barely managed to hold back her tears.

"Did you hear what I just said? I just told you that he wasn't anywhere near here, so there's no way he could hear you. Why would you shout so loudly if you're supposed to be hiding? This isn't a safe area; there are many creatures around here who might wish ill upon you for one reason or another, and the last thing you want to do is attract their attention."

"Sorry."

"All right. I accept your apology, but you should be more careful next time." She began to walk into the next room. "We can only hope that nobody who would want to do you harm heard your shouting."

Little did Silara know that somebody who would want to do her harm actually did hear her shouting. She seemed to have the worst luck with that kind of thing.

Chapter 39

It was Angroo's second day of traveling since his mysterious near-death experience, but he had not gone far. He had yet to completely convince himself that leaving the girl alone was the right thing to do, so as a result of his hesitation he walked very slowly and allowed himself to take lengthy breaks. There was too much at stake to turn back, though, he rationalized. As much as he wanted to stay with the girl, he knew that he had to go home and persuade Molar-Licker and the others to sign the peace agreement. He trudged on. It would have been nice to have had someone to travel with, though.

But why not go back and visit the girl? It would only be for a couple of days. Angroo was weary from all of his traveling the past few weeks, so he could certainly use a nice little break like that; at the very least it would allow him to be well-rested and energized for the trip back to his home in the mountains. He began to seriously consider going back. He figured that he could have traveled four times faster if he had really been trying, so he reasoned that it shouldn't take more than half a day of hard travel to return to the sorceress's cottage. Travel time wouldn't be much of an issue, then. He'd really have to pick up the pace, though, if he wanted to make it back to see the girl before the sun set, but it was worth it. Yeah. He began to turn around.

He couldn't do it. He couldn't bear to think about what would happen if he allowed the humans to unleash the power of their Golden Egg on the orcs. Everyone would die and everything he knew would be lost just because of his little, selfish play date. Maybe it didn't matter either way, though, since it was somewhat hard for him to fathom both sides coming to an agreement just because of something that he did. Nothing that he did ever resulted in something positive.

But why hadn't the humans already used the Golden Egg if they were going to use it? It didn't seem to make sense. If there was only one Golden Egg left and they wanted to protect it so badly, they should have just used it and gotten it over with. Maybe the humans really did want peace, though. Maybe that was the reason they hadn't already exterminated the orcs. Or maybe the orcs have something that Victory City wants. It was all so confusing. Angroo sat down on a big, soggy tree stump and thought about what he should do next, resting his chin on his knuckles.

"Ribbit."

"Who's there?"

"Ribbit." Angroo jumped up. Standing before him were two huge, bipedal frog-like creatures! They must have been at least eight or nine feet tall, and their massive, beady eyes stared down at him without expression. They looked like big, slimy stuffed animals. Angroo drew his weapon.

"What are you doing here?! What do you want with me?!"

"Ribbit. Ribbit." One of the frogmen opened its mouth, and, in a burst of saliva, a huge pink tongue suddenly shot right out at Angroo! He batted it away with his trident, but the other frogman's tongue shot out as well and coiled around the trident, ripping it out of Angroo's grasp and flinging it off into the woods somewhere.

Angroo began to lose his mind. There were too many things that needed to be done for him to die there, so he couldn't let it happen. Not yet. He turned and sprinted away, only to be stopped in his tracks when a wet, sticky giant frog tongue shot out from behind him and grabbed onto his right arm! He tried to rip the tongue off his arm, but before he could make any progress another tongue soared from the opposite direction and stuck to his other arm! The frogs circled around him so that they were directly in line with each other, and then they began to step backwards as Angroo struggled to get free. He soon found himself suspended a foot off the ground as the frogs continued to separate. They were playing tug of war, ripping him in half in the process!

Angroo had to concentrate over the rapidly increasing pain. No, there was no time to concentrate. He had to take action right away or he would be dead. Angroo wrapped his legs around a low tree branch that was dangling in front of him and managed to get his body on top of it. He then maneuvered himself off of the other side of branch, bringing the two tongues down with him and causing them to scrape against the rough bark and bleed. One of the frogs let go at this point, releasing its tongue from Angroo's arm and giving him exactly the opportunity he was looking for; grabbing the other tongue with his now-free hand, he ran under and climbed back over the branch, tying the tongue in a knot and finally freeing himself from the tongue's grasp with a quick, powerful heave. The hapless frogman struggled but was unable to retract its tongue from the branch it was now knotted around. Angroo grabbed a sharp stick and vaulted forward, stabbing the trapped monster repeatedly until it was no longer moving and then turning back towards the other frog, who again tried to catch Angroo with its tongue but missed. Angroo grabbed the tongue out of the air and used all of his strength to heave the frog hard into a tree; he then killed this frog in the same manner he had finished off its friend.

Angroo stood over the fallen bodies of the two frogmen, wheezing and covered in blood. Stupid, stupid frog people. They had brought this fate upon themselves. He tossed the bloody stick onto one of the bodies and glanced around to make sure he didn't have any more amphibious company.

He decided to lie down and rest for a minute. One thing was certain: he needed to be a little more vigilant in the future. That was much too close.

Some leaves rustled in the distance. Angroo leapt to his feet and listened carefully; someone was coming. Someone was definitely coming. Where was the trident?! He looked around and spotted it near a tree several yards away, so he hurried over and picked it up, quickly turning back to face the direction of the footsteps. Who was it? Another frogman? He knew that he wouldn't be able to see his assailant through the dense underbrush until it was very close, so he would have to act fast as soon as he saw something. The footsteps sped up. He felt cold beads of sweat run down his face. He was too exhausted for this right now.

Angroo watched plant leaves and branches begin to give way as somebody pushed through them; the confrontation was imminent. He clutched his weapon and prepared to strike, but he still found himself completely unprepared for what he saw. There, emerging from the bushes like Venus emerging from the clamshell, was a delicate female body. It was the woman. The half-elf fire sorceress. She was wearing her leather armor that he loved so much and she looked more stunning than ever with her wavy brown hair splayed around her beautiful face and dotted with leaves and twigs from her journey through the woods. So natural-looking. It's funny how he had almost completely forgotten about her since he met the elf girl.

"Angroo!? Is that really you?!" she cried. "General! I found Angroo!" The human commander emerged from the bushes right after her. Angroo couldn't help himself any longer; he fell to his knees. He couldn't have possibly been more relieved to see them.

"Are you all right, Angroo?!" shouted the commander.

"It looks like you need medical attention!"

"I'm okay," he muttered back. He suppressed his smile of joy, wanting to make himself seem as nonchalant as possible. "Everything is okay. It is good to see you again, General Richmond. And it's good to see you too, Firelight."

"Why are you covered in blood?" asked the commander. "What happened here?" Angroo pointed to the mangled bodies of the frog people.

"Their blood."

"What the heck?!" gasped the woman in a high-pitched, astonished voice. Her eyes went wide with curiosity. "Is that some sort of toad?"

"I don't know. They attacked without warning, but I took care of them." He crossed his arms. Firelight walked over to the frog bodies and closely examined them.

"Wow. I've never seen this kind of creature before."

"Is the princess safe, Angroo?" asked the commander.

"Yes. She's with Winterfrost right now."

"Excellent work, then."

"Good old Winterfrost. How's she doing now, anyway? I haven't seen her in years."

"Uh, I don't know. I didn't really…"

"She always was a little bit of a stick in the mud. I can understand if you didn't have the best first impression of her, but she's a good person once you get to know her, though."

Angroo wondered why the woman thought so highly of that wretch. Could someone who believed that every orc deserved to die possibly be worthy of his respect? Maybe some people were just ignorant about certain things, he thought, but wishing for his race's extermination was a little tiny bit too extreme of an opinion for his taste.

"How close are we?" asked the commander.

"Half day, maybe," replied Angroo. "A little more than a

half day. Why? Do you want to go there?"

"I don't know. I don't think we have to at this point. Right Firelight?"

"Uh..."

"Why did you come here, then?"

"We were going to pay Winterfrost a visit," explained the commander, "because we were hoping that you were still there. We wanted to catch you before you left."

"You were looking for me?"

"Yes. We need to talk to you, but now that we found you we may as well just go back."

"I don't know, General," said the woman. "We came all the way here. Maybe we should just stop in for a night or two, you know, just to see how everything's going."

"All right, I suppose you're right. Angroo, show us the wa...it a minute." The commander looked around, his expression suddenly grave. "What if we're being followed?"

"I don't think we're being followed," the woman replied. "I haven't seen or heard anyone."

"No, we have to go back. Whoever went after you in the city might be following us, and we can't risk tipping our hand on the princess's location."

"I don't think we were being followed out of the city, though. I'm pretty sure that we weren't."

"We just can't take the risk. We have nothing to gain here; we already found Angroo and we'd just be wasting time anyway. I don't want to put anyone in danger if someone really has been following us."

"Why would anyone be following us? Don't be ridiculous."

"Maybe we should... go... visit," Angroo butted in quietly. Both of the others turned to him. "It's uh... not too far. Not a big hassle. I'll lead you there if you want."

"Yeah, listen to what he says. We're practically there anyway." The commander thought about it for a minute. "And plus, there's nobody following us! Come on."

"All right, we'll visit Winterfrost and the girl, then. But we need to be quick about it. We can't stay there long and we can't bring attention to ourselves." He looked around again. "I don't know why you're so certain that we're not being followed, Firelight."

"I don't know anything for sure. It just seems a little unlikely."

"All right," the commander said, nodding his head very slowly. "All right, let's go. Let's hope that you're right. But I really don't have a good feeling about this."

Chapter 40

Princess Silara was beginning to worry about Angroo. He had promised that he would stay with her for a while but he never showed. It didn't seem like him at all to just make up something like that; what if he was hurt somewhere? Silara waited until it began to get dark, and then she crept out of her window and tiptoed slowly towards the woods. It was a nice, warm night. If Winterfrost had eyes and ears all over the forest as she had claimed, then why didn't she notice Silara sneaking out of her own house? She was probably too caught up in a boring book or something to realize what was happening. Silara began to wonder if this was really the person she wanted protecting her. Where was that big cuddly white orc when you needed him?

She stopped suddenly after hearing something move; the sound came from the dark woods ahead of her. She stood completely still, holding her breath for a moment and listening closely. Completely still. Now it sounded like someone or something was breathing. There was definitely someone there. She turned and began to sneak back to the house as quietly as she could as fear mounted inside of her. She turned her head to look back but didn't see anything; the muffled breathing continued somewhere, though. Her pace steadily increased as she went until she finally began to run hard, throwing away any element of stealth she might have been clinging to as she rushed ahead. She was now in an all-out sprint as she approached the house. Just a little... bit... further!

"Ribbit."

A cold, soaking wet frog tongue came from nowhere and wrapped itself around her head. She tried to scream but couldn't; she couldn't even breathe or see anything with the tongue wrapped tightly over her entire face. A sickening, chemically smell flooded her squashed-open nostrils. Her hands frantically clawed at the tongue, but it just wrapped even tighter as it dragged her quickly off towards the woods. Suddenly, she felt another wet tongue grab her legs, and a third one wrapped around her belly. They were suffocating her. She managed to free one of her eyes with a strong, desperate pull and caught a glimpse of dozens of werefrogs fiercely struggling with each other like frenzied sharks; they must have been fighting over who gets to eat her. It's as if they had all been gathering there for some time, waiting for the opportunity to get to her, but how did they know they would even find her there? She felt herself beginning to pass out from a lack of oxygen.

"Release the girl at once!" shouted Winterfrost. A second-long pause was followed by the sounds of the creatures clumsily and hastily pushing past each other. To Silara's surprise, most the werefrogs were retreating to the woods; apparently the woman's reputation preceded her. Those who didn't escape, however, were soon sorry they had stayed. A blue flash zipped out of the sorceress's fingertip, and in no time the tongue around Silara's face unraveled as its owner plummeted backwards in a halo of blood. Another flash, and then another and another. It was all over in a matter of seconds: four werefrogs lay dead, shards of ice lodged between their gigantic, bulging eyes. Silara gasped for air on the dirty ground as Winterfrost stood over her; she couldn't bear to look up and face the sorceress's angry gaze, instead choosing to bury her face in the dirt.

"What did you think you were doing?! You were nearly eaten alive by those creatures!"

"I was just…"

"You were just what? Looking for that friend of yours?!"

The princess didn't respond. "I told you that he's not in the area anymore. He left. What reason would I have to lie to you about that? What reason?!" Silara covered her face with her hands and began to sob. She felt extremely embarrassed and ashamed.

"I just…"

"I told you that this was a dangerous swamp, but you didn't listen to me. How old are you?! You're not a little child! You're a young lady, and I expect you to behave like one if you're going to continue to live in my house!"

"I'm really sorry! I don't know what got into me!"

"You have some nerve to just come here and expect…"

"I'm sorry!"

There was a short silence.

"It's okay." Winterfrost knelt down next to the sobbing girl and put her hand on the top of her head, combing her hair softly with her fingers. "I understand what you must be feeling. You're worried about one of your friends, and that's okay. You just need to learn to trust me a little bit if I'm going to continue to protect you." Silara nodded slowly. Her face was red from crying.

"Angroo told me he would stay and visit. He always keeps his word."

"I don't know why Angroo isn't here, Princess. I hope he comes also, and if he does come you can be assured that he will be shown my complete hospitality. But we must live in the present, and right now there are a lot of creatures in this swamp who want to make a meal of you. The werefrogs have been especially active these last few days for some reason." She put her hand on Silara's shoulder and leaned her head closer. "You're a very special girl. Believe it or not, you actually remind me a lot of myself when I was your age. I'll do everything I can to make sure that you stay safe, so don't cry.

You just need to have faith in me and trust me, all right?" She gave her a small kiss on her forehead. "Now, let's go inside; I finished washing your dress so you can change back into that if you want to get out of these filthy clothes, and in the meantime I'll heat up some more green tea for you. How does that sound?" Silara smiled and nodded her head.

"Carry me."

"Carry you? But you're nearly the same size as I!"

"My daddy always used to carry me back into the house when it started getting dark outside."

"All right. I'll carry you." Winterfrost hoisted up the princess into her arms and clumsily lugged her back into the house as darkness descended. It was quiet. Things suddenly seemed very peaceful in the swamp.

Chapter 41

"Welcome, good citizens of Victory City, and thank you for joining me on this gloomy evening. As you all know, times are bleak. Our fine city has been plunged in the throes of chaos and uncertainty as we wage war with a vicious, unyielding enemy, while the orc who killed my father roams free and plots his next unspeakable crime even as I stand here speaking to you today. But things will get better. The great city we live in will soon rise to reach and even surpass its former splendor! Mark my word, good citizens! My word is truth!

"I thank you for your applause, but perhaps it is unwarranted. I stand humbly before you a sovereign without a crown. A leader with no official means to legitimize my rule. I remain grateful that you have all placed your trust in me during these difficult times, but the fact remains that the very backbone of our society has been taken from us: the Crown of Victory City! This simple jeweled headpiece represents purity, strength, wealth, and tradition, all that is valued by our society and all that we cherish deeply. I'm afraid that until we recover this heirloom of our city, this monument to our long history of greatness, we will forever be put to shame. My father cannot have a true successor to the throne until this crown is recovered, and you know what? His killer knows this. He knew it all along. My father's killer wants the city to *panic*. He wants chaos; he thrives in it, as all orcs do. But, let me tell you, he has vastly underestimated the resolve of the people of Victory City! We shall remain steadfast, and until the crown is rightfully returned and the threat dispersed, we shall fight on! Nothing shall hold us back!

"Now this brings me to the real reason I called all of you here today, so heed my words carefully and with your full patience. Today I look upon you, and I am nearly brought to tears as I gaze upon your suffering faces; my heart holds the pain that each and every one of you must bear. You are young and old, rich and poor, but you are all fine men and women of Victory City and you are all part of my family. I care deeply about all of you. That is why it pains me to no end when I say that things must take a turn for the worse before they get better. I ask each and every one of you a simple question: can the loss of some good life be considered justifiable if, as a consequence, others may live in eternal peace and our city can be restored to its full glory and legitimacy? Please consider the sheer gravity of the situation and the responsibility that each of us owes to our fine city and to ourselves. Alas, we must live in the present time. I shudder to think that any of the heroic souls of this city might be lost to the ravages of war, but I'm afraid that this is the terrible price that must be paid in order for our way of life, life as we know it, to endure. That is why I have decided to authorize a daring, full-scale raid into the heart of the orc territory; it was easily the most difficult decision of my life. This massive raid will no doubt lead to the loss of the lives of a great many of our soldiers, but it is something that must be done because if we cannot quash the orcish uprising now, it will escalate beyond our comprehension. This attack will take great courage and great dedication, but I know my soldiers will step up to the challenge and do what they know must be done. Men and women of Victory City, heed my words! The crown of our city, the honor of our fathers, hangs in the balance! Our *lives* hang in the balance! Stand by me now, good citizens! We must act now! For the crown of our fathers, we must act now!

"I leave you now with those grim tidings. I thank you for your continuing support during these trying times, and I pray that I will one day lead you into peace and prosperity as king, with the Crown of Victory City firmly planted upon my head. Thank you all for hearing me out and please try to enjoy the rest of your evening if you can; comfort yourselves with good wishes and optimism for what the future will bring. Thank you."

Chapter 42

"Ribbit."

"Who's there?!" shouted the general as he drew his sword. A huge, hulking figure emerged from the darkness in front of them.

"It's one of those frogs!" cried Firelight as she nearly dropped the torch she was holding. "Get him!"

"I prefer the term *werefrog*, actually."

"You can talk?!" squealed Firelight.

"Yes. All werefrogs can talk. Most just choose not to." The werefrog casually leaned against a tree, but he was suddenly forced to put his arms out in front of him in self-defense as the three travelers approached him with their weapons drawn. "Lower your weapons, good folk! I mean you no harm! My name is Frufur von FroggenMcHopper and I'm only here to serve!"

"You're only here to serve?" repeated a confused General Richmond. "Hmm. Perhaps you can help us with something, then. We are looking for Winterfrost, an elf who lives in this area. She's a powerful sorceress. Can you tell us exactly where she lives?"

"Certainly, and I'll even take you there myself."

"That's a relief," said Firelight with a sigh. "Thanks, Fluffer NuttenMcFrogger."

"A frog's honor, my lady."

Back at the house, Winterfrost and Silara were playing a card game by candlelight. Silara figured that it was an okay game, a little boring maybe, but it was kind of complicated and she still didn't completely understand the rules. It was better than doing nothing at least.

"Got any sixes?" she asked.

"Go fish," replied Winterfrost. Before Silara could take a card from the pile, though, her hand was shoved down onto the table.

"Wha... I didn't know that was part of this ga..."

"Shhhhhhhh! Quiet. It's not part of the game. Someone's coming." A shiver traveled down the princess's spine; the last thing she wanted was some more unexpected company barely an hour after that unfortunate incident with the werefrogs.

"Who is it?!" she whispered as she scrambled under the table. Her host didn't answer right away, instead listening carefully to what was going on outside with her ear up against the wall. Silara thought she saw a faint smile flash upon her face for a split second and disappear.

The door opened and a man walked in. The princess was taken by surprise; she jumped up from under the table and backed against the wall.

"Ah, Princess Silara! Well met again! And you must be Winterfrost."

"I am. It's a pleasure to meet you for the first time, General Richmond." She shook hands with the general.

"How did you know my name?"

"Winterfrost!" cried Firelight as she entered the room. "How are you?! It's been so long!" She ran over to hug her old friend. "I hope we didn't catch you at a bad time."

"Oh no, not at all. I heard you coming from far away, so I knew you would be here soon."

"Geez, Winterfrost, you'd think you'd at least have the decency of mind to clean up the place a little bit if you knew you were having guests over, right?" Winterfrost stared at Firelight. "Heh, heh. I mean, um, you have dead werefrog bodies all over your front lawn. That's seriously what I was

196

talking about."

"The werefrogs have been very active lately. Those unfortunate souls whose bodies now lie in front of my house are the ones who attempted to attack the princess earlier this evening."

"You certainly made short work of them," muttered the general.

"Yes, but there will be more. It is only a matter of time before they show up again, hungering for mortal flesh. I was telling the princess that she must be very careful while she stays here. Anything she does or says can attract their attention."

"You could handle them if they did attack, though, right?" said Firelight. "Why don't you let the princess relax a little? She's been through a lot the last few days."

"Yeah!" shouted the princess.

"We must not be foolish," replied Winterfrost. "Our lives are fragile, delicate strands. We must never let down our guard against those who want to take them from us, especially during chaotic times such as these. If we are vigilant, the time for happiness will come, Firelight."

"All right, but just don't go too hard on her."

"You should have seen the test she gave me when I first got here!" said Silara. "She told me all these lies..."

"Oh boy. You gave her one of your *tests*?"

"These are dangerous times, Firelight, and I have to protect myself as well. With things the way they are now, choosing where to place my trust is of tremendous importance for me."

"Yeah, I know. I understand. You always did know how to handle yourself." There was a short pause.

"Well, it's important that I teach Silara how to protect herself as well. I won't always be around to save her from the werefrogs, you know."

"Speaking of werefrogs," said General Richmond, "not all of them are bad. We were escorted here by a friendly one."

"Oh, that must have been Frufur. He's an outcast among the werefrogs. He and I have been helping each other out for a few years now."

"His name's Frufur?!" Firelight snorted. "Man! I've been calling him Fluffer or something stupid like that the whole time!"

"Yes, his name is Frufur von FroggenMcHopper. He comes from a very well-respected lineage, you know. His great uncle Professor Frobert FroggenMcHopper is actually the one who first invented the werefrogs."

"Don't you mean Professor Frobert *von* FroggenMcHopper?" asked Silara.

"No, no. You see, 'von' is Frufur's middle name. It's werefrog custom to leave one's middle name lowercase."

"Oh, I get it now. But I didn't even know his middle name was lowercase because I've never actually seen it written out anywhere."

"As you get older, Princess, I have no doubt that you will. Werefrogs are avid writers who developed writing skills early in their history, and they correspond with each other quite frequently. You will find that their written manuscripts are not difficult to obtain."

"Wow, these werefrogs seem like fascinating creatures that I'm sure we'd all love to learn more about!" Firelight said sarcastically. "Especially Angroo; he's probably chomping at the bit to find out more about the werefrogs' penmanship or whatever after they nearly tore him in half!" There was a sudden silence. Silara looked up at Firelight with keen interest.

"Angroo? Is he okay?!"

"Yes, he's fine," answered the general. "Where is he

now, though? He was traveling with us just a minute ago. Maybe he's being shy." The four of them peered out the front door to see the white orc looking down at the bodies of the fallen werefrogs under the moonlight.

"Angroo!" screamed Silara as she rushed forward, embracing the orc with all of her strength. The others couldn't see the orc's reaction, though, because he was covered in shadow. They were both completely covered in shadow as a cloud passed in front of the moon.

"The princess is very fond of that orc," Winterfrost told Firelight and General Richmond as they stepped back into the house. "She often speaks about him. She sees him as a strong fatherly figure, I believe, or perhaps as an older brother."

"Angroo used to be an adversary of ours, but he has since agreed to help us work out a peace deal between Victory City and his kind," explained the general. "He has a good heart. He spared my life in battle and I owe him a debt of gratitude for that."

"I see."

"So Winterfrost, you don't mind if the three of us stay here for a night, do you?" asked Firelight.

"Of course not. You are welcome to stay as long as you like, although unfortunately I do not have any place for you to sleep except on the floor of the living room. I can retrieve some blankets for you, though."

"That will do just fine," said the general. "I'm afraid we won't be staying for more than one night, though. Maybe we'll remain here for a few hours tomorrow as well but we'll need to be moving shortly thereafter. There is too much that needs to be done."

"I understand. Make yourself at home while you're here and relax. There's a nice, grassy field a couple minutes' walk from here that would make a good camping area; I have some marshmallows, so why don't we start up a campfire?"

"Leave that to me," laughed Firelight. She snapped her finger and a tiny flame jumped up. Winterfrost smiled.

"How has your training with Methuselah been going, Firelight?

"Oh, good. My magic's gotten a lot better over the last few years, so now I can actually make myself useful some of the time."

"That's a serious understatement, my dear," said the general. "She's been invaluable to our efforts from the minute she joined us, so don't be fooled by her modesty. Now if you don't mind, I'm going to go see what the others are up to." He walked off. Winterfrost looked back at Firelight.

"You always had a strong heart, my friend. And you've always had a strong mind. I knew that you would be able to find the power within yourself to become a great sorcerer one day."

"Well, I mean, I'm still nothing compared to you..."

"Don't say that. We sorcerers are a rare breed, Firelight. We are one and equal. You are different from others, and you have to let that show. Bask in your power. You are a rare specimen indeed."

"I don't think..."

"Do not shortchange yourself. You must go out and make a difference. You have a serious talent that can be used to make the world a better place." Firelight was taken off guard by her friend's incessant compliments. She didn't know what to say; she was kind of dumbfounded.

"But... then how come *you* don't go out a make a difference, then? You just stay here and hang around by yourself in the swamp. You're the most powerful sorcerer I've ever seen, and you keep it all to yourself." Winterfrost turned away.

"I don't want to…"

"You're so smart and powerful, Winterfrost. You're talented beyond belief, and you always seem to know what to do in every single situation. Every time. You really should share your brain with the rest of the world."

"Things have been very hard for me!" snapped Winterfrost as she suddenly turned to face her friend. "It's so easy for you to stand there and say that, isn't it?!"

"Didn't you just tell me the same thing?"

"You're different! Not everything comes easy to me, you know, and I'm not better than you at everything. We do things in different ways. You have a spark. I… I don't want to discuss this anymore."

There was a short pause. Firelight looked down.

"Listen. I'm very sorry for what I just said. I didn't mean any of it."

"Let's not talk about it anymore."

"I feel like such an idiot right now. I didn't mean to hurt your feelings at all."

"You didn't hurt my feelings."

"I just have so much respect for you, I didn't know what to say when you told me about my…"

"It's okay. I forgive you. Here." Winterfrost hugged Firelight. "We are different, but the same. Don't you understand?"

"I guess…"

"Continue to be strong, Firelight. You have the power to make a difference. You're still very young, and the good that you do now will one day come back to you." Winterfrost turned away. "Now, let's get the fun started, okay? Everyone is waiting outside for us!" Firelight smiled.

"One campfire coming up!"

Chapter 43

It was getting late. The campfire was weakening now, but the night sky provided ample light, and a comfortable breeze blew in from the north and filled Angroo's nostrils. The moon and stars shined down upon his face as he gazed up at them and reflected their shine. They were so far away. Angroo never really understood things that were far away; he always wanted to understand them, but he never could. Things always seemed too unpredictable from too far away, but he certainly didn't have to worry about those things now. His prize, the little girl who had become a major part of his life in only a week's time, was by his side; all that mattered was right there within arm's reach. She was fast asleep and curled in a ball right next to where he lay, and he smiled as he listened to her soft breathing. She looked adorable in her white dress, which was finally clean, and she was still wearing her leaf moccasins. Did she ever take those shoes off? He stroked her silky hair with his fingers as the two of them lay alone on the grass by the remnants of the fire. Things were good. Tomorrow might bring something new to think about, but tonight this moment was the only thing that mattered to him; it was everything. Tomorrow was so far away, anyway, and he never really understood things that were far away.

It had been a strange evening for Angroo. He had finally met the raven-haired sorceress that he had heard and thought so much about, and he was taken off guard because she was not at all like he imagined. First of all, she was much better-looking than he had thought; she was very thin but also very curvy in the places it mattered, and she had an attractive face as well. Her most striking features were easily her crystal blue eyes, which were so deep and mysterious that they seemed to invite him inside and distance him at the same time whenever he looked at her from across the crimson flames of the campfire. She was probably in her thirties, he decided, but she seemed much older than that from the way that she spoke about things as if she had studied them for many years. She seemed very on-the-ball and focused as she spoke to Angroo and the others around the fire that night, and he liked that. He liked focus. He was *intrigued* by her.

She was still an orc-hater, though. He had heard what she said with his own two ears a couple of days earlier, but he was afraid to broach the subject in front of everybody. Maybe he hadn't actually heard it at all, though; maybe it was just another one of his false memories. It had to be. She really didn't seem like someone who would hold such irrational views. At the very least, Angroo could tell she was committed to keeping the girl safe, and he knew that she was capable of keeping this commitment after he saw the bodies of those werefrogs who had attempted to attack the girl. She must have killed those four monsters without the slightest bit of effort, a far cry from how he had struggled so mightily to fend off only two of the same creatures. She was powerful and committed. That made him feel a little bit better, and it also made him think that, if she really did believe that all orcs should be put to death, she would have been fully capable of killing him and thus would have already done it. She was probably all right.

His mind was a little bit at ease now, and he felt warm inside. For some reason, he felt like a little kid noticing the stars for the first time. He fondly remembered when he and his friends used to sit around the campfire in the swamp when he was a little bit younger; his good memories were filtering to the top for the first time in a long time.

The commander came over and sat down next to him, but he didn't say anything right away. Angroo closed his eyes and laid back to relax, thinking only of the good stuff in life. Maybe things would work out after all. There was no reason why they shouldn't.

"Isn't it a lovely night?" the commander said softly, ending the silence.

"Yes. Lovely."

"You know, Angroo, I always wanted to tell you that you remind me of my son, William. He's probably a couple years younger than you but for some reason I just can't help but see the connection."

"Thank you, General Richmond. I take that as a compliment."

"There's no need to address me so formally. Just call me Charles. Everyone always calls me 'General Richmond,' and it makes it seem as if I am somehow different from everyone else in every situation. It reduces me to a title."

"I understand," answered Angroo as he nodded his head. There was a short pause.

"I joined the army when I was a young man. My father was the head general of Victory City's army back then, and he always wanted me to follow in his footsteps; I was eager to rise in the ranks and earn the trust of those around me, and eventually I fulfilled his dream and mine. I've been the head general now for eleven years, and it has been the most rewarding career I could have dreamed of. But it doesn't define me, and it never has." He paused for a moment as he continued to look up at the sky. "My father is no longer alive, though. Tragically, he was killed in battle about twenty years back when the city was raided by orcs."

"I'm sorry to hear about your father."

"It broke my heart. I still often think of his death to this day; it reminds me of how fragile life really is. My father always taught me to stand up for what is right, and he lived and died by his own advice; he could have retreated when the orcs attacked but he didn't. He stood up to them. That's why he isn't here today, but he and his men killed all of the attackers and prevented them from striking and killing again. He saved many lives."

"You speak fondly of your father. Why do you not hate his killers, then? Why are you telling this story to *me*?"

"Hate is not always the answer, but I admit that I do hate his killers. I don't think I can ever forgive them for what they did. But you were not one of his killers, Angroo. The entire orc race was not responsible for his death; only a few individuals were responsible. It's important for people not to take out their anger on those who are undeserving."

"Orcs are deserving, though. They're just plain vicious; they are born vicious, and as they grow up they are taught to be even more vicious. They're monsters. Why not hate all of them? Any of them could have been your father's killers."

"Don't be ridiculous, Angroo. Are you trying to test me or something?" He paused for a few seconds. "I agree with you that, in general, orcs may have a disposition towards aggressive behavior that is greater than that of most men, but it would be both wrong and foolish for me to try to categorize all of them as monsters, as you say. They're really not so different. Your people and my people have the same goals, and I know that you agree with me deep down." Neither of them said anything for a minute as Angroo thought about what had just been said.

"I'm not sure we have the same goals in this war, though, Charles. There's one real reason why we're attacking your city, and that's to prevent you from unleashing the power of the Golden Eggs of Gotty Gottya on us." The commander seemed surprised by this statement.

"So it's true, then. You really are after the Eggs."

"As far as I understand it, yes. We *fear* the Golden Eggs with all of our souls because we know that they can be used for our genocide."

"All orcs fear the Golden Eggs?"

"Most orcs don't know about the Golden Eggs. Most orcs think we're attacking simply to plunder Victory City, but our leadership knows better. We know that we must strike before the Golden Eggs are used against us."

"Listen, Angroo. I don't know what the Golden Eggs can do, but I do know that if you fear them so much, maybe it really would be best for you to completely call off your attack. I'm sure that whoever knows how to 'use' the Golden Eggs against your kind would be more likely to do so if he felt like he were being threatened."

"I hope that you're right, Charles. I want peace just as much as you do, but the rulers of Victory City have been blackmailing us for years. To tell you the truth, I think the only way for a lasting peace to really come about is if the Golden Eggs were somehow destroyed." The commander gazed up in thought.

"So you're saying that the rulers of my city have been blackmailing you? King Lucius knew about the power of the Golden Eggs during his reign? Hmm. Prince Lucio claimed that he didn't know anything about them, and I would think that if they were so important the king would have told his only son. This is all very peculiar."

"I don't know what to say about that."

"Remember the night several weeks ago when your tribe attempted to besiege Victory City? We held a meeting earlier that night to discuss the possibility of an attack by the orcs, and I remember overhearing McDuff the Great, the leader of the dwarves, speaking about the Golden Eggs. He seemed to dismiss the idea of fighting to protect them, as if they had some kind of sinister nature that was not worth protecting. McDuff is a wise ruler, so I'm sure he knew what he was talking about that day. I think he wanted peace as well, but I don't know the real story with these artifacts."

Angroo nodded. The commander stopped gazing at the stars for a moment and turned to him with a sudden sense of urgency.

"How do the Golden Eggs work? What do they do, exactly?"

"They can be used to kill orcs. I have no idea how, but I've been told by Chief Molar-Licker that they can be used to wipe out every single one of us, and I believe it. Molar-Licker never lies to me."

"That's terrible. I'll have to make sure the truth comes out about those Golden Eggs." He leaned back and stretched out his arms. "Anyway, Angroo, this brings me to why I sought you out here in the first place. The prince said that he would consider peace with the orcs only if King Lucius's killer were captured. The prince seems to be convinced that an orc was responsible for the murders, but I'm not so sure. I thought that you might be able to help me find the killer."

"I already told you, Charles. I don't know who the killer is, but I'll do what I can to make sure that he's turned over to the people of Victory City if he is indeed among our numbers."

"Do you have any idea of who it could be, though? Were any of your fighters unaccounted for the night of the murder?"

"I don't know. I don't really remember."

"All right, I understand. We'll have to leave tomorrow and hurry to get back; Victory City is planning a full assault against the orcs sometime very soon, and we need to try to get this worked out before that happens. We'll need to establish search teams to hunt for the killer."

"I agree. I'll do my best to help out, but we must make sure the time for peace comes."

"I'll make sure that it comes." They both looked up at the stars and didn't say anything else for several minutes. It was starting to get a little bit colder as the campfire died down to a flicker and the wind picked up. The stars were as beautiful as ever, though.

Angroo heard soft footsteps coming from behind him. He turned to see the crystal-eyed woman approaching.

"There you are. How is everything going over here?"

"Not bad," replied the commander. "It's a wonderful night."

"General Richmond, I've been meaning to ask you about the princess. Why is she in so much danger that I'm needed to protect her?" She sat down next to him.

"Princess Silara's father, King Eliazer of Elkanshire, controls a powerful artifact known as the Golden Egg of Gotty Gottya. It was originally one of a set of three, but the other two were stolen. Nobody but Eliazer knows where the last one is hidden, though, so somebody has been attempting to kidnap the princess and presumably force Eliazer to reveal the Golden Egg's location."

"The Golden Eggs of Gotty Gottya? I understand now."

"You know about them, Winterfrost?"

"Yes. I have read about them, but I was unaware that they still existed. They're destroyed quite easily if I remember, right?" Angroo and the commander looked at each other.

"How are they used?" asked an anxious Angroo. "How can someone tap into their vast power?"

"I do not remember, but I'll research it tonight and tell you both about it in the morning before you leave. The book is written in an obscure elven script that is difficult to decipher."

"Are you sure you want to stay up doing this? You

probably need some rest so that you're alert enough to protect the princess."

"It's fine, General. I don't need much sleep anyway." She stood up.

"Speaking of sleep, I'm getting a little tired myself. Angroo, why don't you carry the princess back to the house and then get some rest? We have a long day of traveling ahead of us tomorrow and we'll need our sleep."

"Okay. Just give me a moment."

"Very well. I'll see you in the house, Angroo. Thank you again for your warm hospitality, Winterfrost."

"You're welcome. Once all of this chaos is over, you two are welcome to visit me again anytime. The swamp is much nicer in the spring, anyway." The two of them walked away towards the house, leaving Angroo alone again with the girl.

It was even colder now. Angroo remained on his back on top of the cold grass, petting the girl's hair as the campfire dwindled down to embers. He didn't want to get up because he knew he would have to leave in the morning. He'd have to leave the little girl behind. Would he ever see her again? If he were lucky, he'd see her in a few months, maybe a few weeks if he were very, very lucky. Maybe he'd never see her, though. Could she really be protected? Would both of them survive to see each other again? Even if they did both survive, would circumstances allow for their reunion? He wanted to lie there until the morning with her, but it was cold and he knew that he couldn't stay for much longer. He had to face the facts: night had arrived. He continued to look up at the stars for another minute or two before finally getting up and shoveling some dirt onto the campfire. He then gently cradled the girl in his arms as he slowly carried her down the trail back to the house. He needed sleep, and it was finally time.

Chapter 44

"Come… Angroo…" said a distant voice. Everything was white. "Come… to… me…" Angroo stepped forward, but he didn't move. He couldn't move. There was only white everywhere.

"Come… closer…" He tried to take another step, but nothing happened.

"Closer…"

Angroo began to run. He wasn't really moving but it didn't matter; he ran as fast as he could. He just kept running forward towards nothingness. As fast as he could. He still wasn't moving.

"AAAAAAHHHHH!!!!!!!"

AAAAAAAAAAAAAAAAAAAHHHHHHHH!!!!!!!!!!!!!!!"

What was going on? What was that screaming? He kept running but he still couldn't move.

"AAAAAAAAAAAAAAAAAAAAAAAAHHHHHHHHHHHHH!!!!!!!!!!!!!!!!!!"

He kept running. He was helpless.

Angroo leapt out of his blanket in a cold sweat. What a horrible nightmare.

"What is it?" moaned the commander as he slowly got up and rubbed his eyes. "It's so early in the morning. Is everything okay?"

"Something isn't right." They turned behind them to see the door to the bedroom wide open.

"Firelight, get up. Something's happened."

"Huh? What's going on?"

"Someone's been in the house. Winterfrost! Silara!"

No response. The three of them rushed into the

bedroom, but there was nobody there; both beds were empty. The window had been smashed open and in the dim morning light they were able to see dark red blood spots on the floor.

"Oh no!" cried the woman. "Oh no!"

"Grab your weapons, quick!" shouted the commander as he ran back into the living room and felt around for his sword. "Quick!" Angroo thought he had left his trident next to where he was sleeping but he couldn't find it anywhere.

They scrambled out of the house and found a trail of blood leading from the window off in the direction of the previous night's camping area. Angroo sprinted ahead.

"Wait!" shouted the woman. "Was this one of the dead frogmen that we saw last night? It doesn't look like it." There seemed to be a new werefrog body strewn across the side of the house.

"Werefrogs?!" cried the commander. "Are the werefrogs responsible for this?!"

"Uh… I think it's the good one. It's Frufur." Angroo returned to get a closer look. It was him all right, felled by six stab wounds on his chest. His killer had just thrown him there as an afterthought. There was no time for this now, though. No time! Where was the girl?!

"This way!" screamed Angroo. His entire body was shaking violently. The other two rushed after him as he led them back towards the campsite.

Angroo tore through the familiar path that he had walked the night before. His heart was racing. He forced himself to remain calm, though. He had to stay calm.

The blood trail finally ended at a splotch of long, black hair on the grass. The body was lying on its side several feet away, completely nude and sprawled out over where the campfire had been. The top half of the head was missing. The brain was missing.

"Win…wint…" The woman backed up against a tree; her face had gone completely pale and her eyes were strung open in horror as she stared at the void where her friend's brain had been. It was like a geyser gushing with blood.

The blond soldier emerged from the woods.

"Quite a bloodbath, *isn't* it?!" he screamed. "See, General?! See this?! *This* is what happens when you let a pig-face walk all over you! Are you happy now, General?!" The soldier stepped forward. Angroo was speechless; he was gasping for air.

"Yohannis!!!" roared the commander. "What is the meaning of this?!"

"Why don't you ask your good buddy right here, huh? Maybe he knows a little bit about it? Just a suggestion." The commander stomped forward, his sword drawn.

"You know, you always seem to be going missing, Yohannis! You always seem to be missing whenever something like this happens! Where are you?!" He continued forward. The blond soldier backed away.

"You dare accuse me of this monstrous act?! The orc is clearly the one responsible!"

"Angroo was with us!"

"Was he, now? Then how do you explain… *this*?!" The soldier kicked Angroo's trident, which had been lying on the ground near the body and was drenched in blood. He crossed his arms and shook his head back and forth in disgust. "The repulsive creature's been lying to you the whole time!" he sneered.

"No!" screamed Angroo. "No! You're lying! I had nothing to do with this!"

"You're nothing but a cold-hearted killer! I've been reading the signs all along!" Angroo knew that there was no time for this kind of stupidity now.

"Where's the girl!?" he screamed as he rushed forward in a blind rage.

"Don't take another step, snouty!" yelled the blond soldier as he drew his longbow. Angroo froze in his place; an arrow was being aimed between his eyes, and he knew that the blond soldier was close enough for a sure hit if he released his hand from the string.

"Lower your weapon, Yohannis!" cried the commander. Nobody moved. "I said to lower your weapon!"

"General Richmond, do you see what's happening here?! The orc has been toying with your mind as if it were one of his playthings! Toying with your mind! Because of his tricks, now you trust this horrible, unholy being of filth over one of your own loyal men!"

"No!" shouted Angroo.

"There's so much evidence, General! Don't delude yourself! How else do you explain how the fiend knew *exactly* where to lead you?! How do you think the foul creature's weapon of choice, stained in the blood of his helpless victim, got here in the first place?! Did it just appear here, General?!"

"Lower your weapon!"

"Never!"

"Angroo..." muttered the woman. "Angroo, do you know... how the trident got here?" Angroo turned back towards her to see her kneeling near the body and looking up at him. Was she against him now? Did anyone trust him? He felt the fury quickly building inside of him.

"I've been framed!" he howled. "I was asleep the whole time! I was in the same room as you, don't you remember?! I was framed!" He turned back towards the blond soldier, who continued to hold a bead on his head. "Where's the princess, you murderer?! Where is she?!"

"How should *I* know what *you* did with the princess?!"

"What have you done to her?!" Angroo stepped forward.

"Another step and I'll send you back to whence you came, vile abomination!"

"All right, let's calm down now!" shouted the commander. "Let's not do anything hasty! Yohannis, what do you know about what transpired here?"

"Ask the pig-face!"

"Don't give me that response, idiot!" The commander took another step forward, but the blond soldier didn't move from his position. "I'll ask you one more time. What happened, Yohannis? What did you see?"

"I didn't see anything! I got here moments before you!"

"Are you telling me the truth?!"

"Yes!"

"So you didn't actually see Angroo commit the crime?"

"Is there any doubt that it was him? No, I didn't actually see him commit the crime. But I can see it in his eyes now. He's filled with hatred. General, I think you'd better be careful. I think he's ready to kill again."

"I couldn't have done it because I was sleeping. We don't have time for this."

"Did either of you hear anything during the night? Firelight, did you hear anything? Angroo?"

"Screams."

"You heard screams, Angroo?"

"I thought it was a nightmare. Horrible screams."

"Where were they coming from?"

"I don't know. Far away."

"Who was screaming? When did you…"

"There's no time for this!!" roared Angroo. "We have to find the princess! It's urgent!"

"I said don't move, scum!"

214

"He's right, Yohannis. Drop your weapon right now! We have to look for her!"

"No, General! He'll kill us as soon as I put it down!"

"Drop it!"

"No!"

Angroo made a sudden dash to his left, but the arrow never left the blond soldier's bow because a hand came from behind him and grabbed the arrow shaft right before his grip was released. The bowstring twanged loudly.

"He said drop it!"

"Get off of me, you filthy half-breed!" The woman held on tight to both of his arms as he tried to shake her off his back, finally dropping his weapon in the process. The commander dove forward and snatched it off the ground before the blond soldier could pick it up. Angroo was now running away at full speed.

"We have to find her!" he yelled as he bounded off towards the woods. "SILARA!!! SILARA!!!!!" The blond soldier freed himself from the woman's grasp and stood up.

"You're letting him get away."

"Stay where I can see you, Yohannis. If you really are telling the truth then maybe you can help us find out what happened to Princess Silara."

"The pig-face is getting away!"

"My patience is running out. This is a serious matter."

"Of course it's a serious matter, and I'm disgusted that you're so quick to misplace your trust, General! I'm absolutely disgusted. One day you'll wish you had listened to me about that orc, and it'll be sooner rather than later." He brushed himself off. "All right, then. Fine. I'll help you find the little princess's body."

"Don't say that!" shouted the woman.

"Oh, so you think that we'll find little Goldilocks alive

somewhere?! You really think so?! I'm willing to bet that Angroo took it even one step further on this kill; not only will we find her dead, but every organ in her entire body will be missing! He didn't just stop at her brain! Mark my words: by the time we find her, there will be nothing left of her but a blood-drenched pile of skin!"

Twenty minutes of frantic searching had passed with no new discoveries. Angroo yelled for the girl until his throat was raw; he was tremendously exhausted, but it didn't slow him down. Nothing could slow him down because he was determined to find her, and nothing else mattered. He screamed again for her even though the pain in his throat was unbearable.

The killer had left no trace. There was no trail of blood except the one that led from the house to the campsite, and that didn't tell him anything. There didn't seem to be any new footprints visible. He had to piece it together somehow, but he found it too hard to think clearly; the only things keeping him going were anger and fear, with reason taking a back seat. He had to slow it down and think because the girl's life depended on it.

What if she had escaped, though? This new idea brought a smile to Angroo's face for the first time since the night before. What if she escaped and was now hiding somewhere? No, it wasn't possible. She would have heard him screaming for her if she were hiding. She was probably dead somewhere. He would find her mutilated body and that would be the end of everything. He stomped the ground with rage and turned back towards the murder scene.

That stupid blond soldier. Angroo hated him more than ever, even more than when he had been shot in the chest and left for dead a few days earlier. The mere thought of that stupid bastard made him clench his fists in anger. Was he the killer? Did he kill the girl and hide her body somewhere just to blame it on him? As much as he hated and despised the blond soldier, Angroo couldn't shake the feeling that he was actually innocent. How could he be innocent, though? He was just so *bad*. Nothing made sense anymore. Angroo was helpless again, but this time it wasn't just a dream.

Chapter 45

The sky was red as Prince Lucio gazed down upon his city from the balcony. Twilight. Soldiers ran back and forth through the streets as they prepared for the massive onslaught against the orcs, but they were not just Victory City soldiers; a large army of elven reinforcements hailing from Elkanshire had recently arrived and were preparing to lend their assistance to the strike. Standing next to the prince was King Eliazer, a shadow of his former self. The two of them were alone.

"Something terrible's happened to my little girl. I can feel it in the air."

"Calm down, Lord Eliazer. I'm sure everything will work out and we'll find her safe and sound. Are you feeling any better?"

"How can I feel better, Prince? The orcs…"

"I know that things are hard for you now, but it's imperative that you remain resolute. Do not let those creatures sway you into giving them the Golden Egg."

"I… know. It's much too important, and I understand that. But it's so… hard… for me." He put his hands over his face. "How could General Richmond be so silly?"

"The general has been one of this city's greatest assets over the years. I would trust him with my life, but you must understand that everyone makes mistakes. Still, though, I'm utterly baffled as to why he would simply allow an orc to escape with your daughter." He scratched his chin.

"But he lied to you about it, Prince, and that should concern you. Didn't you tell me that he claimed to have never seen Silara?"

"Yes. His men told me otherwise."

"Not only did he find her, but he handed her over to that

orc! And now he's bolted town! What's going on, Prince Lucio?!"

"He didn't just bolt town; I allowed him to leave after temporarily relieving him of his duties. The general maintains a fundamental difference in opinion from the rest of us regarding the severity of the orcish threat, I'm afraid."

"Its sounds like you just let him off the hook for no good reason! I demand answers!"

"Listen, Lord Eliazer. If the orcs are holding your daughter, there's a strong probability that we will rescue her once we gain access to their lair. The orcs do not suspect such a massive attack, and they will be taken off guard. They have no reason to rid themselves of their biggest bargaining chip by killing her. Do not lose your composure."

"I hope you're right. I really hope... you're right." Eliazer was choking on his tears, and the prince put his hand on top of his shoulder.

"No matter what happens, we cannot give away the Golden Egg. Catastrophe will ensue if the orcs get their hands on it, and you know that. We both know that."

"I know. But I heard your speech yesterday, Prince Lucio, and you'd think by listening to it that the only reason for this whole war is your crown."

"The crown is important, Lord Eliazer. It's an important symbol of this city, but you and I both know that it's not the main reason for all of this. People wouldn't understand if we tried to tell them about the Golden Egg, so we need to tell them something that they can understand. As long as that crown is missing, their beloved city will be without a king. That's reason enough for them to mobilize."

"I hope all of this works out, Prince. I... oh, I can't talk about this anymore. Oh, Silara! Where are you?!" He shook his head and turned to leave. The prince said nothing as the king of the elves left the room.

Several minutes passed as the prince continued to gaze upon his subjects. It was becoming slightly darker outside, though, and the temperature was falling. Another cold night was about to set in. A busy night, also, since there was still much that needed to be done.

"I hope I'm not dropping in at a bad time, sir," said a voice. The prince was startled, but he did not turn around. He knew who it was.

"Rugby."

"You expected someone else, My Prince?" There was no answer as the prince continued to look down at his city, but things suddenly seemed much quieter and darker than they had been a minute ago. It was eerily quiet. Finally he turned around.

"What are you doing here?!"

"I have something for you." The man with the red mustache opened up a box he was carrying and reached his hands in, removing a golden, jewel-studded crown. "Looking for this?"

"You…"

"The people of Victory City need a king, you know. I think it would be unwise to keep them waiting any longer."

Prince Lucio stared Rugby in the eyes. His expression was unchanging.

"I told you not to show that to me until after this whole ordeal had finally ended. It's much too early. Put the crown away and go make yourself useful."

Chapter 46

As darkness set in, Angroo began to despair. Nothing had turned up after an entire day of searching. Absolutely nothing. He stood and stared down at the shape of the sorceress's corpse, which was now completely wrapped up in a blanket and had been moved to the house. What happened to her? After a long day of piecing things together, they had established that she was most likely reading about the Golden Egg just like she had promised she would; a book found on her bed was opened to a page showing an egg-shaped diagram. Did the killer catch her off guard while she was reading? There was certainly evidence that a struggle had ensued inside of the bedroom, and he figured that she must have already been dead before the killer dragged her off through the window.

The killer must have quickly murdered the girl as well, because otherwise she would have screamed and alerted everyone's attention. What was that piercing screaming in his dream, then? Was it just part of his dream? Nobody else heard the screaming, so perhaps it was.

Maybe she was still alive; it made sense that the killer would want to take her alive because he may have wanted to hold her for ransom. Maybe the killer stuffed her mouth while she was still asleep so that she couldn't scream, and that's why they didn't hear anything. What could he have stuffed her mouth with, though? There didn't seem to be any sheets missing. There *was* something missing, though. The night before, Angroo had taken off the girl's moccasins and put them under her bed after he had laid her down, but only one of them had been found there. There was no sign of the other one. It was getting a little darker outside.

He suddenly thought of something.

"I KNOW WHERE SHE IS!!!" shrieked Angroo. "I KNOW WHERE SHE IS!!! FOLLOW ME!!!!" He began to run off towards the campsite, and the others dropped what they were doing and ran after him. His blood was pumping a mile a minute as he dashed through the brush, swatting plants out of his way as he burst ahead. As soon as they made it to the campsite, Angroo stopped running and began searching around frantically.

"What is it?!" asked the commander. "Where do you think she is?"

"Somewhere... around..."

"Excuse me. May I have a brief word, General? I won't take more than a moment of your time."

"What, Yohannis."

"Thank you so much, General." The blond soldier held out his hands in front of his body. "If you don't mind, let's step back and take a moment to consider our situation now. You and mutt-girl here are practically in love with the pig-face, so naturally you wouldn't be expecting any sort of *trap*, right? If he did lead you into a trap, you wouldn't be able to protect yourself because you're not willing to accept the possibility of such an event occurring. Essentially, you'd be helpless. Unfortunately, I also find myself at a similar disadvantage, but for a different reason; you see, I can't protect you if you continue to keep me away from my bow and arrows, leaving all three of us completely at the swine-head's mercy. I *kindly* request that you give my bow and arrows back to me at once so that I may kill the vile pig-face if he tries anything devious."

"Yohannis, you have shown yourself reckless and unworthy of my trust. I will not give you your weapon back until the time is right." The commander turned back towards Angroo, who was looking in every direction. He seemed to be in a trance. "Do you know where she is, Angroo? Do you need our help?"

Angroo didn't answer. He suddenly dashed towards a large, dead tree at the outskirts of the campsite and knelt down next to it. The tree didn't seem any different from the others except that it had a large hollow in its side about eight feet from its base. Angroo pressed his ear against the bark for a few seconds and listened closely.

"What's going on? Is something in there?"

Angroo drove his trident into the side of the tree with several quick thrusts, rapidly chipping away the bark. Finally, once the bark had weakened enough, he dropped the weapon and began to rip it all off with his hands. After one mighty final heave, the entire side of the tree came loose; something fell from inside and landed hard on the grass! The princess! She was still in her white dress, but it was filthy and covered with insects. Her entire body and her hair were black with filth. The grass moccasin was stuffed into her mouth and tied around her head, and she looked up at Angroo with panic in her eyes. She was too weak to move.

"My God!" shouted the commander as a smile ballooned across his face. "She was trapped inside of that tree! Angroo, you did it! You found her!"

"I can't believe it! She's still alive!" cried the woman. "Look! She's breathing!" Both of them tried to run forward, but they were stopped cold as the blond soldier grabbed onto their arms.

"How did you know she was there, orc!?"

"Let go of me!" snapped the commander, who was now standing still. "The princess requires immediate medical attention!"

"How did you know she was there, pig-face!? Answer my question!"

"Yohannis, she's been stuffed in a tree all day!" The

commander turned his head back and glared angrily at the blond soldier. "I don't want to fight you right now, so let go! Be reasonable for once!"

"Are you blind, General?! It's all a setup! He'll kill you next!"

"Yohannis, let go or I'll throw you into the ground. Hard." The blond soldier sneered but finally relented and released his grip.

Angroo stared at the others as they rushed towards him, and he stepped in front of the girl. The sky darkened. A breeze set in.

"Don't come any closer."

"Wha... Angroo? We just..."

"Don't come any closer," repeated the white orc.

"Let us get a closer look at her! She might be hurt!"

"Just go away. I found her. She's safe now." General Richmond and Firelight stood still and watched while Princess Silara gazed up at them with eyes wide from the expression of sheer terror. Beyond terror. What was going on?

"Angroo, let me come closer. You know you can trust me." No response. "At least take the gag out of her mouth! What's gotten into you?!"

No response.

"I'm just going to get a little closer."

No response.

"Let me get closer."

No response.

General Richmond stepped closer.

The orc shoved the trident into General Richmond's face, ripping open the top of his head with one violent upward motion. General Richmond collapsed forward; it had taken only a split second for all life to vanish from his body. It didn't seem physically possible. The orc wrenched the general's brain off of his blood-stained weapon and began to gnaw on it like a mouse.

Firelight and Yohannis were utterly stunned. They couldn't speak. They couldn't even breathe.

The white orc continued to devour the brain as if nothing else were going on around him, completely preoccupied with this activity.

"Angroo!" screamed Firelight as she backed away from him. She was gripped to the core with panic. "Angroo! What have you done?"

No response. The crazed orc finally finished his meal and looked up at them like a rabid animal trapped in a corner.

"What have you done?!" She threw a fireball at his face but he moved his head out of the way; the fireball instead landed on the ground near the tree and ignited the shards of bark that were strewn all over the grass.

At this point, Silara finally began to move her arms. She tried to get up and crawl away but, in the blink of an eye, the orc lunged on top of her and wrapped his arms around hers. He lifted her up into the air without the slightest semblance of effort and rushed away towards the woods.

"After him!" howled Yohannis as he charged forward. He arrived at General Richmond's body, turning it onto its side and jerking his bow and quiver of arrows out of the general's belt. He then quickly readied the weapon, firing several rounds into the distance without coming close to his intended target and then running at full speed after the fleeing orc.

"Yohannis, wait…"

"I knew it all along, you white-skinned freak! I knew it! Murderer! I'll make sure you finally see justice, you ruthless, brain-eating piece of slime!" He continued to run, but he still needed to make up a lot of ground as the orc had been moving at an inconceivably fast pace in his escape. Yohannis was soon out of sight into the woods, and the soft cackling of the fire was the only thing that could be heard. Smoke slowly blanketed the air.

"General Rich...m..." Firelight stumbled over to the body and awkwardly embraced it. Not knowing what else to do, she found herself kissing what remained of his face; his blood seeped through her lips and made her gag. She let herself fall backwards and was soon lying on her back, staring up into the darkening sky with weak, bloodshot eyes. The fire began to grow around her, but she couldn't move. She couldn't do anything. Everyone was dying and she couldn't even do a single thing to help them. All she could do was start a stupid forest fire, and that's it. She was completely useless.

This wasn't how it was going to be. She jumped up and hastily shoveled piles of dirt onto the fire, putting it out before it could spread to the trees. She gazed off into the distance. Something had to be done about all of this.

Chapter 47

"Thank you for agreeing to meet me so late at night," Prince Lucio said to the messenger. "Now what is the word from the front lines?"

"Our troops have made solid progress thus far, Prince. We've suffered heavy losses but the orcs have been hit much harder and appear to be on the run."

"That's all we can hope for at this point." The prince paced back and forth around the throne room. "They haven't found Lord Eliazer's daughter, have they?"

"No, sir."

"What about the crown?"

"No." The prince paused for a second and looked at the messenger.

"You do recall that there was another certain item in the orcs' possession that I requested be recovered. Was that item found?"

"No, sir."

"Are you absolutely positive? It's extremely important."

"Yes, sir. Absolutely positive. The soldiers haven't penetrated into the main lair yet, and at best estimate it will take at least a few days for the brunt of our forces to break through the orc's defensive perimeter and enter their lair. And that's an optimistic estimate."

"Very well. You are dismissed for now, Messenger. Please return to me when you have more news from the front."

"Will do, sir."

"And please reiterate the importance of recovering this item to the front line commanders. And tell them to be extremely careful handling it. Is that understood?"

"Of course, sir. I'll leave at once."

Chapter 48

The sun was rising, but Firelight was already awake. She had not slept at all since the horrible betrayal; it was too dangerous to sleep, and there were too many things that needed to be done. She had spent most of the night digging three deep holes in the soft dirt outside of the house with a shovel that she found, and now she was drained of most of her energy. The bodies of Winterfrost, General Richmond, and Frufur von FroggenMcHopper, each carefully wrapped in sheets and blankets, had been lowered into the holes one by one and then the holes had been filled back up to the top with dirt. The gravesites were then each marked with stones. Closure for the victims was imperative, and this was as close to a proper burial as they could get and it had to be done.

She was so tired. She knew that she had to sleep sometime, so she trudged back to the house to rest up for the long, sad trip back to civilization. This was probably the safest time for her to rest anyway because the werefrogs probably weren't as active during the day. After making sure the door was closed tightly, she lay on the floor of Winterfrost's living room and took some deep breaths as she stared up at the ceiling. Everything that had happened in the last twenty-four hours needed to be blocked out of her mind, but it was hard. Finally, her eyes closed. Her body was ready for sleep, and she began to relax. Everything was peaceful as sleep's gentle hand began to caress her weary mind.

There was a knock on the front door.

Maybe she was just hearing things because of a lack of sleep. It was probably just something else, maybe a woodpecker or something. Nobody knew she was there.

Another knock.

Firelight got up and rushed towards the window, but

she suddenly froze when she heard breathing. There was somebody right outside the window, standing there and waiting for her to leave. A second person. It was a trap.

The door opened. A man wearing a dark hood and a dark cloak covering his entire body entered and looked around quickly. There was nobody in the room. He turned to leave but suddenly fell to the ground as Firelight jumped out from behind the door and clocked him over the head with a footstool. She ran out towards the woods as quickly as her legs could carry her. Could she ever catch a break?

She turned her head back as she approached the trees, but there was nobody following her. The door to Winterfrost's house was still wide open and the grass was peacefully swaying in the breeze as if none of that had just happened. Where were they? She walked quickly through the woods and finally stopped, hiding behind a large tree and catching her breath.

Five minutes passed, but now someone was coming. She heard footsteps getting closer and closer. She couldn't take the suspense any longer; she jumped out of her hiding spot and, wasting no time at all, engulfed the hooded man in flames! He didn't fall, though. He didn't even flinch as his clothing burned and smoked, and he lifted his smoldering hands into the air. Firelight tried to run.

Bzzzzzzzzzzzzzzzzzzt!

A sudden surge of electricity jolted through her entire body! She grabbed onto a nearby branch and leaned on top of it, badly shaken. What the heck? Her attacker must have been some sort of sorcerer as well.

"What do you want from me?!" she shouted while trying to catch her breath. The man didn't respond; his hood and most of his clothing had burnt off, and his hideous face stared down at her with a faint smile. He lifted his hands into the air again, but this time Firelight didn't let him repeat his magic trick; she yanked the branch off with a strong, sudden heave and then whacked the man in the head, knocking him off his feet and cutting him badly. She retreated deeper into the woods.

"That was a close call," she mumbled to herself as she continued to run. Suddenly she stopped short; two more hooded men stood inches away, preparing to strike! She whipped out her sword and threw it in front of her; the lightning zipped out of the hooded figures' hands and discharged harmlessly into the metal weapon. Then, bringing both of her hands down, she blasted the two attackers with bursts of flame. Again it didn't work, as both of the men were completely unfazed by the fire that was now consuming their dark robes right off of their bodies. They looked like they were creatures made out of billowing smoke. Firelight darted in between them and ran off before they had the chance to attack her again, thinking only about how much these fire-repellent goons reminded her of the dog she had fought days earlier. How many of these freaks were there? She didn't want to find out, so she just kept on running.

It was time for a plan. How was she going to get away from these people? Maybe if she continued running she could get away from them, but she didn't know where she was going and the last thing that she needed was a bunch of hooligans on her trail. She could take them, though, even if their skin was somehow resistant to her fire. Easy. She laughed when she thought about how she had just used her sword to draw their electricity right out of the sky; she was actually pretty impressed that she was able to think of that so quickly. Yeah, this wouldn't be a problem. She'd find a way to win somehow. She turned around and began to hurry back towards her attackers.

230

There was no sign of anyone anywhere, so she finally just stopped moving and listened closely to her surroundings. Nothing. The woods had become completely quiet. She began to worry a little bit when she realized that she no longer had her sword, as it was still on the ground from when she threw it earlier. Maybe she shouldn't be running towards danger so eagerly. Maybe she was being a little bit overconfident here; no, she *definitely* was. At the very least she needed to find her sword, and then she could decide how to proceed. She remembered where she had dropped it and began to run in that direction.

Firelight flew forward and landed face-first on the ground. A tripwire. Clever. Very clever. She looked up just in time to see the three attackers, with their tattered, burnt clothing and hideously deformed faces, come at her from three different directions and completely surround her. She leapt to her feet.

Bzzzzzzzzzzzzzzzzzzzt! Bzzzzzzzzzzzzzzzzzzzt! Bzzzzzzzzzzzzzzzzzzzt!

Extreme pain pulsated through every part of Firelight's body as all three of her assailants zapped her at once. She soon found herself back on the ground, her body jerking and convulsing uncontrollably.

Bzzzzzzzzzzzzzzzzzzzt! Bzzzzzzzzzzzzzzzzzzzt! Bzzzzzzzzzzzzzzzzzzzzzzzzzzzzzzzzzzzzzzzzzzzzzzzzzzzzzzz zzzzzzzzzzzt!

Firelight felt like she was about to die. Everything began to go numb. She tried unsuccessfully to get up as she continued to twitch violently on the dirt floor. She flopped around like a fish on dry land for several seconds and then stiffened up. The three men slowly walked towards her, stopping and looking down at her when they were each about a foot away. They seemed to enjoy seeing her in this helpless state.

One of the men dropped her sword in front of her face. Were they playing some sort of game? She reached out her completely numb arm and grabbed onto the blade of her weapon.

Bzzzzzzzzzzzzzzzzzzzzzzzzzzzzzzzzzzzzt!

Somebody zapped the sword, and the electricity flowed into her fingers; she immediately released her grip and rolled over in pain. She was now face-up, watching powerlessly as the three ugly, ugly men laughed at her. They began to kick her and stomp on her, but she didn't feel it because she was completely numb. One of the men reached down to pick up the sword; was he going to try the same little joke again? No. This time, he was going to try to impale her with her own weapon.

Firelight reached her hand out and, focusing her energy, threw a fireball straight up. The killers chuckled, apparently thinking it was meant for them; they were surprised when a flaming tree branch landed on their heads after a couple of seconds and knocked two of them to the ground. Firelight struggled to her feet with the strength that she could muster, grabbing the side of the tree with one of her hands and a low branch with the other and hoisting herself up. Luckily she was a good climber.

Bzzzzzzzzzzzzzzzzzzzt!

She nearly lost her grip and fell back down. She couldn't lose her grip, though. She was too determined as she continued to ascend higher, turning around to kick one of the men in the face and then kick off the first branch so that they wouldn't be able to climb up after her.

Bzzzzzzzzzzzzzzzzzzzt!
Bzzzzzzzzzzzzzzzzzzzzzzzzzzzzzzzt!

Her body again convulsed with the electrical shock, but

she had locked her arms around a branch and this prevented her from tumbling off the tree. The pain was nearly unbearable, but she fought it off. She struggled onto a higher branch that was on the other side of the tree, and now the men couldn't hit her as easily because the tree's trunk stood between them.

She looked down and saw, underneath her, all three of the men coming around to her side of the tree and looking up at her with their hideous, deformed faces. How could anyone be so ugly? Panic set in as she frantically climbed up as quickly as possible, almost losing her grip and falling several times in her recklessness. She grabbed onto a high branch and heaved herself up, and then she pulled herself onto an even higher one. She climbed up several more branches, and by this point they stopped trying to zap her because she was finally out of their range; the lightning wouldn't have been able to reach her without striking something else first.

The branch she was now hanging onto was not strong at all, and it began to give way under her weight. She desperately grabbed onto an even higher branch and pulled herself onto it as the other one snapped under her knees and tumbled down, landing with a thud far below her. This new branch seemed sturdy, but it was narrow and was isolated from any other branches. The bark was irregular and painful as she lay forward on top of it and locked her legs and arms tightly around it. She knew that she would have to maintain this uncomfortable position for a long time because there were no other nearby branches and she was too weak to try anything acrobatic.

She looked down at the men circling the tree below her; they were far away now. She was very high up, and she knew that a fall would mean almost certain death. It didn't matter, though, because her fate appeared to be sealed anyway. She was alone and helpless in a tree. Her armor was blackened and tattered nearly to the point of uselessness, and her body was mostly numb because of brutal electrical shocks that she was amazed she had able to endure. She was completely defenseless against her attackers because they were unfazed by fire and they had her sword. What other fate could there be? It would only be a matter of time before they felled the tree or found some other way to get her to come down. It would all be over soon. She would be dead.

Firelight began to cry for the first time in a very long time. She had held it all in up until that point, but now she let it all out as she pressed her face against the rough bark and wept hysterically. She was going to die because of her stupidity and overconfidence. She didn't belong in this war, but now she was about to become just another casualty in it because she assumed that she could handle anything by herself. What a joke. Now she was letting Winterfrost and General Richmond down by dying so uselessly, mocking their deaths with her own. She was letting everyone down. Her crying intensified now as her entire body began to convulse. She couldn't stop crying. Her whole world was crashing down on her, and there was nothing she could do about it.

Chapter 49

"Remind me of why we're doing this again…" moaned one of the giants he trudged through the mountains.

"If you don't like it, you can blame good old Methuselah and his gambling addiction!" replied Gnarly as he shook his head back and forth in anger. "He owes a *lot* of money to the leaders of Victory City, and they agreed to let him off the hook only if he supplied some muscle for their little spat with the orcs. And that's where we come in. Typical politics."

"He should really see a professional about his gambling problem."

"You're telling me! You should have seen him when…" Gnarly suddenly stopped near a ledge and stood still. A wide grin spanned across his ugly face. "Fellow fire giants, behold! The reason why we came here at long last!" The others came and looked; a large army of orcs was gathered below in a clearing not far from the ledge, unaware of their presence. The giants immediately lifted up whatever they could find – boulders, small trees, the local wildlife – and positioned themselves for an attack.

"March!" shouted one of the orcs from the clearing. "Hup, two, three, four! Hup, two…"

"CATCH THIS!!!!!" wailed Gnarly as he hurled a gigantic boulder high into the air. The orcs panicked and fled in all different directions as the various objects that had been thrown came crashing down to earth. The fire giants chuckled loudly, shaking the ground with their hearty laughter.

"This is going to be a piece of cake!"

"I'll say! Come on, guys! Let's take it to them!"

Chief Molar-Licker, the leader of the orcs, was brooding

alone in the darkness when one of his tribesmen ran in.

"Chieftain! Me come to say that the fire giants attacking now! Coming from east! We get word of attack!"

"The giants of the Fire Realm? I thought they might involve themselves." He did not move from his position, continuing to sit Indian-style on the floor and stare at the wall.

"What we do now, Chieftain? They get here in a few days! We being attacked from all sides at once!"

"There's no reason to worry."

"What you talking about? Are you crazy?!"

"There's no reason to worry. Victory will be delivered to us soon; the spirits have foretold it."

"You crazy." The orc was about to leave when he suddenly noticed a steaming cauldron on the other side of the room. "I have some soup now, okay?"

"No!" shouted Molar-Licker as he jumped up. "That's not soup! Do not drink any of it!"

"But I hungry!"

"It's not soup! Don't touch it or I'll be forced to kill you!"

"Okay, okay." The orc backed off and finally left, and Molar Licker returned to sitting on the floor. It was nice and quiet again, just the way he liked it.

He focused his mind and soon entered a trance-like state.

"Spirits of the night, I beseech you!" he chanted. "Spirits of my ancestors long gone! Deliver swift victory to your mortal kin! Make good of your promise! Deliver! Deliver!"

Chapter 50

There he was. The murderous pig-face mere feet away, carrying the limp elven princess on top of his shoulder as he walked. Yohannis had finally caught up with and had even gotten ahead of the filthy creature after stealthily following him for nearly twenty-four straight hours, and he now hid in the bushes along the villain's presumed trail and waited patiently. The time to wait was ending, though. The time to dispense some long-overdue justice was upon him!

Yohannis hated to kill from hiding; it felt so cowardly. He wanted his victims to know who he was as they drew their last breaths, and after previous careful consideration he had decided against making an exception for this especially horrific life form. He jumped onto the path ahead of the orc.

"Well, well, well," he laughed. "Thought you could just get away with murder, did you?! It's time for you to die, once and for all, you despicable pile of filth!" He aimed an arrow at the orc's head, but the orc didn't seem to notice him as he continued to walk forward in a trance-like state. Princess Silara certainly noticed him, though, and she moaned and made a frantic but futile effort to escape from her captor's iron grip.

The orc continued forward until he was about to walk right into Yohannis, so Yohannis backed away.

"Halt!" he screamed, but the orc ignored him and continued to stride forward. "All right, then. All right. I see where this is going." He pulled back his bowstring and smiled, but he knew something was wrong. He somehow seemed out of his element.

Something was wrong.

"FOR JUSTICE!!!" he screamed.

Yohannis's weapon flew out of his hands in the blink of

an eye and landed in pieces in the bushes alongside the path. He felt the violent impact of the trident shaft upon his face and in no time he found himself on his back with the orc's foot stamping down hard on his chest. The wind was being stomped out of him as he lay defenseless on the ground; he didn't even have time to taste the blood in his mouth.

The white orc raised the trident above his head to strike.

"Go ahead..." Yohannis choked. "Kill me when I'm down... sick... monster......"

It started to rain.

Chapter 51

Firelight was somehow still alive after so many hours hanging onto the branch, but the heavy rainstorm made it especially difficult for her to maintain her grip now. She figured it must have been the late afternoon, but it seemed to be much later in the day because rain clouds blocked the sun and darkened the sky. She stuck her head out to look down at the dark forest floor far below her, but she soon had to brace herself and tighten her grasp as a sudden, strong gust of wind wobbled the branch.

She had spent most of her time in the tree reflecting on what had happened, and the fact the she would never see her dear friend Winterfrost again was finally starting to settle in. It was a horrible shame. Winterfrost was a genuinely good person and a great friend who had so much life in her eyes. Firelight laughed when she remembered all of those times when she had said things that she knew to be incorrect just to get on Winterfrost's nerves. It was all in good fun, though. Wasn't it? It didn't matter anymore. Her poor, poor friend was gone forever. Poor Winterfrost had so many good years ahead of her, and Firelight cringed when she thought about her violent, sudden death. Did she even get the chance to see her attacker? And she was completely disgraced, too: her brain was ripped right out of her head and she was dragged through the woods and just dumped naked somewhere. That wasn't supposed to happen; it made her feel so empty inside whenever she thought about it. But the important thing was that Winterfrost be remembered for her life, not her death, and Firelight promised herself that she would try to block out the memory of that fateful moment when she first turned the bend in the woods and came upon the horrifying sight of her friend's corpse.

She could never forget that, though. She was sure that the horrible image would stay with her and continue to haunt her, but she knew that she needed to separate Winterfrost's death and life. She couldn't define her friend by that horrible moment. The same went for General Richmond as well; there was no way that she would ever forget the horrible clanking sound that the trident made as is penetrated through the poor general's skull with such tremendous force, but she couldn't remember him for that. The general didn't even have time to react to what was going on; he didn't even have time to express pain or surprise on his face. He never even knew he was dying, or who his killer was. It was all over so quickly. At least there was a little bit of consolation in knowing that he had not suffered much, but it just seemed like such an unfitting end for such an honorable, courageous, and genuinely kind-hearted man. This guy still had a family to return to and a city that looked up to him, and now he was just dead in the woods without a brain. She couldn't think about it anymore because it was all so overwhelming.

And then there was that sick orc she had almost trusted. She thought that he was genuinely good, a shining example of someone who overcame extreme adversity in order to really make a positive difference in the world. He had acted in an upstanding manner the whole time she knew him, but there was always the tiniest little bit of doubt in the back of her head about his true intentions. She didn't know why the doubt was there, whether it was because of something she had subconsciously observed or perhaps her own prejudices against orcs, but for some reason it was there. Tears welled up in her eyes as she thought about the monster he had suddenly become. She really wanted him to be good, but it just didn't happen. He could have been something special, maybe even more special than his poor victims. He was never special. Firelight had been dreading something like this for a long time, and her fears came to pass in the most atrocious way imaginable.

Everything had gone so horribly since she had left the Fire Realm, but maybe things would get better. Something had to be done before the orc could strike again, though, and she knew it. Was he going to hurt Silara? She didn't want to think about it; the poor princess had been through so many terrible things, and her nightmare may have just been beginning. Firelight had to save the princess, but how? She wasn't even sure if she could save herself. She didn't know where her attackers were because she hadn't seen them for a few hours, so maybe they were gone. Maybe they decided to leave her alone. That was pretty unlikely, though; they probably just went to search for an axe or something else they could use to chop down the tree. But why hadn't they returned? Firelight was still weak from the horrible ordeal she had faced that morning, but she felt a little bit stronger and the wind was dying down a little, so maybe she could climb to another tree. It would be dangerous, but there definitely were some branches that she might be able to jump to and it was probably her best chance of survival. She had her eyes on one branch in particular, a long one that was about five feet lower than her own branch and extended out from another large tree. The rain poured down on her face as she inched in the direction of that other branch. Moving across the rough bark was tougher than she thought.

Two golden eyes appeared out of the darkness on the other branch, staring directly into hers. She froze; it was a huge animal! Some sort of massive black panther! It crept forward and then jumped right onto her branch with no effort at all, and its powerful jaws were now only a couple of feet from her face!

"Do not be alarmed, little sister. I do not wish to hurt you." Firelight didn't actually hear anything; the message just appeared in her head like she had thought it herself, except she hadn't. The huge cat stopped moving towards her and just looked at her.

"What's going on?" she thought.

"I have established a telepathic link with your mind, Firelight. I can read your thoughts, just as you can read mine."

"A talking cat?!"

"I don't actually talk. I communicate telepathically, you see."

"That's baloney. Why am I thinking all of these things to myself?"

"You're not. *I'm* thinking them to you." This was starting to get really weird.

"You? The cat?"

"Yes."

"And you can read my mind?"

"How else would I answer all of your thoughts?"

"I don't believe it. What number am I thinking of?"

"Seven."

"Oh, really? The correct answer is..."

"You just changed the answer to ten."

"I was going to say…"

"Eight? You just changed the answer to eight."

"This is ridiculous, anyway. Cats don't know how to count." She must have been *really* tired.

"Listen to me, Firelight. I am here for your protection."

"*My* protection? Why?"

"I am bound by honor. You saved my life and so I must make sure that yours continues as well."

"I saved your life? When?" Just then, she remembered what had happened in the castle courtyard in Victory City. She

242

rescued a black cat from the jaws of that huge pit bull. A black cat? Hey, wait a minute…

"That's right. I am that very same feline."

"I knew you looked familiar. Why are you so much bigger than you used to be?"

"When we last met, I assumed a small size so that I could easily watch everything that was happening in the city. Unfortunately, I found myself unprepared to return to my natural state when that canine ambushed me, so there was no way I could have defended myself. You saved my life that day."

"Why were you even watching the city in the first place? Why wouldn't you be doing normal cat stuff instead?"

"What do you mean by 'normal cat stuff?' Felines spend their time watching and studying their surroundings; they are by nature curious creatures."

"I thought curiosity killed the cat."

"Not this time, Firelight. Not this time."

Firelight rolled her eyes.

"Well, I mean…"

"Don't try to be modest. You could have escaped, but you chose not to. You chose to help me, and I am honor-bound to serve you now. Thank you for what you did."

"Oh, it was nothing." This whole communication-by-thought thing was actually kind of fun.

"I don't believe I've introduced myself yet. My name is Ocallin."

"O'Callaghan?"

"Ocallin. I would think you'd be able to get my name right on the first try if it appeared inside of your head."

"Watch your tone with me, furball."

"Apologies."

"I'm just joking. What kind of creature are you,

anyway?"

"A feline."

"Well, yeah…"

"A magical feline from another plane of existence."

"Oh, okay. That clears things up."

"Are you prepared to climb down this tree yet, sister?"

"What about the men down there?"

"They are no longer a threat to you. They were unable to handle the local wildlife and they perished."

"The werefrogs killed them?"

"Yes." Firelight smiled, but she didn't want to get too excited.

"Are you sure?"

"Yes."

"Are you absolutely sure about that?"

"Yes. I saw it happen not long ago."

"They're all dead?"

"Yes."

"How many men did you see?"

"Three, although to tell you the truth I actually knew you were thinking three because I read your mind. But there truly were three. They were ambushed and slain as soon as the sky started to become dark." Firelight looked at him suspiciously. "You can trust me. You must learn to trust me. Here, is this enough proof?" He gave Firelight her sword back, which he had been holding coiled up in his tail the whole time.

"All right, I trust you."

"Climb on my back. I'll take you down."

"What!? No way."

"I knew you still didn't completely trust me."

"Yeah, maybe. This is all so weird, though. You have to cut me a little slack here."

"I understand. But you must learn to trust me if you

want me to help you in any meaningful way. I could have easily finished you off already if I wanted to."

"That makes me feel good."

"I'm sorry if I'm frightening you. Have faith and trust me."

"Are you sure this is safe, though?"

"Yes. Just climb onto my back and hold on tight."

"Okay." The cat knelt down, and Firelight carefully climbed onto the creature's back and grabbed on tightly to its furry skin. It certainly felt a lot nicer than the rough bark she had been clinging to for most of the day.

"Now, prepare yourself. Here we go." Firelight's heart skipped a beat as the cat leapt into the air, but, to her relief, he landed gracefully and stably on a lower branch. She held onto his back even tighter.

"That wasn't so bad actually."

"Only a little bit more." The cat jumped to another branch, and then another. It was a thrill ride for Firelight as they bounced all the way down the tree. Finally, in what seemed like no time at all, they were back on the ground.

"I kind of liked that."

"See? All it took was a little bit of faith." Firelight smiled.

"Thank you for helping me get down, Ocallin. Now I think you've repaid your debt, though, so you're free to go."

"I cannot accept your offer of freedom because I know you could have overcome that situation yourself without my help. I sensed the strength inside of you."

"Oh, that's all right."

"I am dedicated to helping you in any way that I can. Let's go rescue that princess now."

"Really? You'll help me rescue her?"

"If I were lying, you would sense it in my mind. Get on my back; you can sleep on the way there. I'll make sure you don't fall off. Do not worry about anything and just enjoy your rest."

And so the journey began. Firelight laid her head on Ocallin's neck and closed her eyes as the rain fell softly onto her hair. It felt kind of nice. Maybe the good things she did actually did come back to her, just like Winterfrost had told her. Maybe Winterfrost herself had sent this cat down to her as a blessing. Whatever. She still wasn't sure what exactly had just happened, but it was time to accept it. There was no need to think about anything anymore. Too many thoughts. It was finally time... for... sleep........

Chapter 52

The man with the red mustache entered the dark room and closed the door behind him. Complete silence. It didn't seem like anyone else was there, so he turned to leave.

"What news have you now, Doctor?" asked the voice from the shadows. Dr. Rugby froze in place.

"I didn't notice you in here, sir."

"What news do you have for me? Did you hear back from your magicians?"

"No, sir. There has been no word from them."

"Then why are you wasting my time?!"

"It's about King Eliazer, sir. His departure is imminent; he will leave the castle early tomorrow in an attempt to meet with Molar-Licker of the orcs. He wants to negotiate his daughter's release."

"Early tomorrow? I'm not surprised that he wants to do this, but you're absolutely certain he'll leave tomorrow? That's somewhat sooner than I expected. What evidence do you have?"

"I overheard him talking with his neighbors in the room next to his. He told them to come into his room twice a day, starting tomorrow, to feed his dog and let it outside. He even went so far as to label the bag of dog food along with specific written instructions for the serving amounts."

"He must be planning an extended leave, then. You must follow him and make sure that the orcs do not get their hands on the Golden Egg."

"I understand that, sir. I am ready to follow him."

"And be very careful. The integrity of this entire mission depends on this."

"I will not fail. I have invested far too much into..."

Suddenly, the door swung open behind them. Rugby

jumped and whipped his head around as light poured into the room.

"I g…g….got you now, Dr. Rug…Rug…Rug…P….P….P…PRINCE P…PRINCE LUCIO!?!?!?!?"

Chapter 53

"We are gathered here today to remember Chazwick Phinneas Erikhome," spoke Prince Lucio, his eyes filled with tears as he solemnly addressed the crowd of mourners. "Chazwick was killed last night defending his city from murderous intruders who sought to undermine the very core of our government, and he will always be remembered for his noble sacrifice. A lieutenant in our army, he was a dedicated, inspirational leader who overcame a serious speech impediment, weight issues, and embarrassing facial acne to become one of Victory City's finest soldiers. And he was fine human being as well, one who always lived life to the fullest and did what he could to help others and make his community a better place. I am ashamed to admit that I personally once underestimated the good lieutenant, but his surprising *persistence* truly won me over. Chazwick, I am your biggest fan." The prince walked over to Erikhome's casket, where his body lay in state. He held up a small, circular, golden pin for everyone to view. "See this, everybody? This is a badge given only to those who achieve the rank of captain in our city's military. Rising to the rank of captain is no small feat, and it was always young Chazwick's dream. It is with great honor that I finally promote him and bestow this title upon him posthumously; he has truly earned it, and I can think of no one more deserving." With a round of applause from the crowd, the prince pinned the badge onto Erikhome's shirt collar.

"Now I remind all who gather here that we must not let Captain Erikhome's death go to waste. It is our responsibility to ensure that everything that this brave man stood for be kept sacred, and I am therefore authorizing a further increase in the intensity of our strike against the heart of the orc's fortress. Our resolve will be tested like never before in the next few days, but with our newest allies, the fire giants of Flamewind, at our sides, we will prevail. Did you hear me?! We will prevail! We will challenge the orcs on their own turf, and our courage shall not falter! We will eliminate this pestilence from our world once and for all! We will *strike* them dead! We will *strike* them from this earth! Mark my words, citizens: for all that is good, we will have this day! That is all."

Chapter 54

It was a cold, misty morning, but Chief Molar-Licker wouldn't have known it because he had spent the entire day sitting alone inside of his quarters in the cave. He was waiting.

Footsteps could be heard from outside. Very slow footsteps, growing slightly louder with each new step. Coming slightly closer. Even closer. He was finally here. The wait was over now. He was here.

Angroo entered the room and carefully laid the girl's motionless body onto the ground in the corner. He stood and looked at her without expression, while Molar-Licker continued to sit and stare at the wall. Silence persisted for several minutes.

"What... what have I done?" said Angroo in a tiny voice.

"You did only what needed to be done, Angroo. You have performed exactly as planned. You did well."

"I killed people. I remember it now. I killed innocent people for no reason."

"You have served the greater good. You have done nothing wrong."

"I *murdered* innocent people." Angroo suddenly turned around to face the shaman, but all he saw was the back of the shaman's head. "I *murdered* in cold blood! I remember all of it!"

"Calm down, Angroo." answered Molar-Licker. He didn't move from his spot on the floor. "You have served the greater good, and that's the only thing that matters." Angroo stepped forward, clenching his fists as his face boiled over with rage. He was out of control.

"What the hell have I done?! I didn't serve the greater good, Molar-Licker! I murdered innocent people and devoured their brains like some depraved animal!"

"Life is cruel. Now you have truly learned its cruelty."

"Face me!" screamed Angroo. "Look at me when I talk! I'm talking to you!"

"You have served the greater…"

"LOOK AT ME!!!"

Molar-Licker finally turned to look at Angroo.

"Calm yourself. How is the princess faring?"

"Look at what I've become! I'm a murderer! A MURDERER!!!"

"Calm down!" The shaman's expression was unchanging. Angroo calmed down slightly and took half a step backwards. "How is the princess faring? Is she well?"

"She's asleep." There was a short pause.

"Listen…"

"Molar-Licker, what's gotten into me? Why did I do these things?"

"The spirits have entered your body. They have been selectively controlling your actions and your thoughts and they have been manipulating your emotions."

"The *spirits*? Some *spirits* entered my body and made me murder in cold blood?!"

"It was what needed to be done, Angroo."

"*Spirits*?! How did these spirits enter my body, then, huh?!" He stepped forward.

"This needed to be done."

"How did they enter my body?!" There was a short silence. "It was that potion that you gave me, wasn't it? That potion that you gave me, telling me all along that it would cure my skin condition. You monster."

"I did what needed to be done."

"I trusted you for so long. You were the only one I could trust for so long. You *lied* to me. You *betrayed* me."

"Just let me explain…"

"TRAITOR!!!"

"Still your tongue! There was no treachery here!"

"YOU TRAITOR!!!"

"THERE WAS NO TREACHERY HERE, ANGROO!!!! Get a hold of yourself!" Angroo stared into Molar-Licker's eyes with contempt and breathed heavily. "Listen. What you did was for the greater good. The spirits have led you on a bloody path, but it was a path for the preservation of your people. Your kin. The orcs."

"I murdered innocent people because of YOU!!!"

"The Golden Eggs of Gotty Gottya were a serious threat to our existence. The spirits guided you to the Golden Eggs on whatever path they could, and they lent you supernatural strength and agility when you needed it so that you could accomplish your task successfully. I apologize if the path was a cruel one."

"This is absurd. What did I need *supernatural* strength for?! When did I need it *most*?! I needed it most SO THAT I COULD MURDER DEFENSELESS, INNOCENT PEOPLE!!!!!"

"Those people were necessary casualties. They stood in your way, so you had no other choice..."

"I had no other choice? I had no other choice?! That's laughable, Molar-Licker. Absolutely laughable. Absolutely laughable. I had NO choice!!!"

"I'm sorry that this had to happen, but this *was* your choice. This whole thing was your choice. You once told me that you'd give everything to protect your kin, and this was the only way you could protect your kin. This potion was the only way."

"No!"

"The potion provided a medium for the spirits to enter your mind. They have guided you on the path necessary for our race's survival."

"No! I'm not listening to this madness any longer!"

"There was no other way, Angroo. I'm sorry. It was only a matter of time before the Golden Eggs were activated and all orcs were wiped from the earth. Just calm down and think about it." Angroo stood still and looked down at the ground.

"Oh yeah? Well the spirits must've screwed up because one Golden Egg still remains. I only stole two of them. The spirits…"

"The third is currently in a secret location that only King Eliazer of Elkanshire knows about. The spirits determined that the only way to bend King Eliazer's mind would be to kidnap his daughter, and that's exactly what they forced you to do. It was the only way."

"Those horrible things I did to Silara… everything was because of spirits inside of me? Some spirits?!"

"The spirits determined…" Angroo suddenly shoved Molar-Licker to the ground and lifted up his trident above his head.

"What's that, spirits? You said you want me to kill CHIEF MOLAR-LICKER?!?! Oh, okay, if that's what you think is best!"

"Don't be a fool!" shouted the shaman as he stared up. Angroo returned his gaze and they stared each other in the eyes. "It was fate, Angroo. All those people you killed – it was their fate to die and you were the one chosen to be the facilitator. You are fate's champion. But *I* do not share their fate, and you cannot kill me. Put the weapon down."

They continued to stare at each other without moving.

"I… I can't do it," muttered Angroo as he dropped his weapon to the floor. He wanted to turn and look at the girl but he couldn't. He couldn't even look at Molar-Licker. He stumbled out of the room.

Chapter 55

The man with the red mustache stood beside a tree and waited. It was the early morning, and his new contact should have been arriving any minute now. Finally, he noticed a figure approaching him through the thick morning fog. It was a dark-haired, scruffy-bearded man carrying a box.

"You're late, sir."

"Not late, Rugb'. You said to meet y' in the m'rn, and that's what it is n'."

"It doesn't matter. Have you recovered the potion?"

"Pr'lly one of these. Can see for y'rself if you want." He opened the box he was carrying to reveal several vials of differently colored liquids.

"I hope you were careful handling these, Brack."

"C'rse I was." Rugby closely examined each of the vials and then returned them to the box.

"You stole all of these from Molar-Licker?"

"Y'sir. Every one."

"I'll have to go back and conduct some tests on these to make sure that one of them is indeed the Spirit Juice. Then you can receive your payment." Brack stepped closer.

"Don't think so, buddy. I th'nk you're gon' be paying me right ab't now."

"How do I know that one of these is the potion I asked you to retrieve?"

"Don't know. But the last t'me someb' didn't pay me, I got real angr'. When Molar-Licker d't pay up, I got real, real angr'."

"That's because you failed Molar-Licker. He was expecting you to bring him Princess Silara alive, and yet you came back empty-handed. You let her slip right out of your grasp."

"Not m' fault," answered Brack. Rugby smiled.

"You're a bad man, Brack. You're a bad man and they don't come any worse than you. Crista thought you were helping her escort the princess to safety, but you *lied* to her because you thought you could make an extra dime kidnapping her for the orcs instead. And when the orcs refused to pay you for failing at your task, you *pretended* that you were still their friend while you raided their supply of magical concoctions for *me*. You're the most duplicitous scoundrel I've ever seen."

"Are you g'n pay me, th'n?"

"Fine. All right, I'll pay you what I promised. After all, I wouldn't want you turning on me next, would I?" He reached down. "Oh, how very careless of me. I dropped the bag containing your payment around here in these leaves somewhere. Would you mind helping me find it?"

Brack was confused, but he began to look around for the bag anyway.

"Oh, here's your payment! I found it!" shouted Rugby as he leaped at Brack from behind and strung a cord around his neck. "Here's your payment! You deserve this, you duplicitous, lying scoundrel! You deserve this!"

Brack was caught completely by surprise; he struggled as hard as he could to remove the cord from his neck but his assailant's grip was much too strong. After several minutes of fierce resistance, he finally stopped and collapsed to the ground. Rugby kicked his limp body and then lifted the box of potions with a laugh. He turned around and headed back the way he came from, using his shoulder to wipe the sweat off his left cheek as he trudged off.

"A pleasure doing business with you, sir."

Chapter 56

Angroo sat down near the entrance to the shaman's room with his face pressed against his hands. How could this have happened? Why were the spirits inside of his head? It wasn't fair. He got up and returned to the room to find Molar-Licker in his same position on the ground, staring at the wall. It was as if he had never moved from his position at all.

"Why did you do this to me?"

"It was the only way. They would have killed us if you hadn't retrieved the Golden Eggs of Gotty Gottya."

"I couldn't fight the spirits. I failed myself."

"You did what had to be done, and I'm sorry this had to happen." Angroo looked down blankly at the floor, and Molar-Licker suddenly stood up and began to walk in his direction. "Look, it's okay." He embraced him. "I'm very sorry that it had to come to this. I love you very much, Angroo. You've always been like a son to me. The closest thing to a son that I've ever had. I thought about this long and hard but I knew that this had to be done and I knew that you were the best one for it. The spirits called for you." Angroo continued to stare at the floor.

"I didn't have to kill those people. I didn't have to kill King Lucius or anyone else. I could have snuck in and stolen the Golden Eggs without killing anybody if that was so important."

"The spirits do not operate that way; they prefer to wreak as much havoc and sow as much chaos as possible, as all orcs would. They saw those people as threats to the integrity of your mission, and they took advantage of your inner aggression to explode upon them."

"My inner aggression?"

"The spirits unleashed your aggressive tendencies. Your mind was ripe for the taking because the will to commit those acts was already there, deep down."

"I didn't want to kill those people at any level, though. I didn't want to hurt anybody. Honestly."

"Listen. Do you love your people? Do you love your fellow orcs?"

"Yes."

"Then you must accept the truth. Angroo, orcs are violent creatures by nature. Their entire lives are fueled by intense urges of aggression. It's true for every one of us. We're not like the humans, elves, dwarves, or anyone else."

"I don't believe that."

"You must believe it. You know it. The aggressive urge that you've had to go through extraordinary lengths to suppress to become the way that you are today. That hostility and anger. It was always in you. That aggression was always in you, tormenting you constantly, brewing and stewing, and *you know it*."

"No…"

"You know it was always in you, and the spirits knew it as well. That is why they were able to take control!"

"No! You're lying!"

"You can't hide the truth from yourself! The murderer was inside of you all along, and the spirits merely released him from the bounds cast by your artificial, frail moral compass! *You* were the one who killed those people. *You* were the one who ate their brains and mutilated their bodies. Don't you understand now? It was all *you*."

"NO!!!"

"Any orc would have done the same, Angroo. It's who you are. You can't fight the truth."

Angroo stepped backwards. Images of every one of his tribesmen he had ever befriended suddenly sprung to his mind; were all of them murderers deep down inside? Killers?

Were all orcs *evil*? He squinted his eyes and clenched his fists as the anger built up inside of him – that very same anger that had caused him to commit those obscenities. He felt like he was about to throw up.

"NO!!!"

"Easy. It's okay. Just accept it." Molar-Licker tried to embrace Angroo again but Angroo shoved him aside.

"NO!!! IT'S A LIE!!!!!!" He backed off, then turned and ran out of the room. Silence again.

Molar-Licker sat on the ground and stared blankly at the wall.

"IT'S A LIE!!!!!!!!!!!!!!!!!" screamed Angroo, startling the orcs that had gathered nearby.

"Easy, white-skin. What you yelling for?"

"Get away from me, you murderous traitors!"

"Hey! I didn't do nothing! I was just going in to talk with Chief."

"Yah, me too!"

"Yah, and me!"

Angroo suddenly thought of the girl, who was lying undefended in the other room. She was completely defenseless. Completely undefended. He clenched his fists.

"*You* will not take another step! Nobody goes into that room!"

"Hey! Stop yelling!" The orcs backed up as Angroo lunged towards them.

"You will not go anywhere near that room, you sick, lusty animals!"

"What? Why?"

"You know exactly why! Now get out of my sight before I strangle you with my bare hands!" The orcs looked at each other and backed away quickly. They were soon gone, and Angroo sat down on the floor and didn't move.

What was he going to do next? Who were the spirits going to force him to kill next? He couldn't fight them because the murderous urges were already there, so he might as well just accept it. All orcs were that way, right? It was okay to accept it then. Just accept it. He was a monster and there was nothing he could do about it.

He couldn't accept it, though, because the things that he had seen were much too horrible. An idea suddenly came to him: maybe it was time for him to kill *himself*. It was the only thing he could do to stop the spirits from forcing him to kill another innocent. Yes. Yes, it had to be done. He stood up.

Chapter 57

It was almost noon. Prince Lucio was on his way to the dining room for lunch when he suddenly stopped short. He noticed a man wearing a dark blue coat and a large hat skulking nearby; Rugby's disguises never fooled him.

"Get in there!" the prince whispered as he pointed to a nearby room that happened to be empty. The man seemed somewhat surprised. "Get into the room now!" He finally did what he was told and both of them entered the room. The man with the red mustache removed his hat as the prince closed the door behind them.

"I…"

"What are you doing here?! You were supposed to be tracking down Lord Eliazer!"

"I thought that…"

"You were given specific instructions, Dr. Rugby!" There was no immediate answer.

"I'm here because I made a mistake."

"You're bloody right you made a mistake!"

"I thought I had found Molar-Licker's Spirit Juice, so I rushed back to conduct tests and make sure. It turned out that none of the potions that I recovered were indeed the Spirit Juice." Prince Lucio looked him in the eyes, but he averted his gaze.

"So you just let Eliazer get away? He's probably almost there by now!"

"I might still beat him there. He won't know how to find their fortress in the woods and…"

"You *might* beat him there?!"

"I'll leave at once to…"

"Your priorities are all wrong, Dr. Rugby. The Spirit Juice is certainly important, but the Golden Egg is essential.

Do you remember our agreement?" There was a short pause.

"You know what? I've had just about enough of your twisted logic, Prince Lucio! Might I remind you that once we find the Spirit Juice, the Golden Egg loses its value? Did that ever occur to you, *sir*?!"

"I do not appreciate your tone." Rugby stepped closer to the prince.

"Dear Prince Lucio. You and I both know that the Spirit Juice can turn someone into a *monster*. A monster that cannot be stopped. You saw what happened to your father, right? You saw what happened to Milkbone. That monster was much too strong and much too quick to be stopped. Now imagine if you and I, and not the orcs, controlled the Spirit Juice. You could have at your disposal an entire army of unstoppable warriors! We wouldn't need the Golden Egg of Gotty Gottya to hold off the orcs or anyone else! Our city would be triumphant!"

Prince Lucio smiled.

"I've learned to pick up on your lies, Rugby. You would never let anyone near the Spirit Juice if you ever got your hands on it. You want it for yourself; in fact, that's the reason why you agreed to help me in the first place! You would recover one of the Golden Eggs for me so that I could use it to dispose of the orcs, and in return I would allow you to keep some of that potion for yourself." He stepped towards Rugby, and Rugby took a step back. "Victory City cannot thrive, cannot grow... nay, cannot even exist if the orcs continue to threaten it unchecked! You don't care about this city at all, though. You don't care about honoring agreements at all. You just want to turn yourself into a super soldier by drinking a magical potion."

"You're being unreasonable!" Rugby stepped back again.

"You are a disgrace, Dr. Rugby. An utter disgrace. You seemed like such a good servant the whole time I've known you, but your trust was fleeting. Your ego was growing and growing. You really didn't care about your city at all; the only thing you ever cared about was yourself. I bet I would have been your first target as soon as you got your hands on that potion; right? Just so that nobody would ever know about any of this, right? You'd cover your trail perfectly. I would be a dead man, Victory City would go to ruin, and you wouldn't care."

Rugby smiled and looked around. He began to laugh, and something about his appearance suddenly frightened the prince.

"Very good, sir. Very good. You're right, of course. I don't care a lick about you or your moronic city! I've allowed you to shove me around for far too long!"

"Draw your weapon, Rugby! Draw your weapon right now!"

"But Prince, I'm the superior swordsman. This isn't a fair fight."

"I said draw your weapon!"

Both of them drew their swords.

"What kind of weapon is that, Prince Lucio?" gawked Rugby. "Swords aren't for decoration, you know. They're for killing people." The blade of the prince's sword was in a strange zigzag shape.

"This is called a flamberge. Despite its decorative quality, I assure you that it was not purely an aesthetic choice. Would you like to see what I mean?!" The prince lifted the sword up into the air and brought it down as hard as he could. Rugby parried the blow with his own sword, but the weapon sent unexpected vibrations into his weapon and caused him to lose his balance as Prince Lucio kicked him in the stomach.

"You…"

"Doesn't give you a good *vibe*, does it Doctor?"

"Your little gimmicks can't save you now!" Rugby tried to jab the prince, but he was blocked and again the jarring vibrations threw Rugby off of his balance. The prince tried to hit him with another swing, but he missed as Rugby turned and bolted through the door.

"Come back here, you frightened rabbit!" shouted the prince, but Rugby was already all the way down the hall. "As soon as you lose the upper hand you immediately retreat! You're nothing but a coward!" The prince shook his head. "I should have known that you would betray your city someday. I should have seen it much earlier." He sheathed his sword.

Guards came running from all directions towards the prince.

"Your Highness! Is everything all right?!"

"Yes, everything's fine."

"What happened here?"

"Nothing happened. Everything's fine."

"Are you sure, Your Highness?"

"Yes. Everything's okay."

"That's good. Are you ready for your lunch, then?"

"My lunch? No, no. I'm afraid I've lost my appetite."

"Are you sure?"

"Yes. I'm sure. Thank you anyway." The guards left as the prince sat down on the floor. He was alone now. What had gone wrong? It was time for him to reevaluate his situation.

Chapter 58

Angroo hadn't moved from his spot. He reasoned that suicide was too easy, or maybe it was actually too hard considering he couldn't bring himself to do it. Were the spirits telling him not to kill himself, and that's why he couldn't do it? Did they still want to use him as a tool? He didn't want to think about the spirits anymore. Maybe it really was time for him to make sure that those spirits never got to him by ending it all right there. But he still couldn't do it.

One thing he could do, though, was turn himself in. He remembered what the human commander had told him – poor, poor Charles – about how the prince of the human city would only consider peace if the killer were somehow apprehended. It was now in his power to make sure that happened. Yes, maybe that was the way to go; maybe it would save the orcs from certain destruction and prevent any further bloodshed. His own life meant nothing compared to all of those things.

Were the orcs even worth saving, though? If they were all the homicidal monsters that Molar-Licker had told him they were, maybe they weren't worth saving at all. Maybe they really should all die. He didn't want to believe that, though. He didn't want to believe any of it, and he certainly didn't want to kill anybody else.

The choice was clear now: his final legacy would be one of hope, not one of despair and mistrust. It would be a legacy of hope for a future of everlasting peace. He didn't know for sure what was right, but he did know that he had to turn himself in as quickly as possible. He took a deep breath and walked towards the cave exit. He would have to go straight to the prince himself and make everything better.

Chapter 59

It was starting to get late, and the light was dying down. Crista's face became darker and darker as the prince stood above her, stroking her wavy hair. She was lying in bed, still comatose, but still beautiful and peaceful.

"Oh, my dear, sweet Crista. I'm very sorry for everything that's happened." The prince continued to stroke her hair. "It wasn't supposed to turn out like this at all."

He reached down and lifted up the Crown of Victory City, placing it on the bed beside the unconscious woman.

"I wanted to wait until the time was right before I became king. I didn't want to arouse suspicion that I had been conspiring to kill my father, even though it wasn't true; I wanted to make it seem like the orcs had stolen the crown to dishonor our city. How pathetic it all seems in retrospect." He felt the soft skin on her face. "I want you to have it now. If you ever wake up, I want you to lead us. I failed my city because I let all three of the Golden Eggs fall into the orcs' hands, and now it's only a matter of time before those savages regroup and overrun us. I just hope I see you again before that happens." He knelt down and kissed her on the forehead. "Goodbye for now, sweet darling."

He turned and began to walk slowly out of the room. That traitorous Dr. Rugby had ruined everything for him; everything had gone to waste now that the orcs were about to get their hands on the final Golden Egg. All those secrets he had kept, all those lies he had told, all for nothing. He killed Lieutenant Erikhome for nothing. He had justified all of those things because they were necessary for the preservation of Victory City and for the honor of his forebears, but now they were all for nothing. For nothing! He had been the only one who really understood the threat that the orcs posed, especially with that mysterious 'Spirit Juice' that they had developed to make themselves unstoppable, and he knew that the time had come to finally activate one of the Golden Eggs and eliminate the orcish threat for good. His father didn't want to believe him, though; nobody listened to him. Dr. Rugby was the only one who believed him. Or so he thought.

It was time for him to retire to his bedroom for the night. As he walked up the dark stairway, he thought that he felt a cold breeze on his face. The windows weren't opened, though, were they? He didn't think they should have been. He turned and, despite the darkness, he was able to see that the window next to where he was standing was completely smashed open. He felt the sharp shards of glass on his fingers as he touched it.

He immediately turned and looked up; a dark figure stood at the top of the stairs and looked down at him with glowing eyes. Panic set in.

"I, uh…" Prince Lucio whipped out his flamberge and rapidly stepped backwards down the stairs as he gazed up at the figure, who watched him and didn't move. "Who… who are you?"

No response.

"You must be the one who killed my father, and now you're here for me as well. Quite an entrance you made, heh."

No response.

"Perhaps I deserve this for what I've done. Perhaps I had this coming to me, and perhaps you have the right to want to kill me. After all, I always hated your kind. I wanted to kill every orc because I was afraid of what you could do."

No response. The figure seemed to shiver just a little bit.

"Listen, whoever you are. We can work something out. Victory City can make peace with the orcs, if that's what you want. Just look at me: I'm a defeated man. I'm desperate. If you have to resort to coming after me at a time like this, then you must be desperate as well. Let's work something out that both of our sides can agree upon, all right?" His eyes were filled with the tears that he had made no attempt to hold in. He reached out his hand.

No response.

The prince took a step forward. There was no time for him to react as the dark figure lurched down the stairs and the trident penetrated through his face.

Chapter 60

A lone man stumbled through the woods in the pitch darkness. He was very hungry, but he decided against looking for food; sleeping was his top priority now. He had been through enough that day. He finally found a comfortable place to lie down and he closed his eyes.

Someone was approaching. Startled, he jumped up to see a bright light coming his way; it was a woman holding a torch.

"Who's there?!" shouted Firelight. He didn't answer, instead trying to lie down as close to the ground as possible and hide. She walked over and stood above him, looking down.

"Go easy on m', please."

"I think I've seen you before. Aren't you the guy who was escorting the princess through the woods a couple of weeks ago? The ranger? Brock or something like that?"

"Brack. Name's Brack."

"Okay, Brack. I just…" The man suddenly grabbed her leg and attempted to trip her, but she kicked him hard in the face and then leaned over and pointed her sword at his neck. "No funny business, buddy! What are you doing here?!"

"None a y'r business."

"I'll make it my business!"

He moaned.

"Okay, 'kay. Know what? I'm in a giv'n mood r' now. I'll tell y' what I know for twenty gold pieces."

"I don't have any money."

"Fi'teen, then."

"I said I don't have any money. And why is your neck all bloody? It looks like…"

"A'ight, fine. I'll tell y' for free. Seems l'ke nobody wants t' pay me anyth' these days anym'."

"Were you attacked?"

"Yes ma'am. Dr. Rugb' tried to kill m' after I gave 'm what he wanted and asked f' payment."

"Dr. Rugby?! You mean Gorman Rugby?!"

"Yessuh. Thought he killed m', but I was just play'n dead."

"You were just plain dead? But you're alive now."

"No, n', I was just *play'n* dead."

"You were just plain dead?"

"N'! *Play'n* dead!"

"You were pretending to be dead?" He nodded.

"Play'n dead. Now listen closel': the only reason I'm tel'n you this is 'cause I hate Rugb' and I want y' to find him an' kill h'."

"Where is he?"

"He hir'd me t' steal a magic potion fr' the orcs, and I gave h' a bunch that I foun' but I don't thin' any of them w' the one he w' looking f'. They w' too easy to steal to be th' one. He'll pro'ly be traveling back there t' find th' real one."

"To steal a magical potion from the orcs? Are you sure?"

"As s're as can be 'spected. Supposed t' be a pretty powerf' brew, s'far as I heard. Makes y' turn into a monster 'r someth' like that. Rugb' is pr'lly on h' way right n', so you better hurr'. Now leave me to m' sleepin'."

"It turns you into a monster?"

"S'far as I heard."

"What do you mean it turns you into a monster?"

"D' know."

"A monster? Do you know anything else about…"

"N'!" There was a short silence as they stared at each other through the dim light.

"Can you at least tell me where the orcs live? Where's the lair?"

"Here's a map, n' leave me 'lone. Sleeping t'me."

"All right. All right, thanks." Firelight took the map and backed off into the darkness, shaking out her torch as she went. Everything was suddenly dark again.

Chapter 61

It was dark and quiet inside of the cave as Chief Molar-Licker continued to meditate alone in the corner of his room. This time, though, his peace would be short-lived; the quiet was shattered and his concentration disrupted by a sudden, loud commotion outside. He looked up to see several of his tribesmen barge into the room and throw a thin, cloaked figure to the ground in front of them.

"We catch this guy snooping around outside."

"Yah."

The figure slowly stood up and pulled off his hood, revealing the worn-out, tired face of an elf with long, golden hair. It was obvious that he hadn't slept for days. Molar-Licker stood up and turned to face the stranger.

"You must be King Eliazer of the city of Elkanshire. It was only a matter of time before you arrived." The elf stood up and stared at the shaman, the sheer determination in his eyes shining through despite his extreme exhaustion.

"Where's my daughter, you fiend!?"

"She's safe."

"Where is she?! What have you done to her?!"

"I said that she's safe. You will see her shortly if you cooperate."

"I won't tell you where I've hidden the Golden Egg of Gotty Gottya until you let me see her!" Molar-Licker took a step forward.

"You're not in much of a position to make demands, elf."

"How do I know you'll keep your end of the bargain? What if she's hurt?!"

Molar-Licker took another step closer. He was now inches away from the elf and he stared down into his eyes.

"Where is the Golden Egg?!"

"I'm not telling until…"

"Where is the Golden Egg?!"

"I…"

"Strip him naked, warriors. I have ways of procuring this information."

"Wait, wait! Let's be civilized here! I… I'll tell you where it is." Molar-Licker looked at him and smiled.

"I'm listening."

"It's, um… do you have something to write all of this down on?"

The elf was handed a dirt-stained piece of parchment, and he took a few minutes to write out detailed directions while everyone waited. Once he was finished, Molar-Licker snatched the instructions out of his hands and carefully read them.

"Let me see if I understand this correctly. Once we reach the large tree that's shaped like a hand with only four fingers, we make a left, walk for three and a quarter miles and then travel south towards the riverbed?"

"Yes, but remember that it's not the first large tree shaped like a hand with only four fingers that you'll see. It's actually the second large tree shaped like a hand with only four fingers."

"And the location where you buried the Golden Egg is marked with a purple-colored rock?"

"*Violet*-colored. There are plenty of purple rocks in that area, but only one *violet* one. You'll know it when you get there, though. It's quite obvious, I'd say."

"Very well. This will have to do." Molar-Licker turned to the orcs and handed them the paper. "Follow these directions and bring me back the Golden Egg. And be extremely careful handling it." The orcs groaned and left the room, leaving only

Molar-Licker and the elf behind.

"Now can I see my daughter?"

"She's in a different area of the cave. You can see her when my warriors return with the Golden Egg."

The elf looked around. He soon noticed a large, steaming cauldron on the other side of the room and walked over towards it, licking his lips.

"Do you mind if I help myself to some soup? I'm famished."

"Do not drink that soup!"

"Okay! You don't have to yell!"

"Get away from the soup!" The elf stepped away.

"You seem to be very insistent that I don't eat any of this soup." Molar-Licker didn't respond, and the elf stepped back towards the cauldron. "I don't know, though. I'm pretty hungry right now."

"Do not touch that soup."

"I'll make you a deal, Chief. You let me see my daughter, and I won't have any of the soup. Is that a deal?" He grinned.

"You fool. You have no idea what that soup..."

"I'm getting quite hungry."

Molar-Licker stepped forward, but the elf cupped his hands and reached towards the cauldron; Molar-Licker froze in place and stared.

"You'll see your daughter soon. There's no need..."

"I haven't eaten anything all day, Chief."

"You miserable little whelp. Very well, I'll let you see your daughter, but you must promise me you will not eat any of the soup."

"You have yourself a deal."

"Come with me, then. I'll show you where she is."

"Why don't you bring her here instead? As soon as I

take one step away from this soup pot I lose all of my bargaining power, you know."

Molar-Licker snarled and shook his head. His fists were clenched tightly. He walked angrily towards the room's exit, looking back at the elf to make sure he didn't try anything.

"Going somewhere, sir?"

Molar-Licker quickly turned his head to see a blade in his face: a man with a red mustache was standing in the exit way and brandishing a razor-sharp sword! Molar-Licker instinctively swung his fist down and tried to knock the sword out of the man's hand, but the man slashed his wrist and cut his forehead on the follow-through. He then slashed Molar-Licker's abdomen and, avoiding another fist, drove the sword through the chieftain's thigh and all the way into his bone! Molar-Licker howled in pain as he stumbled back into the room, the man's sword now suspended mere inches from his throat.

"Who... are you? What are you doing in my quarters?!"

"Who I am is not important, *sir*. You have something that I want, and I would very much like for you to give it to me." Molar-Licker continued to back into the room very slowly as he gripped his bloody thigh, and the man followed behind him and kept the sword positioned at his neck.

"It's you!" shouted the elf as he finally recognized the man. "Why, you're Gorman Rugby, the thug who threatened my daughter! You're part of the Order of the Filthy Foot and a foul servant of Dinther Footmol himself!"

"You've shown yourself to be quite gullible, Lord Eliazer. The whole charade about the Order of the Filthy Foot was merely a ruse meant to intimidate you; I worked only for Prince Lucio."

"Prince Lucio? Wha... you were helping *us* all along? You were helping Victory City all along?" The man stared at him for a few seconds and then began to laugh, but he quickly caught himself.

"Yes. I was working for the interests of Victory City the whole time. I sincerely apologize for frightening you so much, but it was all in an effort to retrieve the Golden Egg from you so that you wouldn't have to worry about guarding it yourself. You wouldn't have had to protect it from this monster here."

"What are you saying?"

"The orcs were after your Golden Egg, and we knew it. We wanted to take it off of your hands to relieve you of the heartache of having to worry about your dear little girl all the time."

"Wha... really?"

"Of course. I would never try to hurt you or your daughter, but that's enough talk for now." He turned towards Molar-Licker, who was covered in blood and was panting heavily with his back flat against the wall. "Good chieftain, I believe you know what I'm looking for. I'm here for the Spirit Juice that you developed."

"I have... have no idea what you're talking about."

"Oh, I believe you know *exactly* what I'm talking about, sir. You know *exactly* what I'm talking about. You stole the only recipe for it twenty years ago." He held the blade closer.

"H..."

"Oh, and you had better not call for help, sir. I booby-trapped the entrance, so as soon as anyone enters or leaves the room the entire place blows."

Molar-Licker and the elf looked at each other nervously.

"You booby-trapped the entrance!?" shouted the elf. "You dummy! How are we supposed to get out of here?"

"I can deactivate the trap. But nobody's going anywhere until I get what I want."

"Help... me..." muttered Molar-Licker.

"Don't even think about helping the pathetic orc, Lord Eliazer. Make one move and I finish him."

"Finish him then. I don't care."

"Help… me…"

"I'll ask you one more time, *sir*. Where is the Juice?"

"Help…"

"Um, excuse me, Dr. Rugby. I don't know anything about this 'Juice' that you speak of, but I think I might know where he's keeping it." The man suddenly turned his head.

"Where?!"

"He seemed awfully adamant about not letting me drink this soup. Maybe it's mixed into the soup." The man whipped around while maintaining his sword's position at Molar-Licker's throat.

"Are you sure about that?" He reached into his coat pocket and pulled out a small vial of liquid. "Listen carefully, Eliazer: pour a few drops of this liquid into the soup, and it should tell us whether or not the Juice is really in there. Smoke will rise if the Juice is there. Catch it!" The elf caught the thrown vial.

"Why do you want this Juice so much?"

"Do it or I'll kill you."

"Oh, I'm sorry. What did you want me to do?"

"Do it right now! Pour it in!"

"Oops, dropped it." The vial shattered as it hit the ground and its contents were spilled. "How dare you speak to me like that?! You're nothing but a filthy liar, Doctor. I guess you'll never know *where* that Spirit Juice is now!" He laughed as the man stared at him.

"You're a treacherous idiot, sir. I brought another bottle of that concoction with me."

"Uh… oops. Sorry then."

The man reached into his pocket and pulled out

278

another tiny vial, flinging it towards the cauldron of soup; it smashed against the inside of the pot and the liquid dripped in. Green smoke billowed out of the pot, the symbol for a successful reaction.

"So you really did mix the Spirit Juice into the soup. Very, very clever of you." He smiled gleefully as he turned back towards the wounded Molar-Licker. "I'm afraid I have no more use for you now, unfortunately. Do you have any last words before I slice your neck, sir?"

"Help!"

"Pathetic. How many times will you…"

"Angroo, why won't you help me?! You've been sitting there the whole time ignoring me!" The other two began to look around the room. "Don't pretend you can't hear me! I knew you were here the whole time! I need your help!"

"You're delirious! There's no one there!"

"I'm afraid Dr. Rugby's right, Chief. I don't see anyone else here."

"Angroo, help me!"

"There's nobody else here!"

"Angroo!"

"There's nobody here!"

"Angroo!" The man rolled his eyes and moved the blade closer to Molar-Licker's neck.

"This has gone on long enough! Die, sir!"

"Angroo!"

Angroo emerged from the shadows. The man with the red mustache whipped his head around, his eyes wide with overwhelming fear; he dropped his sword and backed away, shivering wildly, convulsing with panic.

"You. I saw you when I murdered King Lucius. You were there."

"I was just…"

"You were dressed as a guard, helping yourself to the poor king's treasures as I was leaving with the Golden Egg. You're just a common thief."

"I was..."

"Why are you here now?"

"I..."

"You want to steal the potion? Is that why you're here? You want to go through the same living hell that I have to go through?"

"I was..."

"It wouldn't work for you, anyway. It only works for orcs. Only orcs possess the inner hatred that the spirits feed off of."

"No, I..."

"I don't think you heard me. I said that it only works for the orcs, you imbecile."

"I..."

"IT ONLY WORKS FOR ORCS!!!!"

"I wasn't..."

"Go ahead, take some then. I don't care. Drink it. I'll let you."

"Angroo, don't let him drink the..." Molar-Licker tried to move forward but Angroo fiercely shoved him against the stone wall. The man stood still and didn't move.

"Are you deaf?! I said drink the soup. Move it."

"Oh, o..."

"Shut up and drink the damn soup. Soupy. Soupy. Drinky. Drinky."

"Heh, okay. Okay, sir." He began to walk slowly towards the soup.

"Go faster."

The man took another step forward.

"Faster."

Another step.

"Faster."

Another step.

The white orc sprung forward and landed on the man's shoulders, grabbing onto the red mustache with both of his hands and violently heaving his arms backwards over his head as the two of them fell to the ground. The man's head, neck, and spinal cord looked like a dripping wet baby tadpole with a human face, blood slopping around the room like slime as the polliwog sprouted from the man's torso and torpedoed off into the darkness. Thud.

It was all over so quickly. It was too quick and too easy. Silence.

Angroo stumbled back towards the corner. He clutched his face with blood-stained hands and sunk back into the shadows from which he had emerged.

Chapter 62

Molar-Licker's guards returned from their brief trip into the cool night; it had become evident after a short time that the directions they were given were completely fabricated, since none of the landmarks they were told to look for even existed. The elf king had obviously lied, and their frustration began to boil over.

"This be bad situation for us," muttered one of them.

"Yah. What we going to do?"

"We losing war. Big time."

"Stupid puny humans and puny elf-men! They be cutting through our force!"

"Stupid, stupid, puny humans!"

"No, humans and elf-men not the problem. It be the stupid, *stupid* fire giants! Not can giants be beaten! They walk through us as if we not even there, squishing us under their feet!"

"Yah! Ever since stupid giants join battle, I, I just, ARRRGGGGHHHHHH!!!!!" The orc lifted his axe high into the air and then slammed it into the ground in a sudden burst of rage.

"Easy there, Snork. You should take out anger not on floor. You take it out on Chief Molar-Licker. *He* be the one holding us back."

"Yah!"

"Chief? You no go near Chief!"

"No, no. Glorkus right, Plokk. Chief be leading us to path of defeat! He need to step down. Hard way."

"Yah, Plokk! I sick of listening to his orders!"

"Yah!"

"Yah! Kill Chief!"

"Yah!"

"No! You no touch Chief! I go tell him what you say!" The dissenting orc was immediately cut down by the others, and his bloody corpse was left alone to rot in the cave.

"We go kill Chief right now!"

"Yah!"

The orcs hurried through the corridor towards their chieftain's room. They hadn't gone far when they suddenly heard soft, muffled crying coming from a different room; it sounded like a wounded animal. They stopped in their tracks and listened.

"What that sound be?"

"Prisoner, maybe?"

"Oh. Oh, that be it. Yah, I thought Chief Molar-Licker be keeping something away from us."

"Yah."

The orcs shuffled into the entrance. They were taken back in surprise when they saw Princess Silara alone on the other side of the room, her hands and legs tied and her mouth gagged. She was wearing a wet, soggy dress caked in dirt and her face was red from crying. The orcs mobilized towards her like rats after garbage.

"Oooo. Very nice."

"Very pretty elf girly. What your name, pretty girly?"

"She not answering. She must be very shy."

"Ha. Yah."

As the orcs approached, Silara made a sudden, fierce effort to break free from her ropes. It was unsuccessful. The orcs were closing in fast.

"Me think you very, very pretty."

"Yah."

"Get away from her! All of you!"

The orcs stopped in their tracks and turned around to see a young woman with long, brown, fluttering hair standing near the entrance to the room. She gripped a short sword tightly in her right hand as if she were afraid somebody would try and pull it away from her. The orcs looked at each other with confused expressions, and one of them turned to speak.

"Oh yah? What you going to do if me don't want to listen, huh?"

"You have no idea what I'm about to do to you! All of you get away from her right now!"

One of the orcs held a machete to Silara's throat.

"Drop your weapon, girly, or *this* girly be dead!"

"Don't you dare touch her!"

"I say drop the weapon or she be dead! Ten! Nine! Eight! Six! Five! Four!"

The sword clanged as it hit the ground. There was a short silence.

"You make smart, smart decision."

"I'm not done with you! Leave her alone, pigs!" shouted Firelight as she stepped forward. The orcs looked at her and didn't move or say anything. She took another step forward and put her hands out in front of her, slowly raising them and twisting her fingers. "You guys always seem to underestimate m…"

A big, green hand came around from the side of her head and shoved a greasy rag into her mouth. She tried to burn her attacker but a huge orc suddenly bull-rushed her from the side and wrapped his cold, warty arms around her, pinning her arms to her body and nearly breaking her bones. She let out a sudden, muffled squeal.

"We not done with you, either!" laughed one of the orcs.

She couldn't breathe; the gigantic orc's embrace was much too tight. She kicked frantically until another orc came forward and held her legs together. All of the orcs came forward.

"We know about you, Sorceress. We hear about you frying our buddies, and we be ready for you."

"Cat!" she thought to herself. "Cat! Help me!"

"We ready for you."

"Cat!"

She was in an incredible amount of pain as the huge brute squeezed her even tighter, and all she could do was squirm helplessly. She couldn't take this any longer.

"Cat! Hurry!"

The unbearably tight grip continued to press any remaining air out of her lungs; it was as if she were caught inside of a tightening vise. Meanwhile, she felt thumbnails dig into her lower back as one of the orcs grabbed onto her hips from behind, and she was powerless to kick him away. She was in so much shock that she didn't even hear the sound of all of them laughing hysterically at her at the same time as they closed in on her.

Why did she think she could handle all of them at once? It was her overconfidence kicking in again, that same stupid cockiness that had nearly gotten her killed back in the swamp. But wasn't she over that now? Hadn't she finally learned her lesson? Maybe she would never learn; it was if she were being controlled from the inside by her own pride, blinded by delusions of ability that she didn't have and powerless to let rational thought take the reins.

"Cat! CAT!!"

"RREERRRRR!!!!"

The big orc released his iron grip and fell backwards as Ocallin's jaw locked onto the top of his head. The other orcs were struck with sudden terror; some scrambled clumsily towards their weapons while others tried to flee. Firelight wasted no time in climbing to her feet, letting instinct take over as she immediately torched an orc attempting to run past her and watching with scorn as he stumbled to the ground, the last seconds of his consciousness melting away with the rest of his burning body. Another one tried to get past her, but he met the same fate as Firelight doused the creature in flames. She quickly scanned the room; one of the panicking orcs was a bit too close, but he wasn't even looking at her and was instead concentrating on the cat. It didn't matter; she descended upon him anyway and burned him to death. Everyone else was far enough away now, so she finally took the opportunity and used both hands to pull out the rag that was stuffed all the way down her throat.

The pathetic orcs continued to scurry around the room like frantic, hysterical mice. She made eye contact with one of them, and the image of Winterfrost's naked body suddenly flashed in her mind. The anger was growing. She clenched her teeth and stomped towards the wretched animal, searing his face as he screamed in agony. But she wasn't done, though; she went after another one in the same way. And another. She thought she heard the horrible, soft chewing sound of the general's brain being eaten all over again as she burned another pathetic orc. Not even the ones already mauled by the cat were spared from her fiery wrath. And why should they be? Firelight torched everyone she saw with a nonstop burst of flame that spewed from her hands like water from an out-of-control garden hose and lit up the entire room, leaving not a single orc alive. There was so much fire everywhere that it seemed as though the orcs' splattered blood must have been made of kerosene.

A few seconds of silence passed. Firelight held her head and collapsed to the ground, taking a few moments to catch her breath as the carcasses smoldered around her.

"Cat! Where were you?!" Firelight thought in an angry tone of voice. There were tears in her eyes.

"My name isn't Cat," answered Ocallin.

"I don't care. That's what I'm calling you, unless you'd rather have me call you Stubborn Ass."

"Well, I'm sorry about taking so long to get here. I was trailing too far behind and I had a hard time finding you inside of the cave."

She was too exhausted and too relieved to be angry anymore.

"It's okay. Thank you so much, Ocallin. I owe you everything for helping me." She got up slowly and walked over to the princess, ungagging her mouth and untying her arms and legs. Once free, the princess immediately began to crawl away as quickly as she could.

"It's all right. Come here, Princess. I won't hurt you."

She ignored her and continued to crawl away.

"I won't hurt you! It's me, Firelight! Remember?"

"Fi...Fire...light...?"

"Are you okay?"

"I think... so."

"I'm sorry for what just happened, Princess Silara. You shouldn't have had to see that." The girl cringed and leaned against Firelight, who slowly sat down next to her on the floor and gave her a soft hug. "I'm sorry for everything that's happened to you, but it's okay now. Everything's gonna be fine."

The princess buried her face into Firelight's leg and cried softly for a few minutes. The room was silent.

"Stay low to the ground. You don't want to breathe in any of the smoke."

"What about... what about... my... daddy?" she finally asked.

"Your father? Is he..."

"I... heard his... voice..."

"Uh oh. He must be here to surrender the Golden Egg of… whatever it's called." Firelight looked Ocallin in the eyes, then stood up and turned back towards Silara. Her confidence had returned in full force, bringing her new life. "Looks like we don't have much choice, then, Princess. We have to help your dad."

"You'll… you'll help my daddy? Good, good! Let's go help him! I think I know what room he's in — I'll lead you to the entrance!" The girl jumped to her feet.

Firelight smiled.

"He'll be bursting with joy to see you again. I promise."

Chapter 63

It was getting darker as the torchlight began to subside. Angroo and the elf sat on opposite sides of the room, averting eye contact with each other and not saying anything, while the wounded Molar-Licker did his best to carefully examine the floor in the small hallway leading out of the room.

"No one goes near the exit," he muttered as he tried to stand up on his good leg. "That fool dumped a layer of highly reactive powder all over the floor and walls. As soon as a warm body comes into contact with the powder, it will ignite and start a chain reaction; there's enough of it here to trigger a massive explosion that would kill all of us and cause the entire room to cave in. The mountain walls are very thin in this section of the cavern; we're near the top of the peak."

"How do we get out, then?" asked the elf. "How can I get to my…"

"Quiet. There's no way out. There's no way to stop the reaction."

"What?! That's crazy! Then how…"

"The powder will become impotent after maintaining contact with the air for twelve hours. We'll have to wait."

"But didn't the doctor say he would disarm it, though?! How did he intend to escape?!"

"Perhaps the doctor thought that the potion would give him the speed necessary to run through before the chain reaction completed, or the strength necessary to withstand the blast." Molar-Licker finally climbed to his feet and limped back towards the others. "How foolish of that man to think that! Why must humans be so eager to tamper with things that they cannot comprehend!?" He stomped the ground in rage.

There was silence.

"That's a pathetic thing to say, Molar-Licker," spit

Angroo. "You had no comprehension of the potion either."

"I knew what I was doing. It was the right thing to…"

"You knew nothing, Molar-Licker. You wouldn't have given it to me if you knew what would really happen. You can't even begin to scratch the surface of understanding the depth of misery you've put me through. And all for what? A scheme? A plot to steal the Golden Eggs of Gotty Gottya? You probably don't even understand how those work, either."

"Angroo, you…"

Angroo stood up.

"I what? How will you justify my murdering sprees this time?! Enough with your logic! Enough!"

"Angroo, listen to me. You…"

"No, you listen to…"

"NO YOU LISTEN TO ME!!!!" screamed Molar-Licker as he leapt to his feet in a sudden burst of anger. "Sit down, Angroo! Sit down! You of all people should know about the Golden Eggs!" Angroo finally sat down.

"What the hell does that mean?!"

"Why do you think you are the way you are right now?!" Angroo returned his glare.

"It's because of the potion you made me drink!"

"No. Why do you think your skin is white? Why do you think it burns all the time? You think you were born that way!?"

There was silence. Molar-Licker calmed down and slowly took a seat.

"You've never heard the Legend of Gotty Gottya, have you?"

No response.

"I'll tell you, then. Many, many years ago there existed a rare plant known as orcsbane that would instantly eat through the flesh of any orc that touched it; it was harmless to other forms of life. The horrible plant was filled with negative energy and would wither if it came into contact with water. Some believe it originated from another world."

"Get to the point," muttered Angroo through clenched teeth.

"Our ancestors were a proud people, much more powerful and widespread than we are today. The humans back then couldn't accept their own inferiority; they spent all their time plotting against us and trying to keep us down. But we continued to thwart their pathetic efforts to stand in our way of expanding our borders."

"If, uh, if I may interrupt for just one second, Chief, but I think you're telling a biased version of the story," interjected the elf. "They weren't just killing the orcs without reason, you know. The orcs had razed countless villages to the ground and were a constant military threat to all of their neighbors, if I remember the history books correctly."

Molar-Licker turned and stared.

"Yes. You're right, elf. Our ancestors were brutal and savvy in the ways of war. They left much destruction in their wake, something that we still take pride in today. But the human scum and their allies wanted to wipe us off the map, exterminate us completely. They decided that if they could gather all the orcsbane plants in the land, they would be able to kill us all outright by burning the plants and polluting the air with its toxins. They sent forth their three most terrible, brutal warriors to accomplish the task, a trio of lance-wielding cavalrymen known collectively only by the name of the infamous, fear-striking war cry that they would shout while on patrol: Gotty Gottya. The three cavalrymen roamed the land, killing all who stood in their path and snatching up hundreds upon hundreds of the horrible flowers to use against our people."

"Well, technically you could have made a more

impressive statement and said that they gathered thousands upon thousands of the orcsbane plants. And, from a strict botanical standpoint, they weren't actually flow…"

"You will not speak unless spoken to, *Eliazer*! Am I clear?"

"Uh, yes. Yes! Of course! Ha, silly me."

"I was just saying that they collected thousands of these horrible plants. Using their knowledge of magic that they had accumulated throughout their travels, they were able to combine all of these plants into three, golden, egg-shaped orbs after many years of work."

"The Golden Eggs of Gotty Gottya!"

"I told you not to speak, you moronic elf! Yes, the orbs were obviously known as the Golden Eggs of Gotty Gottya, and each of the men sculpted one of them. They then distributed one to the dwarves, one to the elves, and one to the men; the men's descendants would go on to found Victory City later in their history. All that is needed to unleash the power of the Golden Eggs is a small amount of fire; the smoke from the burning orcsbane would tear holes in our lungs."

Angroo stared at his mentor.

"So you're saying that, if one of the Golden Eggs were burned, it would dissolve into the atmosphere and kill any of us who breathe it in?"

"Yes. Now you're beginning to understand. The orcsbane in each of the Golden Eggs is so highly concentrated that a single one could potentially wipe out our entire race after a couple days, and the three of them were distributed to orckind's three greatest enemies so that they would forever have the upper hand against our people." Angroo's eyes widened.

"Now wait a minute, Chief!" shouted Eliazer. "They were created as a deterrent to the vicious and unrelenting orcish threats, and nothing else! They were never intended to be used!"

"You're wrong! It was only a matter of time! You and the humans and the dwarves thought you could bully us until we couldn't take it anymore, and then one of you would crack. It's easy to see what would have happened, and that's why desperate measures needed to be taken to ensure that they were doused in water before they could be burned. If a Golden Egg were submerged in water, it would immediately disintegrate and become worthless."

Angroo looked down and didn't say anything.

"But Chief, what made you so sure they would become activated?"

"That's where Angroo comes in. Twenty years ago, King Lucius of Victory City and a number of his men entered this cave under the false pretense that they would be negotiating some sort of pact with us. I don't remember many of the details, but it turned out that he came merely to taunt us and threaten us into relinquishing our borderlands, bringing his Golden Egg with him and demonstrating its powers on a hapless child lying nearby, the maniac. A poor infant. He rubbed the Egg all over Angroo's body, causing the outside of his skin to be eaten away by the horrible orcsbane."

"No!" shouted Angroo.

"Yes, and that's why you're like this. You've always possessed a deep, deep-seated, subconscious hatred of the Golden Eggs since then, and I knew that I could tap into your hatred with the potion recipe that I was forced to steal from the humans. I knew that we needed to act, and this was the only way!"

"No!"

"Yes!"

"NO!!!"

"Let me get this straight, Chief. So you put Angroo, a poor, innocent member of your tribe, through all of this just so that you could destroy the Golden Eggs?"

"Yes, I did. And he's done well so far; we've already destroyed two of them by submerging them in the river."

"You don't think there were other ways to obtain the Eggs, though?"

"There were no other ways!"

"What if you had simply asked for them?"

"That's a joke, Eliazer!"

"Is it?" The elf reached into his coat pocket and pulled out the Golden Egg of Gotty Gottya. "I had it all along. Here, it's yours now." Molar-Licker and Angroo looked at each other. It seemed as if the room suddenly became silent.

"Give it here!" shouted Molar-Licker as he snatched it out of the elf's hands, but he just as quickly dropped it to the ground and yelped in pain; the green pigmentation on his hand withered away, and his hand became completely white.

"Here, I should probably hold onto that for now. Heh." The elf picked up the Golden Egg.

"Give it to me."

The elf turned towards Angroo, who was staring intensely at him. Were his eyes blood-red like that a minute ago?

"Wha..."

"Give it to me now."

"But you just saw what happened to the chief! It will burn your skin!"

"Give it to me."

"It will burn your..."

"I said give it to me." Angroo stood up. The elf immediately scrambled to the other side of the room.

"Take it easy now. Do you want it? Here."

Angroo was only able to stare. The spirits were taking control of his mind, and he was helpless against them.

"Do you want it or not? Take it!"

Angroo tried to say something but he couldn't open his mouth.

"Here it is! Take it please!"

His skin burned.

"Please just take it!"

No response.

The elf stepped forward.

"Daddy!"

"Silara!?"

The elf dropped the Golden Egg onto the floor and turned around.

"DADDY!!!"

The Egg was rolling away.

"No, sweetie! Don't come any closer! Don't come near the door!"

It was rolling away.

"DADDY!!!!!!!!!"

Angroo threw himself onto the Golden Egg as the entire room exploded in a massive burst of flame.

Chapter 64

Heavy wind swept in. Dark clouds swirled ahead of the rising sun, but the clouds weren't enough to prevent the sun from seeing Molar-Licker's dark room for the first time; a huge chunk of the mountain wall had collapsed as a result of the explosion, creating an opportunity for the sunlight to finally enter and illuminate the room. There was nothing to see but piles of rocks, though. But what about the Golden Egg?! It was still there. Angroo shook the rocks off his back and jumped up, holding it up to his eyes. It didn't seem like it was affected by the fire, but he didn't have any time to examine it closely because he was forced to drop it to the ground; his hands felt like they were about to fall off after holding the horrible thing for only a matter of seconds.

Angroo rubbed the dirt off his forehead. He had not been seriously injured in the explosion because he had been far enough away from the entrance, although his hands and chest still killed him from touching the Golden Egg and his back was badly bruised from falling debris. Where was everyone else, though? Where was the girl?

It didn't take him long to find Molar-Licker. The poor shaman's body was badly burnt and was almost completely buried by a pile of rocks; his now-white left hand reached out towards Angroo and the charred remains of his face gazed up as if he were crying out from beyond the grave, desperately begging for help. It was too late for help, though. Poor Molar-Licker was gone now, and maybe he deserved what he got. Yes, of course he did. He had it coming to him. Angroo looked away.

He had to find the girl, but where was she? He furiously dug through some fallen debris without success, then he turned and scoped out the rest of the area. Where was she?

Was she okay?! He had to find her, but he couldn't find her anywhere; he was at wit's end.

Golden hair extended out from behind a pile of rocks. It was her. Angroo rushed over to find her lying face-up, with ash-covered skin and clothing that was burnt and ripped but surprisingly intact given the circumstances. Apparently, she had been thrown to the edge of the room by the force of the explosion, managing to escape most of the falling debris in the process. Her eyes were closed. Angroo felt for her pulse – she was alive. She was breathing. He pulled his hand away.

At least someone would live through this, he thought. He got up and began to pace around weakly. What should he do now? He was a monster; he needed to kill himself. It was the only thing he could do. But could he just leave the girl there, alone and ready to be ravaged by one of the other orcs? No, he couldn't let those animals anywhere near her. He hated his kind. All orcs were monsters, not just him, and now he knew it. Any orc would have committed the same atrocities that he had; it was in their blood and it could not be helped. It was in all of their blood. Orcs were a blight on the world. They made the world worse for everyone else and for that they all needed to die. He had denied it for the longest time, but now he finally accepted it as fact. He knew it. He absolutely knew it.

There was still some doubt in his head, though. Maybe Molar-Licker had been wrong about the potion. Maybe the spirits didn't simply enable murderous urges that were already there but instead instilled these urges for the first time. He looked over at sweet little Silara lying on the ground and remembered her beautiful singing; she was the most innocent soul he had ever encountered. He smiled when he thought about all the wonderful times he had spent with her wandering the wilderness, but the smile quickly turned into an angry grimace. He went to touch her but quickly pulled his hand away. He couldn't touch her because he was a homicidal monster and he didn't know what he would do next. He was so helpless.

She was such an innocent, innocent little girl who saw the good in everything. So much different from the horrible orcs, right? The polar opposite. A terrible idea suddenly shot through his mind. He cringed at the mere thought of what he was about to do, but it was something that needed to be done. He was desperate. He needed to know right then if Molar-Licker had told him the truth.

Angroo scooped up a handful of the terrible soup and funneled it into the girl's mouth, making sure she swallowed all of it. He waited for a minute, falling back onto the ground and watching intently like some kind of starving rat staring at a crumb: nothing happened. She was still the same beautiful little angel sleeping peacefully. Nothing. His heart sank.

Angroo stood up.

Some loose rocks slipped from the top of the large pile near where the room entrance had been, and he slowly turned around. It was the woman – Firelight. She was standing triumphantly at the top of the pile of debris looking down at him, her hair blowing like crazy as she stood ringed with the open sky. She gripped her sword tightly as she stared at him without expression, and he returned her blank gaze. Somehow, he knew she would come. And he knew it would come to this.

"Kill me," he said as he picked up the Golden Egg and held it out in front of his face. "Burn me right now! Burn me!" He tried to ignore the horrible pain pulsating through his hands as he waited with bated breath for her response.

Her expression suddenly changed to one of extreme anger as her stare intensified.

"You murderer."

"Burn me right now!"

"Why did you do all of this, Angroo?! Why did you kill Winterfrost and General Richmond?!"

"Just burn me!"

"They trusted you. We all trusted you. Why did you betray all of us?!" She took a step down the pile of rocks.

"Don't come any closer! Just burn me!" She stepped closer. "I said stay back! Get it over with and kill me right now!"

"I don't know what kind of trick you're trying to..."

He lifted his trident off of the ground, released his grip on the Golden Egg, and lunged forward in a single, swift motion, but she was ready for him. A massive burst of flame enveloped his body as he leapt forward, but he simply emerged from the fire a split-second later with the same crazed look in his eyes and his entire body ablaze, coming down at her as though nothing had happened to him.

Firelight dove to the side as he thrust the trident all the way through the pile of rocks with a loud, horrible noise; it sounded as if the metal itself were screaming as it pierced through the solid rock that she had been standing on less than a second before. He got up and stomped towards her.

She threw another fireball at him, but this time he didn't continue forward. Instead, he dove to ground and shielded the Golden Egg with his body, taking the entirety of the fireball himself. He stood up again and came towards her, completely aflame.

"I won't let you beat me!" she screamed as she let the fire pour out of her hands and pulsate through the orc's entire body. His face writhed with pain but he acted as if he felt nothing. He lunged forward at her again, attempting to grab her with his flaming hands, but she jumped over his head and dashed away.

He turned towards her, his entire face engulfed in fire. He stared down at her.

"Why are you doing this!?" screamed Firelight. "Why are you attacking me like this?!" The orc didn't answer her but continued to stare without moving. She backed away from him.

Something suddenly changed. He began to frantically wipe the flames away from his face as if he had suddenly realized for the first time that he was on fire. He banged his head several times on the rocks and clawed at his entire body like a lunatic.

"KILL ME!!!!!" he wailed. "JUST KILL ME BEFORE I KILL YOU!!!!!!!!!!!!!"

"You're completely mad!!"

The orc walked over and grabbed onto a chunk of the remaining cave wall, ripping it off with a violent heave and collapsing most of the rest of the wall in the process. More light shone into the room. He walked towards her slowly, carrying over his head an enormous slab of rock that would normally be impossible to lift and breathing heavily as he went. He was like a deranged animal. She held her sword in front of her.

"KILL ME!!!!!!!!!!!!!!!!!!!!!!!!!!!!!!!!!!!!"

They stared at each other. Angroo finally dropped the massive slab of rock onto the ground in front of him and let himself fall backwards onto the hard floor.

"Why did you kill Winterfrost and General Richmond?!" No response.

"Why did you kill them?!"

"For this," answered Angroo as he motioned towards the Golden Egg. "It was all for this."

She looked at him but didn't respond.

"It was made to kill orcs. As soon as it burns, it will fill the atmosphere with a poison that kills orcs from the inside out."

She stared into his eyes.

"This was the only way to get it. It needed to be doused in water to be destroyed. I needed to..."

"You fiend! This wasn't worth *murder*!"

"I had to..."

"You murdered innocent people for this! There were other ways!"

"I couldn't help it!"

"You *could* help it, you..."

"I COULDN'T HELP IT!!!!!!" he screamed. "IT'S NOT FAIR!!!!!! I CAN'T CONTROL MYSELF!!!!!!!!!!!!!!!!"

"You killed..."

"I CAN'T CONTROL MYSELF!!!!!!!!!!!!!!!!!!!!!!!!!!!"

Neither of them spoke for a minute.

"You murderer."

"The spirits are in my head, Firelight. They've taken control of my mind. It's not fair! I can't control my own actions!"

"Spirits?"

"The potion that I was given allowed the spirits to enter my body. The potion..."

She tried to step closer, but he quickly jumped up and startled her.

"Don't go near me!"

"You're controlled by spirits? You're *possessed*?"

"My ancestors control my actions. Cruel spirits of orcs before me. I can't tell what they'll force me to do next."

"You're blaming spirits for the sins that you've committed?"

"No, I... no. It was me. The urges were already there. The spirits just released them. The spirits let my homicidal urges pour forth."

She stared at him.

"Listen, Firelight. All orcs are killers like me. All of them. Every single one of them. We make the world a more hideous place." He pointed to the Golden Egg at his feet. "Just do it. Burn it right now. We don't deserve to live."

"It wasn't right to kill innocents for this, Angroo. Winterfrost and General Richmond didn't need to be killed for this."

"Yes they did. I felt the need to kill them."

"You know it wasn't right."

"As much as it hurts me to say it, I really did think it was right. Deep down, I thought it was right, but it doesn't matter anymore. The only way for you to make sure that it never happens again is to burn the Golden Egg right now."

She stepped forward.

"Just get it over with right now."

"You didn't want to kill any of them. You didn't want to hurt the princess, either. I know you didn't want that." She took another step forward.

"Get it over with."

She stepped forward again. And again.

"Hurry up. I'm losing control!"

She knelt down and reached over to pick it up.

Every fiber in his body screamed for him to dive and grab it away from her. He held his hands over his face.

She picked it up.

"You're sorry for what you've done, and I know it," she said.

Angroo stood up.

"Burn it."

"Both of us are outsiders."

"Burn it!" He stepped towards her.

"Both of us are outsiders here, Angroo." Her voice

cracked.

"Just burn it quickly! I'm losing control of myself!"

He stepped towards her.

"We don't belong here. Who are we to control the fate of others?"

He lunged forward.

She stepped away from him and chucked the Golden Egg over the fallen cave wall. Both of them watched as it plummeted towards the river below, getting smaller and smaller until it finally disappeared into the slow-moving currents. It was all over.

He looked into her eyes. The wind was raging.

"Why did you do that?"

The wind howled.

"Because it was what needed to be done. It's what you really wanted."

He stepped closer as he tried to hold himself back. He had to hold himself back.

They stepped towards each other. Her sword slipped out of her fingers and clanged against the ground.

She wrapped her hands around his head and pressed her lips against his as the wind raged behind them. He was at once overwhelmed by the warmth of her soft flesh pressed against his face as their lips locked, and he felt her hair all over him like tiny wisps of fire as the wind blew hard against his back. His eyes widened. What was this? What was going on? He wasn't sure but somehow he liked it. He suddenly felt a rush of adrenaline as he leaned into it. Closer. It wasn't fast enough. Closer!

Angroo grabbed the back of her head and pulled her into him. He was pulling her too close now, and she tried to pull away. He gripped her head. Closer. He was about to crush her skull, and her pathetic, frantic efforts to pull away were for nothing. Her attempts to burn him were for nothing; he didn't feel any of it even though his body was on fire again. She was overwhelmed with pain, but he didn't feel anything at all. She was screaming deliriously. He felt nothing.

She escaped from his grip and fell hard on her back. He lunged down after her, howling feverishly like some kind of crazed beast, but his descent was interrupted. The dark shape of a large animal suddenly sprung into his field of vision, the unexpected impact of the creature's sharp claws against his flesh knocking him off his balance and causing him to trip over his own foot and stagger backwards. His helpless body spun like a top as he tumbled head-first over the wall, plunging all the way down the mountainside in a freefall and crunching hard on the rocks next to the soft, rolling river.

Chapter 65

He was still alive. Somehow, he had survived the fall — what horrible, horrible luck. His entire body was mangled and overflowing with pain. It felt like all of his bones were broken as he lay on the jagged rocks in a pool of his own blood. His skin was almost completely black from his head to his toes from the burnings he had received. The pain overwhelmed him as he suffered alone on the cold, damp rocks, unable to move. At least he felt something.

The spirits were responsible for this now, right? The spirits had gotten him into this mess and had literally driven him over the edge. They were gone now, though. The Golden Eggs of Gotty Gottya, all three of those horrible things, had finally disappeared from the world, and everything was good once again. Something started to happen inside of Angroo; he suddenly felt free again, liberated from those horrible spirits that he couldn't control. He felt like everything was open now. He was as near to death as he had ever been, and yet he felt more alive at that moment than ever. He couldn't hurt anyone anymore, and that was enough for him. But he had hurt so many already.

The entire day melted past as he remained alone at the base of the mountain, reminiscing about his life. The sound of the river nearby was so soothing, but yet there was still something missing from the picture. He still wasn't free. Something was still holding him back and keeping him from being at peace.

He heard some people walking towards him, getting closer. He couldn't see the people but he was relieved to know that they weren't in any danger from him; he was completely incapacitated, so he wouldn't have been able to do anything to them even if the spirits wanted him to. Take that, spirits! He figured that it was a small victory.

"Wha!? Get a load of this!" shouted a man as he stood over Angroo. Another man stood next to him. Simple human soldiers from Victory City, no doubt.

"I don't believe it!" shouted the other soldier. "Is it still alive?"

He tried to tell them that he was still alive, but he couldn't. His mouth didn't work.

"Look! It's breathing!"

"Let's kill it!"

"Yeah!"

"What's going on here?!" Angroo recognized that last voice but wished he hadn't.

The blond soldier pushed past the other two and looked down at him. He stared stunned and confused for a moment, but then a smile ripped across his face. His eyes brightened. He momentarily looked back at the other soldiers and laughed with disdain – he was back to his old self. The sky was suddenly a little bit darker.

"Well. Well. Well. If it isn't my favorite pig-face." The blond soldier loaded an arrow into his bow and took a deep breath. "Looks like the tables have finally turned, slimeball."

"You know this orc, Yohannis?"

"We have a little bit of history, yes." The blond soldier paced back and forth. "Looks like it's finally time for you to get what's coming to you, maggot. You dirty, muck-encrusted creature of filth. It's finally time for you to get what's coming to you."

Angroo couldn't say anything or move at all. He simply stared up at the blond soldier without moving a single muscle in his body.

"Should we kill it, Yohannis?"

"Yeah! Can we?!"

"Hold off. I need to have a little *talk* with him first." He turned back to Angroo and pulled his arrow away. "See, pig-face? Civilized people talk. They use their words."

Angroo was very tired as he gazed up at him with his disfigured face.

"So many people died because they trusted you, scum. They died because you somehow convinced them to trust you. I don't know how you did it, but I certainly know *why* you did it. You did it because you wanted to see the look on their faces when you suddenly turned against them and sent your filthy, muck-covered pitchfork right into their foreheads. You *delighted* in their misfortune. You enjoyed the taste of triumph in every bite of their brains. You lived to kill because you hated everyone else, you hated the world. Do you have anything to say about that, you perverted, remorseless animal? Do you have anything to say at all?!"

Angroo had nothing to say.

"So much irony, you wretch. So much irony."

The blond soldier loaded the arrow back into his bow. He stepped on Angroo's head and aimed the arrow directly between Angroo's eyes. He stepped down harder. He drew back the bowstring.

Nothing happened. The blond soldier dropped the weapon and backed away.

"I once vowed that I'd kill you by sending an arrow through your head," he muttered in a softer, almost monotone voice. "I swore to it, and right now there's nothing I'd rather do than uphold my vow. But you know what, pig-face? I learned something from you when you spared my life that day. I learned that it isn't always best to let your rage make your decisions for you, no matter now justified it is. It's not my place to decide whether or not your life ends right now, you murderous piece of trash, because I'm better than that. We'll let the judicial system of Victory City make that decision. We'll let the people decide your fate." He looked down and made eye contact with Angroo, his lips folding into a faint smile. "I don't know why you didn't kill me that time or what demon possessed you to make that decision not to kill me, but you've got some nerve." He began to walk off.

"Should we kill it, Yoha…"

"If you even think about laying a finger on him, you stupid moron, I'll send an arrow right through your stupid face! Carry him back carefully. *Carefully*! Let's go!"

The two men picked him up and carried him away. He would face justice for what he had done, and he would finally be free from his overwhelming guilt. Or, at the very least, the guilt would be alleviated a little bit; he knew that he could never take back the terrible things that he had done, but this was closure at least. He breathed easy and watched the sun set. It was all kind of nice. This was the best thing that could have happened to him; it was his fate.

Chapter 66

A week had come and gone. It was a sunny and mild afternoon, and Firelight entered Rurik's shop to find him behind the front desk as usual. For someone who used to make a living as a sneak, he sure was predictable.

"I finished analyzing the soup that you found," he muttered.

"Really? What did you discover?"

"You probably won't believe this, but it's actually a fairly simple chemical compound. Temporarily increases metabolism, physical strength, reflexes, alertness, energy and aggression in anyone who drinks it. Nothing that I haven't seen before."

"Are you sure? It seemed like…"

"Well, it's a fairly potent mix. It's not something you see every day, but at the same time I don't think that it's anything *really* special."

"That's weird. I thought it was something a little bit more powerful than a simple chemical compound."

"I doubt it. It seems quite standard to me."

"It can't be."

"I don't know what else to tell you."

Firelight shook her head but didn't have anything left to say about the soup. These last couple of weeks had been so uniquely bizarre that she had learned to just accept things as they were and move on.

"So you hear about the whole situation with the succession?" Rurik asked.

"I sure did. That was really unexpected. Queen Crista was the prince's wife the whole time?"

"Apparently, she was. They uncovered papers that proved she had married him several years back and, now that the Crown of Victory City was finally recovered, she was next in line for it. I don't know why he would want to keep his marriage a secret for so long, though."

"He probably feared for her. He knew that she was an asset to him as an agent, and he didn't want her to become a high-profile figure."

"Yeah. Pretty strange; she seemed to wake up from her coma just in time, didn't she?"

"I hear she always did have a knack for timing."

Firelight looked out the window.

"Well at least this city has no reason to worry about the orcs anymore. They were routed, and most of the survivors were driven off to faraway lands."

"The fire giants just demolished them, right Rurik? It was a completely different ballgame after they entered the fray. Maybe it would have been better if we had just waited for them to arrive and take care of the orcs all by themselves."

"I don't know about that. The giants were certainly powerful allies, but the orcs had the most at stake. They would have fought to the death at every turn and would not have gone down easily. However, the whole tribe really seemed to lose its inner fire when Chief Molar-Licker was killed in that explosion. They were disheartened and disorganized, and there was no way they would have even stood a chance against the combined forces of Victory City, Elkanshire, and Flamewind at that point."

"Did the orcs ever end up naming a new chieftain?"

"I heard a funny story about that, actually. After Molar-Licker's demise, many of the orcs apparently rallied around a very young, charismatic leader and former prisoner of war named Orkianu. Though he was inexperienced and, from what I heard, somewhat slow-witted, he was unwavering in providing a message of hope and enthusiasm that many of the orcs identified with. He was chosen as the new chief, but after a bunch of serious tactical blunders over the span of a couple of days he resigned from his position. There had been nothing but chaos among their ranks ever since."

"Heh. I guess they really beat themselves from the inside." She smiled, but it was a smile that didn't last more than a second as she realized that what she had just said about being beaten from the inside could also apply to something else. She looked out at the empty street.

"I forgot to ask you how your injuries have been healing."

"Oh, it's fine. I wasn't hurt too badly. I had a mild concussion."

"It's lucky that you weren't hurt any worse than you were. And King Eliazer and his daughter made it out without serious injuries as well. It was a miracle after what happened out there."

"It was pretty miraculous, yes."

"What ever happened to that orc that did those things to you?"

"Angroo?"

"Yes, the white one. They caught him, right?"

"They caught him the next day."

"Good. I'm glad that killer was finally captured. He was a menace."

"I agree, but there was something about him. I don't think he was all bad."

"Well if he wasn't all bad, you wouldn't be able to tell that from his list of accomplishments. He murdered King Lucius, he murdered Prince Lucio, and he even murdered Winterfrost for crying out loud. Winterfrost the unkillable. This orc has left behind a legacy of murder and destruction."

"You're right; he was a killer. But even though he tried

to kill me as well, I did my best to make him feel special when we were alone on that mountaintop. I tried to put him at ease after all of the chaos and all of the madness that had pervaded his soul for so long. I only hope I got through to him somehow."

Rurik seemed confused and didn't respond right away.

"Well, I'm just glad that he can't hurt anyone else anymore," he muttered. "So what's happening to him now, anyway? He's probably locked up deep inside a prison somewhere, I'm sure."

"No."

"No?"

"They hanged Angroo this morning." She closed her eyes. "He's dead."

Chapter 67

It was a dark, peaceful night. Silara gazed out the window with tear-filled eyes as she strummed her harp softly and very quietly; after all, she didn't want anyone in the castle hearing her.

Her father entered the room and slowly sat down next to her. He patted her on the back as she continued to look out the window.

"I don't know why you decided to put on a black dress tonight, darling. You look much nicer in lighter, brighter colors that match your eyes."

"I... I don't want..."

"There, there. Why are you so sad? Is it because of Angroo?"

"I..."

"This is the way the world works, dearie. You kill innocent people, you have to face justice. It's the only way."

She didn't answer; she seemed disgusted that he had even mentioned that name.

"Listen, sweetie. Angroo was a killer. I understand that he had a good side – I even saw it myself when we were in the cave – but this is what has to happen to killers. He put you through so much terror. I... I don't know what else to tell you."

She continued to look out the window.

"Now you should continue packing your things. We're leaving for Elkanshire tomorrow." There was a short pause. He began to turn around.

"Daddy?"

"Yes, darling?"

Silara ripped the strings off of her harp and leapt straight up into the air, wrapping them around her father's neck before he even knew what was going on.

"SilARA!?!?!?"

She didn't answer him. She was too busy strangling him.

"HELP!!!!" he gasped. Two of his bodyguards rushed into the room, and both were stunned by what they saw. They tried to pull her arms away but they couldn't because she was much too strong.

"What are your orders, My Lord!?" shouted one of the guards. They held their swords to Silara's chest.

"G...gggrrrrr..."

"What are your orders?!"

"Gggggg..." Eliazer's face was completely purple. He couldn't breathe anymore; their king was dying before their eyes.

"What are your orders?!"

"Sir, what are your orders?!"

She continued to strangle him without the slightest hint of slowing down. She was completely absorbed in the killing. The determination in her eyes blasted right through the tears.

The guards stabbed her with their swords. She dropped the strings and fell back onto the bed, gasping for air just like her father had been seconds before. She was covered in her own blood, a wounded animal.

King Eliazer was stunned. He knelt down next to her bed.

"Noooo!!!" NOOOOOOOO!!!!!!!!!!"

"Dad...dy..."

"NOOOOOOOOOOOOOOOOOO!!!!!!!!!!!!!!!!!!!!!!"

She closed her eyes. She stopped breathing. Her heart stopped.

Eliazer felt her face. He felt her hair and collapsed on top of her. His eyes sunk. He was gripped with horror.

"No....."

He stood up and clenched his face with both of his hands.

"Silara. What happened?! Why did this happen!? WHY DID THIS HAPPEN!!!!!!!!!!!!!!!!!!!!!!!!!!!!!!!!!"

Silara's arm suddenly rose up. She placed her hand over her chest, and as if by magic she was able to immediately stop the bleeding. Her wounds closed up. The color returned to her face. She was breathing again, and her heart was beating. She was suddenly alive.

"Silara? Silara?!"

"Careful, Lord. Don't go near her."

"Silara, my dear?! Silara?!"

"Sir, don't go any closer!"

"Silara!"

The two guards moved in. She sat on the bed and stared at them as they held their swords out at her.

"Silara! What have you become?!"

She didn't answer. One of the guards stepped closer, and she grabbed onto his sword's blade and ripped it out of his hand in the blink of an eye. With two quick swings and two horrible screams, both guards crumpled to the ground. She was covered in blood. There was so much blood everywhere.

She picked up the sword that the other guard had dropped and was now holding one in each hand. She looked up.

"Silara!"

She looked her father in the eyes as he backed away from her.

"Call me Silly. That's my nickname."

28211988R00177

Made in the USA
San Bernardino, CA
22 December 2015